THE MISSING BOYFRIEND

ALEX STONE

Boldwood

First published in Great Britain in 2025 by Boldwood Books Ltd.

Copyright © Alex Stone, 2025

Cover Design by Lisa Horton

Cover Images: Shutterstock

Every effort has been made to obtain the necessary permissions with reference to copyright material, both illustrative and quoted. We apologise for any omissions in this respect and will be pleased to make the appropriate acknowledgements in any future edition.

A CIP catalogue record for this book is available from the British Library.

Paperback ISBN 978-1-80549-900-8

Large Print ISBN 978-1-80549-896-4

Hardback ISBN 978-1-80549-895-7

Trade Paperback ISBN 978-1-80656-026-4

Ebook ISBN 978-1-80549-894-0

Kindle ISBN 978-1-80549-894-0

Audio CD ISBN 978-1-80549-901-5

MP3 CD ISBN 978-1-80549-898-8

Digital audio download ISBN 978-1-80549-892-6

This book is printed on certified sustainable paper. Boldwood Books is dedicated to putting sustainability at the heart of our business. For more information please visit https://www. boldwoodbooks.com/about-us/sustainability/

Boldwood Books Ltd, 23 Bowerdean Street, London, SW6 3TN

www.boldwoodbooks.com

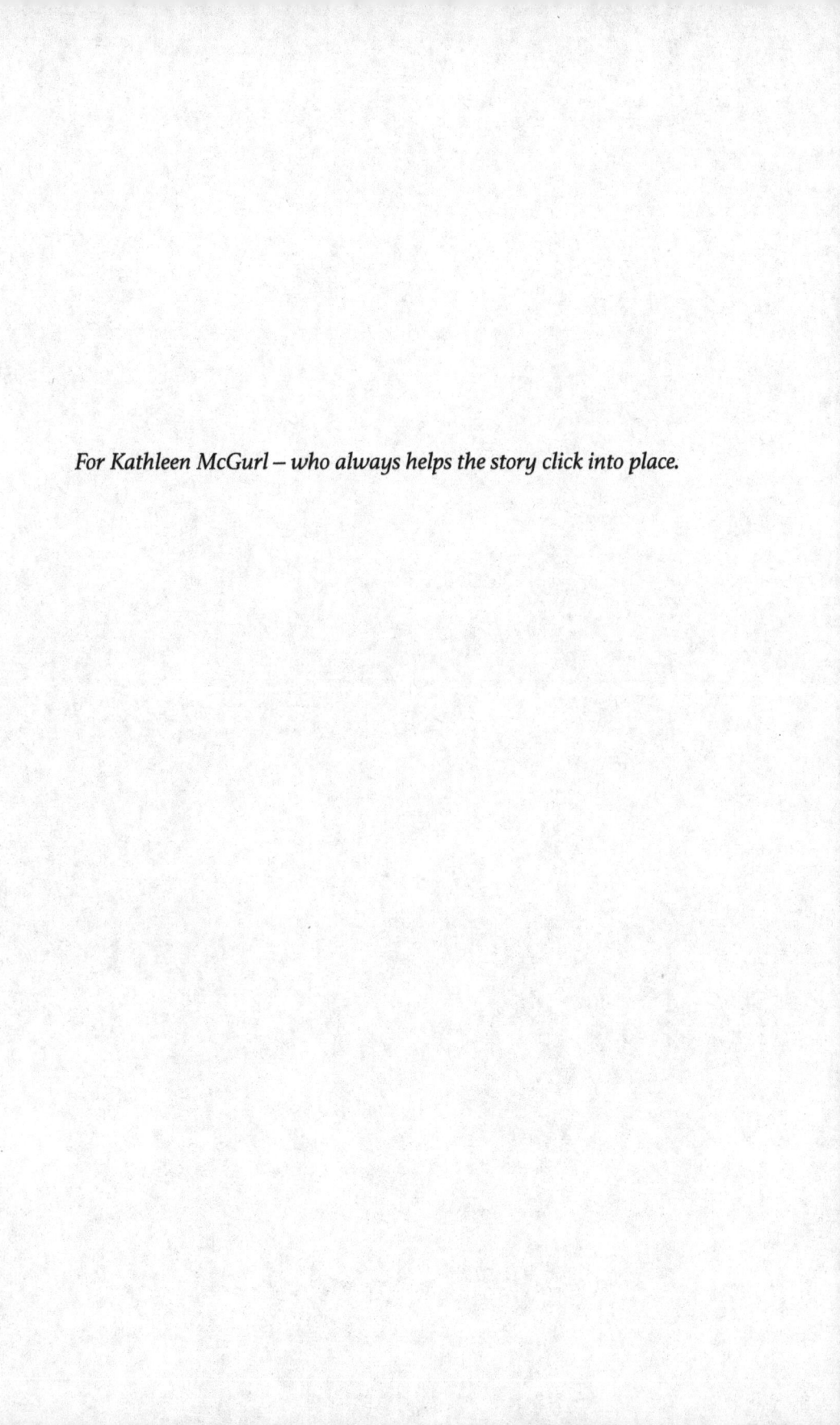

For Kathleen McGurl – who always helps the story click into place.

1

NOW

December

Not him, too.

The words sprang into my head before I could stop them. But it wasn't the same. It couldn't be. And yet, my heart raced as I stared at the empty space in the wardrobe where Callum's clothes had hung next to mine. They'd been there this morning when I'd left for work. *He'd* been here.

'See you tonight.' Callum's parting words repeated in my memory. *'I love you, you know that, don't you?'*

I'd nodded. I knew. It was the first thing I'd truly known for certain in years.

'I love you, too,' I'd told him.

Those four little words had once seemed so impossible for me to feel again. But the last five months had changed that. *He'd* changed that.

Except now I was staring into a half empty wardrobe with no sign of Callum.

A surge of desperation hit me like a charge of electricity, jolting my body into action. I yanked open the dresser drawers one after another in search of his clothes. They had to be here somewhere. They had to be.

And yet they weren't.

I'd run out of drawers to search and all I'd found were more empty spaces.

I pivoted in circles, surveying the room as though his clothes would suddenly reappear. As if I'd simply overlooked them, and they'd materialise in plain sight if I looked hard enough, or long enough. The way my car key did when I missed it in a rush. Except I wasn't rushing now, and Callum's clothes were a lot larger and harder to misplace than a key.

Besides, the flat wasn't that cluttered that it would hide *all* of his clothes. My gaze shifted to the far corner of the room. That space had become Callum's unofficial laundry basket, the existence of an actual basket in the bathroom always seeming to somehow elude him. I couldn't remember the last time the carpet had been visible there.

Until now.

In fact, the room was immaculately tidy. The way it always used to be.

'*Everything has a place.*' Mum's voice echoed in my head.

It was one of her rules that had seeped into my core. *Keep things tidy. Controlled. Predictable.* As though our lives here were part of a plan.

Callum's arrival had chipped away at the charade. He definitely hadn't been part of the plan. And yet for once, I didn't care.

So what if he didn't use the basket? His laundry pile was still separated into darks and whites. He just had his own system, that was all.

It jarred against the structure that had become so essential. But it was also kind of comforting. It was a reminder that now it was the two of us—

I froze. At least it *had* been the two of us.

Tears welled in my eyes, but I blinked them away. I couldn't fall apart. I had to stay strong. I had to figure this out. I knew better than anyone that things weren't always what they appeared to be. And despite evidence to the contrary, I wasn't ready to accept that Callum had just left me.

I couldn't. Accepting that would mean accepting that I was alone.

Again.

I shook my head, refusing to allow my thoughts to slip down that path. I had to stay strong. Stay focused. There had to be another explanation. A *better* explanation. After all, it wasn't the same as last time. *He* had no reason to leave me.

None that he knew of anyway.

I grabbed my phone from my pocket and selected Callum's name in the contacts list. There was one way to find out what was going on. I pressed the phone to my ear, waiting for the ringtone.

'The number you have called is not in service,' a recorded woman's voice informed me, without any emotion for the gravitas of the news she was imparting.

I shook my head. No, this wasn't right. His number had been working this morning. He'd WhatsApp messaged as the Sunday brunch crowd thinned.

Just like normal.

We'd exchanged the usual pleasantries. The questions about each other's day. The emojis that had become our shorthand. Affectionate and personal.

I swiped the screen, my finger instinctively moving to the WhatsApp icon to message him. I froze. My gaze locked on a tiny red notification bubble.

One unread message.

Callum?

Hope surged through me as I hurriedly tapped the screen.

> I'll explain everything later. I promise, I'm going to fix it. I love you. More than you know.

I stared at the message, rereading it over and over again.

Fix what?

I shook my head. There was a more pressing question. My fingers flew over the keypad.

> Where are you?

I hit send and the message turned green with a single grey tick in the corner. Just one.

I stared at it. Willing the second tick to appear. The one that would tell me my message had been delivered.

But it didn't.

I lowered the phone with a shaking hand as my gaze automatically drifted to the wall opposite the bed. Bile rose in my throat as the phone slipped from my hand, landing with a soft thud against the worn carpet.

Blinking, I attempted to refocus my view of the stark white wall ahead of me. Immaculate except for one single nail protruding from the plasterboard.

But it wasn't the nail that bothered me. It was the absence of what used to hang from it. A framed photo. The only one I had displayed anywhere in the flat.

Us.

2

THEN

Three Months Earlier
September

The bell above the door jangled again, but I didn't even have time to look up.

'Flat white, extra hot.'

'Latte with oat milk.'

'Espresso please.'

The orders bled together as I darted from the counter to the coffee machine. I barely had a second to breathe before spinning back to the till, tapping in prices and plastering on a polite smile for the next customer.

'That'll be £3.90.'

The woman handed over a £5 note, and I hurriedly fumbled for her change before pivoting back to the coffee machine.

I grabbed the portafilter and knocked the used coffee grounds into the bin.

Tap, tap, tap.

The sound vibrated through my pounding head as the tightly packed puck of coffee fell from the metal basket. I twisted the portafilter back into the grinder and pressed the button to fill it with fresh coffee grounds, wincing as the sound drowned out the soothing lull of the soft rock playing on the radio.

The rich, bitter scent filled the air as I levelled the mound of coffee off and reached for the tamper, pressing down with firm, practiced pressure. With a twist of my wrist, I locked the portafilter back into the machine and pressed the button to start the shot.

'Espresso,' I called out as I set the drink down on the counter beside a flat white that still sat untouched. I glanced up, scanning the busy café, trying to remember what the guy who ordered it looked like.

The bell jangled again, and as I turned towards the door, I noticed a guy outside pacing the pavement in front of the café's large windows, a phone pressed to his ear.

Was it his?

I squinted at him, trying to recall, but I barely looked at the customers when it was busy like this. All I heard were their voices. Their demands.

'Cappuccino with hazelnut syrup, please.' Another order cut through my thoughts, and I drew in a deep breath, nodding as I put the order through the till. I had too much to do to worry about a customer who couldn't be bothered to pick up his drink. That was his problem.

I fell into a well-practiced rhythm – grind, press, lock, brew, steam, pour – again and again.

'This is cold,' a man's voice snapped behind me. I turned as he slammed his cup on the counter. 'You'll have to do it again.'

I stopped mid-pour, my fingers tightening around the milk jug.

'Excuse me?' My voice was tight, but I fought to keep my indignance from showing on my face as I realised it was the neglected flat white.

'I ordered it *extra hot*,' he snapped. 'But I had to take a call. You left it sitting here, so now it's cold.'

My stomach twisted at the sharpness of his tone.

'It's *undrinkable!*' he barked, shoving the cup towards me, sloshing coffee over the rim.

I stared at it in stunned silence. It hadn't been there that long for it to be that cold.

'It's unacceptable,' he barked.

I could feel the other customers watching. Waiting.

My chest tightened as a familiar wave of panic washed over me. There was a time when I had loved being in the spotlight, everyone's attention locked on me. But that was so long ago, it felt like another life now.

* * *

My fingers flew across the piano keys, my breath rising and falling in sync with the melody, as though it lived within me.

Finally, I lifted my hands, the final notes fading into silence. For a moment, it was as though time stood still. A millisecond where nothing moved. Nothing breathed. Especially me.

And then like a wave rolling in, applause swelled through the auditorium.

I took a deep breath as I stood slowly, my eyes instinctively seeking out Daniel as he stood off to one side. His beaming smile resonated with pride as he roughly brushed a tear from his face with the back of his hand. He'd told me once that I had a way of transporting the audience with me into the music. They didn't just hear it. They felt it. Because I did.

My attention shifted to the audience as they clambered to their feet still clapping, nodding and smiling at me, as though we were connected. As though I belonged. My chin lifted as I savoured every moment, before bowing with practiced grace, unable to restrain my huge grin any longer.

* * *

The memory of it caught me off guard. It was a different life. A life I had buried.

I pressed my lips together. 'Let me finish making this cappuccino and I'll—'

He exhaled sharply through his nose, shaking his head. 'You charge nearly four quid for a coffee in this place, and you can't even get the temperature right?'

'I'll make you another,' I said, fighting to keep my voice calm. 'I just need to finish this order first.'

But he wasn't listening. 'Absolutely *ridiculous*,' he continued, his voice rising. 'I waste my whole lunch break in a queue because there's never enough staff, only to get an overpriced, cold coffee from someone incompetent.' He snorted. 'Make a fresh flat white, extra hot, or I'll leave a review telling everyone this place is expensive, slow, and serves cold coffee.'

My hands trembled as I hurried to finish making the cappuccino.

A bad review could destroy the café. Even this *scene* could be enough to scare customers off. It was barely staying afloat as it was.

But I couldn't afford to annoy a second customer by making him dissatisfied with my service, too.

'Hey, I get it,' the man waiting for his cappuccino said. 'Nobody likes a luke-warm coffee.'

My stomach plummeted. It was too late. Now he was frustrated too.

I braced myself for another complaint, another person ready to add to the pile of problems weighing down on me.

But instead, the man turned slightly towards the angry customer, his hands held open, his tone carrying an easy, unthreatening warmth. 'But she made you a hot drink. *You* let it go cold, not her.'

The customer scoffed. 'She should have known I'd got called away.'

The guy chuckled, a soft warm sound. 'She's a barista, mate. Not a psychic.'

The customer's scowl deepened. 'She—'

'You said it yourself,' the man continued, his voice still calm, still in control. 'She's on her own back there, dealing with a long queue. There's no way she can keep track of every customer's movements and make all these drinks. Nor should she be *expected* to.'

A murmur of agreement rippled through the café from the other customers, igniting a flicker of hope within me.

'But—'

'She's already offered to remake your drink for you,' the man interrupted smoothly. 'Which, given that she's done *nothing* wrong in the first place, is actually pretty *impressive* customer service. So maybe...' He tilted his head slightly, his voice still light but firm. 'You could try thanking her instead of berating her and causing a scene?'

The café was silent.

The customer's lips parted, and I braced myself, waiting for his next outburst. But there was just silence.

His shoulders stiffened slightly as his lips tightened into a thin line. He let out a sharp exhale. 'Fine,' he muttered. 'Just... make it to go.' The demand had lost its edge.

'Thanks,' he added, in a quiet mumble.

I blinked, caught off guard by the sudden change.

He took a few steps away from the counter, pulled out his phone, and locked his gaze on the screen as though nothing had happened.

Conversations around me seemed to resume simultaneously, and the low hum of the café felt almost deafeningly loud by comparison.

I took a deep breath and set the cappuccino down on the counter, my fingers still trembling slightly.

I glanced at the man in front of the counter. 'Thank you,' I murmured, the two words feeling insufficient to fully express my gratitude.

He flashed a warm, easy smile. 'No problem,' he said with a casual shrug, as though going head to head with an angry customer was just another part of his day.

Then, as he picked up his cappuccino, he met my gaze and added, 'And thanks for this.'

Before I could respond, he turned and carried it to an empty corner table.

I mustered a smile as I glanced at the next customer in line. 'I'll be right with you,' I assured them, before turning back to the coffee machine to start on remaking the drink.

'Flat white,' I called out as I set the piping-hot drink down on the counter, pressing a lid onto the takeaway cup.

The angry customer stepped forward, grabbed his drink without a word, and gave me a sharp, short nod of acknowledgement.

An uneasy truce.

I exhaled as he walked away, my gaze flickering – just for a second – towards the corner table.

The cappuccino guy's laptop was open in front of him, but he wasn't looking at it.

He was watching me.

No, he was watching the angry customer, to make sure his intervention wasn't needed again.

'What can I get for you?' I asked the next customer as I tried to shake off the strange sensation that settled in my chest – a mixture of gratitude and indignance.

'Americano, black.'

I tapped the order into the till, before turning back to the coffee machine, my hands moving through the motions on autopilot.

On one hand, it was nice having someone in my corner, someone willing to back me up when a customer crossed the line. That wasn't something I was used to.

But at the same time, I'd handled difficult customers before. I *could* have handled this one. His interference, however well intentioned, made it seem like he thought I *needed* rescuing.

And maybe that was what unsettled me the most. Because I knew better than to rely on anyone but myself. At the end of the day, there was only one person I could count on.

Me.

I set the Americano down on the counter, forcing a small, polite smile as I called out, 'Americano, black.' The customer stepped forward to grab it, and I turned back to start the next order.

But before I did, I stole a glance towards the corner table.

The cappuccino guy had turned his attention to his laptop, seemingly absorbed in whatever was on the screen.

And a puzzling wave of disappointment washed over me.

3

NOW

December

My stomach twisted as an overwhelming sense of confusion closed in around me.

'Please don't be broken,' I murmured as I rushed towards the wall, my gaze dropping to the floor.

I braced myself, expecting to find shattered glass and a cracked frame. An inescapable sign of the fear I couldn't bring myself to face – that something between us might have fractured.

That Callum might not be coming back.

But the carpet was bare.

The frame hadn't been damaged. The photo, just like everything else, was gone.

Despite my plea for it not to be broken, disappointment engulfed me. Somehow missing felt even worse.

Then again, maybe it *had* broken. Maybe that was what Callum meant. He was going to fix the frame. That's why it was gone. Except, why would he take everything else?

I promise, I'm going to fix it.

Callum's message repeated in my head. Silent, but deafening.

Fix what? The question circled again. Everything with Callum and me was good. Nothing needed fixing.

A cold chill tickled my skin as that thought jarred against something inside me.

Was it entirely true?

I took a shaky breath. The room suddenly felt empty and cold. Every sign of Callum's existence had disappeared, as though he had never been here.

I staggered backward and collapsed onto the edge of the bed, my gaze locked on the empty nail. My breathing was fast and short. I blinked once. Twice. But nothing changed. The wardrobe was still half empty. The framed picture of us was still gone. *Callum* was still gone.

And yet, none of it seemed real. The Callum I knew wouldn't do this. He wouldn't just pack up and leave. Not like this. Not without telling me why.

My stomach lurched. Unless he thought I already knew why...

I swallowed hard, forcing that thought down. That couldn't be it. Things between us were good.

But if that was true, then...

'Callum, where are you?' I called out, my voice shaky and taut with desperation.

I knew there wouldn't be an answer, but I couldn't stop myself from hoping. I strained my ears, longing for the familiar creak of the floorboards under his weight. For his hurried footsteps rushing towards me, his arms ready to pull me into a hug the moment he saw me.

Coming home had always been comforting after a gruelling day at the café. But these days it wasn't the solitude I looked forward to, it was Callum's presence. There was finally someone other than Alexa to hear me announce I was home. Someone who actually cared about my arrival, and was just as happy to see me as I was to see him.

Until today.

Now the silence of the empty flat felt even more claustrophobic than it ever had before. Callum's presence had disrupted everything, but it had also revived me. After a twelve-hour shift, Callum's beaming smile and the feel of his arms around me had a way of making everything else fade.

Without him, everything felt heavier.

That's what love was. That safety. That sense of completeness. Of finally being whole.

In such a short space of time, Callum had become almost essential to my well-being. But that was normal in a relationship.

Wasn't it?

Maybe our relationship had moved faster than most. But it was right. We were right.

It wasn't as though I was obsessed.

Not this time.

I shook my head with small rapid movements as I tried to shake that thought away. I couldn't let myself go there. Especially not now. This was about Callum.

Not Daniel.

I forced myself back onto my feet. I couldn't just sit here in defeat. I had to keep looking. There had to be something here. Something I'd missed.

I hurried to the bathroom. But the second I swung the door open, my breath caught in my chest. The cluttered shelf above the sink, once a source of frustration due to his disorganised sprawl of toiletries, was empty aside from my abandoned toothbrush. His razor, toothbrush, deodorant, cologne, and comb were gone.

I hurried across the hallway to the second bedroom that had become his makeshift office. I hesitated for a moment, steadying myself against the door frame, before I pushed the door open.

The small desk was completely empty, the chair slightly askew, the faint scent of his cologne still lingering in the air. It felt as though he could be back at any moment. The only thing missing was his laptop. All of his work was done from there. He didn't have files or notebooks.

'I'm a digital guy.' The memory of Callum's voice, full of amusement, taunted me. Another reminder of our differences.

I turned abruptly, desperately needing to escape the space that felt like him. But I froze as something caught my attention out of the corner of my eye. I pivoted back, my gaze shifting to the plug socket beside the desk. A black cable snaked across the floor from the socket. I crouched down and reached for it, my fingers gliding over the smooth thin phone cable.

Callum's phone cable.

The one he used for his cheap, basic phone that was so out of place against his expensive top-of-the-line laptop. It never seemed to quite fit with his digital guy persona who loved all the latest tech.

Did it?

I unplugged the cable and retreated back to the bedroom, my gaze still locked on the cable in my hands as though it held the answers.

I *needed* it to hold the answers.

I needed it to be a sign that he was coming back. That he hadn't really gone. But what did one tiny cable really prove?

It felt as insignificant as I did. I turned my head towards the half-empty wardrobe. All of his stuff was gone. I knew what that implied.

But I still wasn't ready to accept it. There would have been signs, surely. I would have known something was wrong. If he was unhappy.

I shuffled uncomfortably. What if there *had* been signs?

My instinct screamed at me to push that thought away. I couldn't afford to let it take hold. But this time my brain refused to comply. Like that morbid compulsion to keep watching the screen during the scariest parts of the films Callum liked, flashes of memories replayed in my head, and I couldn't turn away.

The questions I'd evaded. The last-minute absences. Cancelled plans.

The argument...

I swallowed. I'd told myself that things were fine. That *we* were fine. The brief silences. The times he turned away, unable to quite meet my eyes. The difference of opinions. They were normal. Just teething problems that every relationship had.

But what if they weren't?

What if I'd driven him away, like I had with Dad?

* * *

'Dad!' I called the second I stepped inside the flat. 'Dad!' Excitement bubbled inside me. He was going to be so happy.

Happy with me.

That thought ramped up my eagerness. It had been so long since he'd been happy about anything, especially anything I'd done, that the anticipation of his reaction sent a warm rush through my body as I clung tighter to the piece of paper in my hand.

The open-plan living room and kitchen was empty, so I veered towards the bedrooms. I reached my parents' door and tapped on the wood. 'Dad,' I called, bewildered that he hadn't answered by now. He hated it when I made too much noise and disturbed him. He'd be so mad at me for my behaviour now, but I knew it would only be temporary. Once he knew why I was excited, once he understood what I'd done, then he'd be excited too. More than that, though, he'd be proud of me.

I frowned as I stared at the closed door. 'Dad?' My voice wavered uncertainly. Why wasn't he replying?

I'd already been to the café downstairs, expecting to find him and Mum both there. But Mum was alone. She'd said he was in here, in the flat. So...

I rapped my knuckles against the door, louder this time. Still no answer. I reached for the door handle and turned it slowly. 'Dad?' I repeated as I pushed the door open a crack. I peeked inside, but the room was empty.

My shoulders slumped as my hand slipped from the door handle in disappointment. Clearly I was going to have to wait to tell him my news, but... I frowned as the door swung wide open, and I froze in the doorway.

The room was a mess. No, not just a mess. A disaster.

The wardrobe doors gaped open, a tangled heap of hangers strewn across the floor in front. I took a hesitant step inside, my gaze darting around the room. The drawers were all open, some barely hanging on to their runners. One had even been completely wrenched free and lay upturned on the bed.

Someone had broken in. Panic gripped my stomach. Someone had ransacked my parents' belongings searching for valuables. And yet...

Wouldn't Mum have heard a break-in from downstairs in the café?

I turned my head, surveying the living room behind me. Mum's laptop sat open on the coffee table and the TV still hung on the wall untouched. The door had been locked when I entered the flat. There was no sign of anyone breaking in. The only things that were missing were clothes.

I stepped forward into the bedroom, crouching beside a pile of discarded sweaters. My fingers trembled as I picked one up, then another...

They were Mum's.

I glanced up at clothes still hanging in the half-empty wardrobe.

They were all Mum's.

The only things missing were Dad's.

I clutched Mum's sweater to my chest, clinging to it as I realised, this wasn't a break-in.

Dad had left.

There was an unsettling sense of inevitability to it. It wasn't as though I'd *expected it exactly, but I wasn't really surprised either. I'd known he was unhappy here. Unhappy with this life. He resented it.*

Resented me.

I'd known it ever since we had arrived here. I knew that he blamed me for everything he'd lost. Everything I'd cost him.

If he could have waited a little bit longer, though, he'd have realised how hard I was trying to redeem myself. How hard I was trying to make him happy.

I stared at the slightly crumbled piece of paper in my hand.

A in English. A in Maths. And Bs for everything else.

I inhaled deeply. Perhaps it had been naïve to think my GCSE results could change anything. But this was what he'd always wanted for me. Good grades in subjects that mattered. Subjects that weren't music.

I had done what he'd wanted. I had listened. I had changed for him. I had worked for something sensible, something stable, something that could give me a future. If I could get a good job, then I could help my parents get back on their feet too.

It would take time, but it was a start...

My shoulders slumped. Except he would never know. He hadn't waited long enough to find out that I was trying to be the daughter he wanted.

And now, it didn't matter.

I gritted my teeth as disappointment twisted into a sharp, burning anger inside me. But who was I really angry at? Him, for leaving before I had the chance to redeem myself? Or me, for failing all over again?

* * *

I puffed out my cheeks, exhaling deeply as I tried to let go of the past. Dad's departure had made sense. I hadn't seen it coming, but with hindsight I knew I should have. His discontentment had been practically tangible.

But with Callum it was different. Things might not have been perfect, but we were happy.

It wasn't as though he'd just flung a few things in a bag and disappeared, needing some space. He had taken everything.

Who did that?

It wasn't normal.

Except...

I swallowed. In my world, maybe it was.

Once was unusual, but twice felt like something else.

And the common denominator was me.

Callum's voice replayed in my mind, clear and certain: *'I love you. You know that, don't you?'*

I did know it. Even now, confronted with his absence, I still knew it. I nodded, silently agreeing with myself, reinforcing my conviction.

I looked back at the wall.

The empty nail. The missing photo.

He'd taken it.

Our photo.

If he'd left because he wanted out of our relationship, wanted to get away from me, then why take the photo of us?

Dad hadn't. He'd taken everything practical or valuable. But he'd left anything that didn't have a purpose. Photo albums. Scrapbooks. Mementoes of my childhood. All abandoned, as though he didn't have space for them in his new life.

But Callum? He'd taken something sentimental. Personal.

Why would he want that reminder unless our relationship still mattered to him? Unless *I* still mattered?

People didn't take mementoes if they were trying to forget. They took them to remember.

I nodded to myself again, that realisation strengthening my certainty. Callum would never just leave me. Not like this. Not without telling me. He wouldn't just disappear. Especially given he knew it was what Dad had done and how much it had hurt me.

But then, where was he?

My phone lay discarded on the floor where I'd dropped it. With a sudden surge of resolve, I lunged forward and snatched it up. I'd try calling him again. Maybe there was a fault last time. Maybe the line hadn't connected properly. Maybe I'd dialled wrong.

Christchurch didn't have the best 4G signal. Maybe the WhatsApp message hadn't even gone through. Maybe none of it meant what I thought it did.

I was grasping at desperate hope. I knew it, but it was all I had.

I carefully selected Callum's name, biting the tip of my tongue as I double-checked to make sure I had it right this time.

My stomach plummeted as the automated message played again.

'The number you have called is not in service.'

Even though I'd expected it this time, it still crushed me.

I hung up, unable to listen a second longer. I didn't need it to tell me what I already knew.

Callum was gone.

I scrolled down through the contact list and stopped at Lucy's name. She was the one person left in my life I could still call. The only one who'd never left.

She'd befriended me when I first arrived in Christchurch at fourteen and had stuck by me all these years. Though I still couldn't fathom why. Maddie too, though I suspected her presence was more because of Lucy than me. I still couldn't help but wonder if she resented my arrival intruding on their friendship. Not that she'd ever say it. Maddie might be blunt, but she wasn't cruel.

Knowing Lucy, she would drop everything and dash round, pull me in a big bear hug, assure me I could get through this and promise to help me figure it all out.

But I couldn't do it.

'Don't confide in anyone. Problems should always be kept private. Never expose your weaknesses. Your failings. It'll only lead to more heartache.' Mum's voice echoed in my head.

She'd been right. People could be judgemental. They used your mistakes as a reason to turn on you. Or worse, to walk away.

Mum's words kept me safe.

I couldn't trust anyone.

Not even my only friend.

4
THEN

September

'Can I get you another cappuccino?' I asked the guy seated at the corner table. I didn't usually ask; if customers wanted another drink they ordered it at the counter. But after his intervention earlier, I felt like it was the least I could do. Besides, there was something about him, a kind of air of sadness, that made me feel like he needed someone to talk to. Even if it was only to bring him a second cup of coffee.

'Erm...' He blinked, his gaze shifting from his laptop screen to me. He'd been staring at it blankly for a while, his fingers poised above the keyboard, unmoving.

'Sorry, I didn't mean to startle you,' I said.

Never interrupt the customers. Mum's voice scolded in my head.

I shouldn't have intruded. It was Mum's rule, one of many.

The guy shifted. 'No, it's fine.' He laughed awkwardly. 'I guess I was just lost in my thoughts.'

I nodded. 'I get it.'

He tipped his head to the side. 'Yeah, I guess you do.'

I shifted. It wasn't *what* he said. It was *how* he said it. Soft. Knowing.

Too knowing.

I kept my face neutral, but my pulse quickened. What did he mean by that? He didn't know me. He couldn't. No one in Christchurch did.

I'd made sure of that.

I'd worked hard to blend in, to belong here, in this town, in this café. Or at least to look like I did.

I kept my hands steady, gripping the edge of the tray, but my mind raced through the possibilities. Had I said something? *Done* something to make him suspicious?

No. That was ridiculous. He was a stranger. Just a customer. He had no reason to—

'I mean, now that it's quiet like this' – he signalled the otherwise empty café – 'you must get kind of lonely. In moments like this you probably have a lot of time to think.'

I let out a slow breath, relief flooding in. Even after eight years, the fear still lingered, tight and unshakable. One wrong word, one careless glance, and everything I'd built could unravel.

I didn't have much now. The café, which I resented. A couple of friends who barely knew me. But the thought of losing them, of starting again, was terrifying.

And this time I wouldn't even have Mum to stand by me.

I'd be completely alone.

I forced a small, uneasy laugh. 'Yeah, I guess I do.' But the tension in my chest didn't fully fade. 'The quiet does give you a lot of time for thinking about...' My words trailed away as memories surged through my mind, like sand swirling across the beach in the wind.

* * *

The familiar scent of vanilla hung in the air. The delicate fragrance of a scented candle, barely flickering on top of the piano.

But beneath it was something sharper. Stronger. The unmistakable stench of fuel. Thick and clinging.

For a split second, the two scents merged, intertwining in the stagnant air, a contradiction of comfort and destruction.

Then—

Whoosh.

The fire ignited.

My heart pounded as I watched it, mesmerised by the speed at which it engulfed the piano and swept across the room.

It was so fast. Too fast.

I should have moved. I should have run.

But for a single, terrifying heartbeat, I didn't.

* * *

'About?' His voice snapped me back to the present.

I blinked, disoriented for a second before realising he was staring at me, curiosity arching his eyebrows.

I shook my head, trying to shake myself free from the past that refused to let go. 'Just stuff,' I replied, injecting a forced lightness into my tone.

But it wasn't 'just stuff', and his curious, disbelieving expression told me he knew it too.

I needed to change the subject. To put distance between me and the past.

'So, what brings you here?' I asked, my voice a fraction too bright.

I knew why I was in a practically empty café with only my thoughts for company. But he was different. He could leave.

'Erm...' His gaze shifted towards the door.

'Are you waiting for someone?' I asked.

He chuckled as he glanced at his watch. 'After two hours I think it's safe to say I've been stood up.'

'Ouch,' I winced. 'Sorry.'

'It's fine. It was a blind date, so you know' – he shrugged – 'it's always a risk.'

I frowned as I studied him. 'Then why agree to it?'

I could imagine Mum's reaction if she could see me now. Interrupting the customers was disapproved of, so quizzing them on their life choices would be unforgivable.

'You've gotta take a few risks in life to get what you want.'

He sounded so certain. As though it was obvious. Clearly, he didn't understand what going after what you wanted could cost.

'Otherwise, you'll end up stuck,' he added.

I flinched as his words dug into me, like hundreds of tiny needles piercing my skin.

Stuck.

That one word felt like it summed up my entire existence. My job. My home. My life. It had all been defined for me.

I hadn't thought about what I wanted in so long.

I couldn't.

Chasing after what I wanted was what had got me in trouble before. It had destroyed everything. *I'd* destroyed everything.

And yet, if Mum's rules were meant to keep me safe, why did I feel like I was suffocating?

'Are you okay?' Concern radiated from him.

'Yes,' I replied, feigning surprise as to why he would ask. Yet I could see my reaction had betrayed me.

'You need to toughen up, Olivia.' Dad's voice reprimanded in my head. *'You let your feelings show on your face.'*

He was right. But there had been a time when that had been a strength, not a weakness.

'I guess I'm just not much of risk-taker.' I smiled ruefully. 'Not any more.'

I used to take chances. I used to believe the risks were worth it. The end goal was all that mattered. All I could see.

And I'd been blindsided as a result.

I couldn't go through that again.

I could sense his curiosity grow as his lips parted.

'Well, I should get you that cappuccino,' I said quickly, before he could speak, vaguely aware that he hadn't actually asked for another.

But I needed to get away from the direction the conversation had taken. I didn't want to talk about the risks I'd taken before. Or the reason I no longer took them.

5

NOW

December

I walked to the living room, my body drained of energy, yet something inside me kept me moving. I knew if I sat and did nothing, despair would take over and I would give up.

I'd been there before. It was a path I couldn't let myself go down again.

At least not yet. Not while there was still hope.

I paused. Was there still hope?

My gaze drifted around the open-plan living room. Modern and minimalist, it was designed for simplicity rather than comfort. It had never bothered me before, but right now, it felt cold. Impersonal.

There was nothing here that reminded me of Callum. Barely anything that even reminded me of myself. Not the real me. My life and my home both lacked personal touches. The things that most people took for granted.

Was that the problem? Had Callum felt as disconnected and irrelevant here as I had?

I should have made him feel more welcome. The flat wasn't just somewhere for him to stay any more, it was his home. *Our* home. So why hadn't I made it that way?

Resentment bubbled inside me as I realised I knew why. It was the way Mum had made it.

Anything that wasn't critical to our new life had been sold or left behind in Portsmouth. Anything personal. Anything *me*.

'It's exciting,' Mum had assured me. '*A chance to leave the past behind and make a fresh start.*'

Her enthusiasm had sounded forced and fake. A fresh start held no appeal, not even to her. She wanted the same thing as Dad and me; not to move forward, but to go back. Back to the lives we'd had before that one moment had changed everything.

If we could have done that then Dad would never have left. She knew it and so did I. Even if neither of us said it.

* * *

'He'll be back,' Mum said firmly as we stood side by side in the middle of their bedroom, surveying the emptiness.

'He took everything,' I pointed out flatly. I'd sat on the floor and sobbed alone before she'd arrived home.

I had no more tears left in me now. I felt deflated and detached, as though I'd stepped out of my body and was simply observing the fallout. Incapable of anything more.

'Not everything,' Mum said as she walked to the dresser and picked up a silver photo frame. 'He took his clothes. Things he needs for now.' A weak smile formed on her lips as she stared at the photo in her hands. Their wedding photo. Her fingers traced the outline of his face. A face that was younger and unburdened by stress and financial worries. 'He left the things that matter.'

My throat tightened, and I struggled to swallow. To breathe.

Witnessing her quiet denial was worse than if she had broken down in tears. I could have handled tears. I knew what to do with them. A hug. A cup of tea. Anything to provide the tiniest sliver of reassurance that she wasn't alone.

It wouldn't solve anything. It never did. But it was what I'd needed, what I'd craved, for months. Yet she hadn't been able to provide that for me.

I understood why. Sympathy and comfort weren't compatible with blame and resentment.

* * *

I'd known she was wrong; that Dad wouldn't be back. I'd felt it with such certainty that to me there had never been any doubt.

But Callum...

I ran a hand through my hair, curling the ends like I had done as a child when I was nervous before a performance. It was a habit I'd grown out of a long time ago, but right now the familiarity of it was comforting.

The rhythmic pattern of my twirling seemed to slow my racing thoughts. I had to be logical. If Callum's phone wasn't working, there must be another way to contact him.

He had no friends here. At least, none he'd mentioned to me. His family had cut him off completely and the one chance he'd had of reconciling with them I'd ruined. I'd thought I'd been protecting him. But now, I wished I had a way to reach them. At least I could check if they'd seen or heard from him.

Surely if they knew their son was missing, they would help?

Wouldn't they?

I nibbled my lip as doubt seeped into my thoughts. I knew sometimes you couldn't count even on family to come through for you. Sometimes the people who were supposed to love you walked away when you needed them the most.

The only person Callum had was me.

I couldn't let him down too.

I lifted my phone and opened Instagram. For the first time, I cursed myself for my lack of interest in social media. I'd set up a profile for the café years ago, but I barely used it. Just the occasional post about opening hours, special offers, and my half-hearted attempts at marketing. If I'd been more active, maybe I would have thought to connect with Callum. But I hadn't.

Lucy and Maddie always teased me about my lack of online presence, but I preferred it that way. At one point I'd craved the spotlight. But being publicly praised for your successes was different to being judged for your perceived failings. Having your life dissected by strangers made you value privacy. Besides, there weren't that many people in my life to keep track of. If someone wanted to reach me, they'd text, call or stop by the café. I didn't need to stalk them on social media to feel connected.

There was another reason I avoided it, though, I remembered as I scrolled through the random assortment of posts. I avoided the trap of comparison. I didn't need another reminder of what my life lacked.

I already knew.

I forced myself to focus on the task at hand and typed *Callum Hayes* into the search box. A list of Callums appeared, but none of them looked like my Callum. I shook my head. Maybe I was approaching this in the wrong way. There was no guarantee that Callum was even on Instagram.

I switched to Google instead, retyping his name, and this time adding *Portsmouth* to the end. As much as I hated to admit it, Callum's life was mostly there. The only thing he had in Christchurch was me.

I stared at the letters on the screen, my fingers hovering over the enter key. But it blurred before me until it wasn't his name I saw.

It was mine.

6

THEN

September

The clock above the counter ticked loudly in the silence: 4:45 p.m.

Close enough.

I sighed softly and ducked into the kitchen, filling a bucket with hot water and disinfectant, grateful for something productive to do.

Hoisting the bucket out of the sink, I grabbed the mop and carried it back to the café.

'Closing time?'

The voice from the corner made me pause mid-step.

I glanced his way. 'At five.'

He nodded and scraped his chair back as he stood.

'You don't have to rush off,' I assured him. 'You still have ten minutes or so yet.' I hated it when the café was empty. Not that I particularly liked it when it was busy either. I wasn't really a people person. A clear sign that I was in the wrong profession. But for some reason, when the customers left, I actually found myself missing them.

Not them exactly. Their presence. The quiet reassurance that I wasn't completely isolated. That I wasn't alone.

When they left, it wasn't the emptiness that bothered me. It was a reminder that people didn't stay.

'No worries,' he said as he picked up his empty cup and placed it on the counter. 'Thanks for the coffees.'

I smiled at the thoughtful gesture. 'Thank *you*,' I replied. 'And thanks again for your help earlier.'

He waved my gratitude away with a dismissive flick of his hand. 'I didn't do much. Besides, I'm pretty sure you'd have handled that guy without my intervention.'

I blinked. My earlier indignance that he'd thought I needed rescuing melted away.

He hadn't thought that at all. He'd seen me as capable.

'Probably,' I replied, a small smile tugging at the corner of my lips. 'But it was nice not to have to,' I admitted quietly.

I set the mop and bucket down, expecting him to leave and allow me to get on with cleaning. But he lingered, as though he wanted to say more.

'It must get really frustrating dealing with customers like that all the time,' he said finally.

I shrugged. 'Thankfully, it's not all the time. Most people are pretty friendly.'

'Hmm,' he murmured. 'That's good.'

I cast a sideways glance at him. Was there a touch of disappointment to his tone? I shook my head. I was being ridiculous. It wasn't as though he'd want me to have to deal with difficult customers.

'But still...' he added, looking thoughtful. 'It must put a real damper on your day, when someone berates you over a cup of coffee.'

I paused. He seemed really fixated on the difficulties of customer service, as though my feelings mattered. I smiled again. I liked that. Even if it was just a fleeting conversation about work, somebody cared about my well-being.

At least about this.

'I've survived worse than someone yelling about the temperature of their coffee,' I assured him with a heavy shrug.

His eyebrows lifted slightly, like he wanted to ask what. But that was a conversation I wasn't willing to have.

I cleared my throat and turned away. 'Have a good evening,' I said as I lifted a chair and placed it upside down on the table in front of me.

Soft scraping behind me caused me to turn back. I'd expected to hear the bell chime above the door as he left, but instead...

'What are you doing?'

He froze with an upturned chair in his hands. 'Helping.'

I blinked. In the eight years Mum had owned the café, a customer had never offered to help close up before.

'Why?' The word slipped out before I could stop myself. I cursed my bluntness. He was doing something nice and instead of being appreciative, I was questioning him.

But I couldn't help it. I was alone in an empty café with a guy I didn't know. And he didn't seem to have any desire to leave...

I swallowed, resisting the urge to take a step back. I couldn't let him see any signs of unease. Of weakness.

And yet, the undercurrent of fear that had taken hold didn't shift.

'I'm not sure.' He placed the chair on the table, hesitating. 'I guess I figured I owed you after taking up a table all afternoon.'

'That's what cafés are for,' I said, the crease in my brow betraying my confusion.

He chuckled, a soft sound that seemed to fill the empty café. 'True. But it doesn't feel right leaving you to handle all this on your own.'

I tensed. But this time it wasn't fear. It was indignation. Had his offer been made out of pity?

'I always have to do it alone now,' I replied tersely. But the truth of my words was like a weight in my chest.

I'd been closing up the café alone for six months and yet I'd felt alone a lot longer than that.

'You don't have to. Not today. And to be honest' – he lowered his gaze to the floor – 'it feels good to actually do something useful.'

The resistance that had been rising within me faltered as the confidence he'd displayed earlier slipped. For all his talk of risk-taking, in that moment he seemed as lost and anxious as I felt.

He looked up at me hesitantly. 'So, is it okay if I help?'

I tipped my head to the side as I assessed him. Maybe his eagerness to help wasn't out of pity. But even so, letting someone help me felt strange. I'd learnt a long time ago that it's not what people did.

'What would my mum say about me putting her customers to work?'

I inhaled sharply as I heard my own words. They weren't her customers. Not any more. They were mine.

'Erm...' He looked at me nervously. Perhaps he envisaged Mum marching in and scolding him for his interference.

I smiled slightly at that thought. I wished she could. Not just because it would mean she was still here, but also because I was curious. How would he have reacted? Would he have stood his ground?

I never did. Not any more.

But then again...

'Actually,' I said, my smile widening, 'I would love some help, thank you.'

I felt a surge of triumphant energy surge through me, as though accepting his help had been some sort of victory. Maybe it was. For the first time in a long time, I'd made a decision for myself.

One Mum would disapprove of.

He nodded and hurriedly resumed putting the chairs on the table as though he was afraid I'd change my mind.

'Hey, you don't have to do them all,' I teased as he moved on to the next table. 'Leave some for me.'

He laughed. 'I'm committed now,' he said, flashing me a grin. 'Besides, I figure this counts as a workout and since I haven't joined a gym here yet, I'll take it.'

'Well, in that case, I won't deprive you of your workout,' I said, holding up my hands as I stepped back from the chairs. 'I'll start mopping the floor while you deal with the chairs.'

He nodded again and we fell into a companionable rhythm of the soft scrape of chairs and the gentle swish of the mop.

'Are you new to Christchurch, then?' I asked, my curiosity piqued.

'Yeah.' He nodded. 'I arrived a couple of days ago from Portsmouth.'

Portsmouth.

My stomach tightened as that word ricocheted through me. It was crazy to blame an entire city for the issues in my life. But the two had become so entwined. After all, wasn't that the reason we'd left, because that city, those people, would never have allowed me to forget?

'So, uh' – I cleared my throat – 'what brings you to Christchurch?'

He shrugged. 'A job opportunity.' There was a heaviness to his tone, which jarred against his casual movement.

I frowned. 'You don't seem very enthusiastic about it.'

'No, I am,' he assured me a little bit too quickly. He scrunched his nose. 'It's just it's kind of my last chance.'

'What do you mean?' I was too invested now to even pretend to care about Mum's rules.

He leaned against the back of a chair. 'I lost my job back home.'

'Oh.' I cursed my prying. 'I'm sorry.'

'It was my own fault. I—' He let out a weary sigh. 'Well, let's just say I made a stupid mistake. One I should have known better than to make.'

'Ah,' I murmured, not trusting myself to say more. I knew all about costly mistakes. And I also knew how it felt to be quizzed for details.

'This opportunity is kind of a long shot to prove I'm still capable.'

There was a desperation to his words. He needed this to work out. To redeem himself. I glanced around the café. Maybe he'd have better luck than I had.

I gave myself a little shake. I couldn't allow myself to go down that path. I couldn't allow his troubles to remind me of mine.

'I'm Olivia, by the way.'

'Cal-Callum,' he stuttered, no doubt caught off guard by my sudden shift in conversation.

I smiled. 'It's good to meet you, Callum.'

'You too, Olivia.'

Heat crept into my cheeks and I turned away from him, hoping he didn't notice my reaction to hearing him say my name.

I rolled my eyes. Just because he'd stayed to help didn't mean he liked me, and even if he did—

'What about you? Have you always lived here?'

'No,' I admitted without thinking. I was usually more careful. I'd allowed myself to be distracted. Complacent.

'Have you been here long?'

I swallowed. 'We moved here when I was a kid.' My grip tightened on the handle of the mop as I willed him not to ask where I'd moved from. I should have lied and let him think I was a local. At least then he wouldn't be able to find out what had happened.

'And the café?'

I let out a heavy breath. It wasn't the question I had feared, and yet it was still a painful one. 'It was Mum's.' I swallowed, focusing on the floor. 'We used to run it together, but' – I hesitated – 'she passed away a few months ago.'

'I'm sorry.'

I nodded, managing a tight smile in return. It was all I could do without falling apart.

'You must miss her.'

I froze, his statement piercing into my heart.

Did I?

The answer wasn't simple.

I'd missed her for a long time. Long before she died. I missed the mum she used to be. But then, she probably missed the daughter I used to be too.

'We were all each other had,' I said finally. It wasn't really an agreement, but it was the truth.

Living and working together day in and day out didn't mean we were close.

Not like we used to be. Before everything had changed. Before we'd had to abandon the lives we'd known, the lives we'd loved, and come here.

Mum had stuck by me, unlike Dad. But that didn't mean she'd ever forgiven me.

7

NOW

December

I squeezed my eyes shut, trying to block out the screen in front of me as bile rose in my throat. But the problem wasn't on the screen.

It was inside me.

The memories I'd fought to bury had broken loose. And now they were free, I couldn't hold them back.

I pressed my hand to my head as tears escaped from my closed eyes. Like the memories, persistent and unwelcome.

* * *

My chest tightened and my breath caught in my throat as I summoned the courage to hit enter. I'd searched for my name before. But usually, the nerves were edged with anticipation and accompanied by a silent prayer for a good review of my latest performance.

This time there was no excited anticipation. Only dread. For the first time I was hoping that my search would be empty. My desire for the spotlight, for success, for fame, had been overridden by a desperate need for anonymity.

Past performances filled the screen, and I finally breathed again. I hadn't been named. Not yet. I was too young. That's what Dad had said. The press couldn't release my name.

Social media, however, was another matter.

The kids knew my name. They whispered about me. They posted about me. They always had. But this was different. This was wider reaching. More scathing. It was no longer cruel teasing because I didn't fit in. It was a complete dissection of my character. My sanity.

Mum had made me close my accounts. She thought it was for the best. That it protected me from it.

But she couldn't protect me from my own curiosity.

I deleted the search criteria, and this time typed: fourteen-year-old pianist, fire, Portsmouth.

I stared at the first headline:

Child Prodigy or Problem Child?

It was the same paper that had run an article last month. They'd called me a prodigy then too.

I'd revelled in it. The sense of pride that word brought with it. It felt like validation that all the work, all the sacrifices, had been worth it.

Now, though, that same word had become a criticism. My success was tied to my downfall. The story had sparked endless debates:

Are Our Children Under Too Much Pressure Too Achieve?

Does Success Cause Instability, Or Does It Mask It?

I wasn't a prodigy any more. I was a statistic. A problem.

* * *

I snorted. I'd fought for so long and so hard for people to see my potential. And then, just when I was finally starting to get somewhere – recognition, prospects – everything unravelled.

People were quicker at labelling me as unstable and dangerous than they had been to call me talented. And even then, my success had come with caveats. Unspoken questions lingered beneath every compliment: How long will it last? How far can she really go? Who'll be the next rising star to surpass her?

But failure... It was endless.

It still came with questions, but a different kind. This time they wanted explanations. They wanted to know how to prevent their children from turning out like me.

Perhaps they were right to wonder.

I always did.

I closed my eyes for a moment, trying to collect myself, before I scanned the new list of Callums. Facebook profiles. Newspaper articles. Personal blogs. But they all had one thing in common: none of them were my Callum.

Adding 'marketing consultant' to the search box, I tried again. It didn't help.

I tried to shrug off the growing sense of failure, but it was unavoidable. I had run out of places to look. And the only thing I had gained from my search was the realisation that I barely knew him.

How much of Callum's life had I actually seen? No friends. No family. No social media. No trace of him online. He and I lived in a bubble. Our lives centred around the flat and the café. We only ventured beyond that for walks on the beach, day trips to the New Forest, or romantic dinners together.

It had never bothered me before. I had learned long ago to accept the confines of the safe little life Mum had created for me here. But why had Callum been so content to accept it too?

Shouldn't he have wanted more?

I'd tried to include him. To introduce him to my only two friends. But somehow it never happened. Something always came up.

A reason.

An excuse.

The correction stole the breath from my lungs. Had they been excuses? Had he simply not wanted to meet my friends yet?

Was that why he'd left? Had I pushed too hard? Pressured him for too much, too soon?

If I was honest, my desperation for him to meet Lucy, Maddie and their partners wasn't solely for Callum's benefit. It was for mine.

I wanted them to see us together. To see him with me. He was physical proof that someone had chosen me. Wanted me.

I was sure they only tolerated my presence because Lucy insisted. But I was always the odd one out. Always on the edge. Alone.

Callum would have changed that. His presence would have legitimised mine. Not just because I was finally part of a couple. But because they would like him. I knew they would.

And if they liked him, if they wanted him there, then by extension they'd have to want me there too. And maybe, just maybe, his likability would rub off on me.

Had Callum realised my motives? Had I made him feel used?

Questions stacked up one on top of another. Like a giant game of Jenga, one wrong move could bring everything crashing down.

All the odd little things that I'd dismissed as trivial started piling up. It wasn't just my friendships that raised questions. It was his too.

I knew why I hadn't met any of them. They were in Portsmouth, we were here. But I'd never seen him speak to them either. No video calls. No phone calls. The only text messages he ever received were from work.

How could I of all people possibly have more friends than he did?

Work.

The thought burrowed into my brain. Another anomaly. He worked mostly remotely. I loved that; it meant we spent more time together. But why move to Christchurch at all if he could work from anywhere?

Even on the rare days he said he was going to a meeting, he never talked about it afterward. He didn't talk about his office. I didn't even know where it was. Did he have his own desk? A hot desk? A corner office?

I didn't know.

I didn't even know who he sat next to. I didn't know a single name.

How was that possible?

My heart hammered as my thoughts raced. I knew the café's delivery drivers. The ladies at the hair salon across the street. The guy at the corner shop. We weren't close, but I knew the basics: birthdays, holidays, family dramas.

Callum must have known that kind of stuff about his colleagues too. Surely he'd have talked to me about them. Surely I'd have asked?

Hadn't I?

I blinked rapidly, trying to catch hold of a single thread of something. Anything. A trivial detail from his day. His job. His life.

I shared stories with him all the time about customers, strange orders, leaky taps. The little things that made up my day.

But I couldn't think of a single story from Callum's world.

What else hadn't he told me? What else hadn't I asked?

My stomach sank as the undeniable truth hit me. There was a lot I didn't ask. Not because I didn't care. Not because I didn't want to know.

But because there were things I didn't want *him* to ask *me*.

8

THEN

September

I leaned back against the counter, grateful for a rare moment to catch my breath. Autumn always brought a lull in trade as the tourists vanished, but the lunch rush was still relentless. It had been manageable when there were two of us, but now it was just me.

The café looked disorganised and messy. Crumbs and coffee stains marked nearly every surface, and a few tables still held abandoned plates and cups cluttering them.

For a split second, I could see Mum standing by the counter, hands on hips, shaking her head. Disappointment radiating from every pore. I blinked and her image disappeared, but the weight of her disappointment hung in the air.

With a weary sigh, I picked up a tray and started collecting everything.

'Bye,' I called as a couple of regulars tugged their coats on and headed towards the door with a wave. I wiped my forehead with the back of my hand and lifted the now rather heavy tray.

'Need a hand?'

The familiar voice made me spin around, a wide grin spreading across my face. He'd come back.

'Hi,' Callum said as he stood by the door, his hands shoved deep into his pockets.

'Hi,' I replied, aware that I was still grinning at him like an idiot. Did his offer of help mean he hadn't just come back for the coffee? After all, he could have gone to any café for that.

But he was here.

Did that mean—?

I swallowed, suddenly feeling a strange, restless energy fluttering in my stomach. Could he have come back because of me?

I forced my voice to stay light and playful. 'How good are you at clearing tables?'

Callum's shoulders seemed to relax and he smiled back at me. 'Let's find out,' he said, reaching out to take the tray from me. 'Put me to work, boss.'

Boss.

The word caught me off guard. I'd never been the boss of anything, especially not the café. Even now, with Mum gone, it still felt like hers. The café ran exactly as it always had. Nothing had changed except for the lack of her presence.

Though... I glanced over my shoulder towards the counter. Sometimes even that felt questionable.

'Olivia?'

I gave myself a quick shake as Callum's voice pulled me from my melancholy.

'Right,' I said, pretending not to notice the flash of concern in his eyes as he studied me. 'Let me show you where to put those.'

I led him to the kitchen, grateful he couldn't see my smile as he followed behind me. I might have pretended otherwise, but the fact was I had noticed his concern.

Noticed it and liked it.

* * *

I wiped the already spotless counter for the third time, my gaze locked on Callum as he sat at the corner table. I'd expected him to leave after we'd finished clearing up after the lunch rush. But instead, he'd returned to his spot in the corner.

His spot.

I smiled. I liked the sound of that. It felt like he belonged here.

I surveyed the quiet café, illuminated in a golden glow from the soft lighting as darkness set in outside. In the eight years I had worked here, I'd never had a favourite spot, a place that felt like mine, like I belonged.

'Shall we get started?' Callum asked, abandoning his corner and heading towards me.

I stared at him blankly. 'Started?'

'Closing up,' he said, jerking his head towards the clock above the counter.

'Wow, it's four forty-five already?' I asked, staring at the clock in disbelief. An afternoon had never gone so fast. Usually, time dragged after lunch. But today... I turned back to Callum. Somehow, it hadn't.

We fell into a familiar rhythm as Callum started moving the chairs while I mopped the floor. There was something almost rhythmic about working with him, like a well-choreographed dance.

'How's the new job going?' I asked.

For a second, a shadow seemed to flicker across Callum's face, his expression unreadable. Then he shrugged.

'It's okay.'

I arched an eyebrow. 'That didn't sound very convincing.' I swallowed as I realised I was hardly in a position to judge someone else's lack of enthusiasm for their job.

'At least I get to work remotely a fair bit,' he said with a coy smile.

Ah, so that explained how he could be spending so much time in the café. I'd wondered what he was working on so intently on his laptop in the corner.

'What do you do?' I asked, intrigued.

'I'm a, er, marketing consultant,' he replied, his words slightly hesitant.

'You don't sound very sure about that.'

'Ah...' Callum scrunched his nose up. 'To be honest, I guess that all depends on how well this new job goes. I'm kind of out on a limb here trying to earn back my reputation.'

'Because of your mistake?' I asked, intrigued.

Callum nodded. 'I trusted someone I shouldn't have,' he admitted, his expression contorting, as if the words tasted bitter. 'Rob,' he added after a beat. 'My best mate.'

'Oh.' The word felt small, inadequate.

I knew how it felt to be let down by someone you trusted. Someone who was supposed to be on your side.

Instead, they'd turned away. Or more accurately, they turned against you.

It had taught me one thing: you couldn't even trust the people closest to you. A chill prickled my skin. There was something so destabilising about knowing that.

I'd always believed that knowledge was strength. As long as you knew the truth of what you were up against, you could overcome it. But this kind of knowledge was different. It didn't strengthen you. It left you hollow.

And for all their ignorance, I couldn't help but think, those who hadn't learned this truth were better off.

I swallowed, gripping the mop handle a little tighter. It had been years, but the sting of betrayal never really faded. I focused on the steady rhythmic motion of my hands as I swiped the mop back and forth, grounding myself in the task. *It's in the past*, I reminded myself. But the wounds still felt fresh and raw.

'That must have been hard,' I said, my voice quieter now, the words carrying more weight than I'd intended. Because I wasn't just talking about him any more.

Daniel.

The name ricocheted through my brain. Unwanted. Unshakable.

Callum exhaled. 'We'd known each other since we were kids,' he continued. 'Went to the same uni and stayed close even after that. He's pretty much known me my whole life.'

I tipped my head to the side, trying to imagine what that felt like. To have someone who'd been through everything with you, who knew you that well, and still stayed. That was more than my own father had done for me.

'I trusted him,' Callum said. 'We'd always had each other's backs. But then he sent me an email saying he'd uncovered major corruption in the marketing consultancy where *we* worked.'

I frowned slightly. Was it my imagination, or had there been a slight shift in his tone as he said 'we'?

'It was really detailed,' he continued smoothly, 'outlining how the firm was falsifying product details to create misleading advertising campaigns.'

Callum ran his hand through his hair. 'The data he provided was from a project he was leading on. He was terrified that if the campaign went live, he'd be incriminated. I believed him. Of course I did. It was Rob. He begged me for help, so I ran with it. I made accusations. I tried to bring it all down.'

'Without double-checking his claims?'

'Yeah.' Callum shook his head. 'Stupid, right? But I trusted him. And I really believed I was doing the right thing. That I was, I don't know, making a difference. But it was all a lie. Every word of it. And the second I acted on it, everything fell apart.'

My stomach lurched. The bitter taste of betrayal, familiar and nauseating. Yet I edged forwards, completely absorbed. 'What happened?'

'I lost my job of course, but I made enemies of some pretty powerful people. They made sure no one else would hire me.' Callum snorted. 'I'd tried to bring them down and destroy their reputation, but they ended up obliterating mine.'

I drew back. His words pierced so deep, it felt like they'd hit bone.

Fighting to keep my composure, I swallowed. 'Do you think Rob knew that he was wrong? Did he mislead you on purpose?'

'He must have done. There's no way he could have made a mistake like that. He *wanted* me to go after the firm, to ruin my reputation, my career.'

'Why?'

Callum shook his head sadly. 'That's the part I haven't been able to figure out. I mean, what did he gain? If I'd revealed him as my source, I could have ruined his career too.'

'But you didn't.'

'What for?' Callum asked. 'It wouldn't have changed anything for me.'

'You could have at least taken him down with you. Don't you think he'd have done the same if your roles were reversed?'

'Probably. But that's the thing. Our roles would never have been reversed. I would never have done what he did.' He exhaled. 'Besides, Rob didn't get out of it unscathed. His girlfriend dumped him when she realised what he'd done.'

'Good for her.'

'Yeah. Ace turned out to be the only bright spot in all of it.'

'Ace?'

Callum chuckled. 'It's what Rob called her. They met at a poker night his mate was hosting. She crushed everyone. She's got this way of reading people. It's kinda unsettling sometimes, actually.' Callum gave a quick shake of his head. 'Anyway, the name stuck.'

'She sounds cool,' I said, feeling a twinge of jealousy at the way he spoke of her.

'Yeah, she is. She stood by me, helped me pick up the pieces. Hell, she's the reason I'm even down here. She was the one who got me this job. It was a bold move to take a chance on me like that, when we'd never really known each other that well. But it means starting at the bottom again and doing whatever it takes to get a shot at doing something worthwhile. Something right.'

I nodded. 'I get it.'

I did. I understood what it meant to work so hard for your dream. To have passion, drive and determination. To not allow anything to stand in your way.

I'd been like that too once. Part of me missed it. Missed who I'd been, what I'd accomplished, what I *could* have accomplished.

But I'd made the wrong decision. Trusted the wrong person. And I'd lost everything.

Just like Callum.

Perhaps that's what drew me to him.

Making friends wasn't something I did easily. Or well. I was pretty sure Maddie only stuck around because Lucy did. And Lucy was just too kind to walk away when it was so blatantly obvious I had no one else.

But even she would leave if she knew my past.

And so would Callum.

* * *

'We're not having this conversation again, Olivia.'

'But, Dad,' I protested, but he held his hands up.

'You're fourteen. You're too young to make a decision that will affect the rest of your life. You need to finish school, get your GCSEs, and then we'll talk about what you do next.'

'But I'll be so far behind then! The Royal School of Music Junior Academy accepts kids when they're twelve. I'm already two years behind. If I wait until I'm sixteen—'

'You'll have benefited from a normal childhood,' he interrupted.

'Maybe we should at least let her audition,' Mum said tentatively.

'And put her through all that stress?'

'She does exams and performances already. An audition isn't that much different.'

'Not that much different?' Dad repeated Mum's words slowly, his eyes wide. 'Of course it's different. She's been obsessed with getting into the Royal Academy of Music for years. Ever since that piano teacher put the idea in her head. She's built it up into *this lofty goal that everything depends on. Can you imagine the pressure she would put on herself if we actually agreed to let her apply? Do you really want her to go through that?'*

'I can do it.' I urged him to believe me. 'I can handle the pressure.'

'And what happens when she doesn't make it?' Dad continued, his attention locked on Mum as though he hadn't even heard me. 'She's fourteen. She's not old enough to deal with her dreams shattering around her.'

'She might make it.'

Dad didn't reply.

'She might,' Mum insisted. 'You've heard her play. She's incredible. Daniel believes in her. He sees her potential.'

'All Daniel Sinclair sees in her is himself,' Dad said bitterly. 'He's using our daughter to achieve his own dream – one he failed at himself. So now he's talked Olivia into believing it's what she wants.'

'Maybe it is.'

'She never talked about being a concert pianist until she started taking lessons with him. He filled her head with that idea. He's the one pushing her.'

'That's not true,' I interrupted. Resentment coursed through my veins. How could he stand in the way of my dreams like this? How could he just dismiss what I wanted? What I'd worked for? 'I've always wanted this, I just never thought I could actually—'

'She used to have friends,' Dad said, slicing through my objections. 'Do you remember that? Do you remember how different she was? How happy she was? How the sound of laughter filled this house? Now the only sound we ever hear is that piano. She's become obsessed with it. It's like she doesn't exist without it.'

'She's passionate,' Mum said, giving me a lopsided smile.

I stared at her, trying to decipher what it meant. It felt like a mixture of pride and pity, but that didn't make sense. Being passionate about something was a good thing, wasn't it? Why would she pity me for that?

'Maybe we should never have let her take lessons with Sinclair.'

'No!' I objected. How could he even say that? Lessons with Daniel were what kept me going. I counted the hours at school, knowing that I just had to make it to the final bell and then everything would be okay. He'd make it okay.

He saw me in a way no one else did. Not my parents. Nor my teachers. And certainly not the other kids. He actually listened, not just to my music, but to me.

If it wasn't for my lessons...

'Everyone says he's the best.'

'The best?' Dad scoffed. 'If he's the best, what's he doing teaching piano from his living room? Why isn't he out there playing at Carnegie Hall and all those other places he's filling Olivia's head with?'

* * *

I let out a weary sigh.

Callum was stronger than me. He had the courage to start again, even if that meant starting at the bottom.

Whereas I'd given up. Crawled into the shadows and hid behind a coffee machine.

The realisation made my stomach contract.

Thanks to him, I couldn't deny it any longer.

I'd avoided examining my own life too carefully, because I hadn't felt like I could change it. But Callum's determination stirred something within me. A discontentment that refused to be stifled and locked away any longer.

9

NOW

December

Frustrated, I tossed the phone onto the sofa beside me, glaring at it as though it were to blame. It wasn't just Callum's belongings that were missing, it was every trace of his life.

No colleagues. No friends. No social media. No trace of anyone who might know him – except me.

It didn't make sense. How could he have just vanished so completely? How could there be no trace of him online? The articles I'd found proved that *I* couldn't fully disappear, despite Mum's best efforts.

So how had Callum?

'It's kind of my last chance.' Callum's words from the day we met replayed in my mind.

He'd done the same thing I had. Fled a life that had turned on him. *People who had turned on him.*

I made enemies of some pretty powerful people.

What if... I swallowed, barely able to finish that thought. What if the past had caught up with him?

I shook my head. No, I was overreacting. He told me what had happened. He hadn't done anything wrong.

Then again, I'd said the same thing too.

I cracked my knuckles. The sound sharp in the silence, the sensation strangely satisfying, grounding me back in the present.

There had to be something I knew.

Wave Media.

The name sprang into my mind. It was the only name I knew. The only concrete detail he'd mentioned about work.

I tapped my fingers against my leg, playing an invisible keyboard. It had been years since I last touched a piano, yet my fingers still recalled the movement, the rhythm, the familiar sense of calm and control that came with it.

My instinct was to reach for the phone and look up Wave Media. But I hesitated. Everything was already starting to unravel. Did I want to keep digging?

Wasn't I proof that some things were best left alone?

If I carried on, what would I find? Something I didn't want to know?

What if *he* had dug into *my* past? What if he'd found the parts I'd omitted? Was that why he'd left?

And if it was, did I want to know?

I sucked in a deep breath and let it out slowly. What choice did I have? I either accepted Callum had gone, and learned to live without him, as I'd had to do without Dad...

Or I kept searching.

You've gotta take a few risks in life to get what you want.

I grabbed the phone and typed *Wave Media, Christchurch* into Google Maps. Nothing came up.

I tried Google instead. At least this time a website popped up, but the moment it loaded, unease sank to the pit of my stomach.

It was so basic. *Too* basic.

I frowned. Even my feeble attempts at managing the café's website put it to shame.

There was no logo. No testimonials. No 'meet the team' page? Just a couple of abstract photos of Christchurch and a vague blurb about 'innovative marketing solutions.'

That was it.

My stomach tightened, a slow, creeping dread uncurling within me. Something wasn't right. A marketing company should have more, surely?

There was nothing here to make it feel *real*.

Everything I thought I knew was slipping away.

Callum. Our life together. Even his job.

Each certainty I had clung to now felt fragile, slipping through my fingers like sand.

A creeping familiarity wrapped around me, making the air thick and heavy in my lungs. It was happening again...

No.

I shook my head, forcing the thought away. I couldn't let myself go there. I had left all of that behind in Portsmouth. The betrayals, the loss, the feeling of the ground crumbling beneath me.

This was different.

It *had* to be different.

Callum *loved* me.

I squinted at the website, scanning every detail for something I'd missed. I scrolled to the bottom, heart pounding, until I found an address in tiny, barely noticeable print.

It was something.

I copied it into Google Maps and searched again.

Still nothing.

Maybe they'd rebranded or were in the middle of it; that could explain the sparse website. Right?

The question hung unanswered in my brain.

My pulse quickened as I deleted *Wave Media* from the search bar and tried again with just the address.

This time, I got a result.

But it wasn't an office. It was a charity shop.

I stared at the screen, my breath catching in my throat. My thoughts raced as I tried to make sense of it. There had to be a logical explanation.

Maybe I was right, perhaps it was a new website. Maybe they'd moved offices too. Maybe—

My shoulders slumped. Maybe I was grasping at straws.

A cold prickle of doubt crept over my skin. My mind replayed every conversation I'd ever had with Callum about work. The vague descriptions. The meetings that always seemed to be somewhere else. The way he brushed off my questions, changing the subject as though his job wasn't important.

At the time, I hadn't thought much of it. Why would I? I'd trusted him.

I nibbled my lip. What if I'd misunderstood? Maybe I'd got the name wrong. Maybe they were part of a big conglomerate?

But the more I tried to make it make sense, the less it did.

What kind of company didn't have a proper website? No photos, no staff, no clients?

And why had I never questioned that before?

Could I honestly say I hadn't noticed the gaps and inconsistencies? Or had I chosen to overlook them?

And if so, was it because I genuinely thought they were minor? Irrelevant? Or had I just wanted them to be?

Life with Callum was so much better than my life had been without him. Had that made me complacent? Or just protective?

But whatever part of me, conscious or subconscious, that had chosen ignorance out of fear of losing him, it was no longer relevant. He'd already left. Now the question was: how was I going to get him back?

And in order to do that, first I had to find him.

I clutched the phone, my fingers tightening around the edges as my pulse thudded in my ears.

'The simplest explanation is usually the correct one.' Dad's voice echoed in my memory as he quoted Occam's Razor. I'd lost count of how many times he'd referenced that principle in the aftermath of everything that happened in Portsmouth.

But what was the simplest explanation here?

I squeezed my eyes shut. I couldn't let my mind spiral.

I needed more information.

I needed to *see* for myself.

There was only one way to know for sure.

I had to go there.

10

THEN

September

'I'm sorry that you've had to go through all that,' I told Callum, touched that he'd felt able to open up to me about everything that had happened to him due to Rob's betrayal. I admired him for that. His ability to let me into his life. To trust me.

It had been a long time since anyone had done that. Once people viewed you as unstable, they no longer trusted you with anything.

'Thanks,' Callum replied, his voice thick with emotion. 'The worst part was everyone I thought I could count on, colleagues I worked alongside every day, friends I'd known for years, all just went quiet. They wouldn't help. They wouldn't even talk to me.'

A lump caught in my throat. 'I know how isolating that can feel.'

'You do?' Callum tipped his head to the side as he studied me.

I dropped my head, automatically busying myself scrubbing the patch of floor in front of my feet with a sense of urgency, as though somehow that small act was critical.

My words had been honest. Unguarded. Foolish. I ground my teeth, cursing my unaccustomed openness. Unlike Callum, I didn't share my emotions. My past. I'd worked so hard to leave that behind in Portsmouth.

Just like Mum had taught me.

It had been difficult.

I drew in a slow breath, steadying my pulse.

But it had also been necessary. 'I hope people will let you move on,' I said quietly. I truly did. And yet I knew that it wasn't that easy. Some people were good at holding grudges.

I was one of them.

I resented Dad for abandoning me, not just the way he'd packed his stuff and disappeared from my life, but the fact he'd never believed in me. In my abilities. My dreams.

Only one person had truly believed in me: Daniel Sinclair.

And nothing would quell the hatred I felt for him.

Callum nodded slightly, but his movement lacked conviction. It seemed he shared my reservations.

I glanced around the café floor, surprised to realise that I had mopped it all already. That wasn't right. The slow lull before closing usually dragged, minutes stretching seemingly endlessly as I went through the motions, exhausted and counting down until I could finally lock the door.

But today, time had slipped through my fingers.

I turned my head, watching Callum as he started setting the chairs back onto the clean floor, his movements easy and confident, like he belonged here.

I'd spent so many evenings doing this alone, the silence pressing in on me, making every task feel heavier. But tonight, with him here, the usual monotony had disappeared. And now that we were almost done, a sharp pang of disappointment settled in my chest.

He'd be leaving soon.

I shouldn't care. I barely knew him. But somehow, the idea of him walking out the door and the café returning to its usual stillness felt unbearable.

Trying to push the thought aside, I forced a light cheeriness to my voice. 'You're becoming an expert in café closing duties.'

Callum chuckled, setting the last chair back in place. 'What can I say? I'm a quick learner.'

'Clearly,' I teased. 'I might have to put you on the payroll.'

Reality crashed down on me as I heard my words aloud. I couldn't afford to put anyone on the payroll. Including myself.

This wasn't the life I'd dreamed of. The one Daniel had promised me. The one we'd been working towards. Together.

Or at least, I'd thought it had been together. But maybe that had been the problem. We had different goals. Perhaps we always had.

Because for all his promises of what my life could be, the reality was he'd still shaped it. Just not in the way I'd imagined.

Dad had always distrusted Daniel. I used to think it was because he didn't understand him, didn't understand what music meant to us, or the future it could offer me.

But maybe he'd understood better than I ever did.

Maybe he'd seen what I couldn't.

* * *

'Music isn't a stable way of life,' Dad said, repeating his familiar argument.

'And running a restaurant is?' Mum arched an eyebrow.

I tried to hide my smile as Mum scored a point in my favour. The restaurant was doing well now, but I knew it hadn't always been the case. They'd both worked hard to make it happen. Long hours. Sacrifices. Stress. It had all been part of their journey.

But they'd done it.

And so could I.

'No, it's not. Which is why I don't want our daughter to face the hurdles we have – to constantly be fearful of one bad review, one critic who has the ability to tear your entire future apart in a few sentences. I want more for her than that.'

'You can't protect me from everything,' I pointed out.

'But we can protect you from this. At least for now.'

'You don't believe I'm good enough to make it.'

'It's not that,' Dad said softly, resting a hand on my shoulder. 'I know you're talented and dedicated. Even someone tone-deaf and musically naïve, like me, can tell that. But it doesn't guarantee success. I don't want you to look back someday, stuck in a life you aren't happy with, and regret all the things you missed out on because you gave everything up for music.'

'I'd regret not trying more,' I assured him earnestly.

Dad shrugged. 'You think that now.'

'It's not just me who thinks it,' I insisted. 'Daniel says—'

'Daniel,' Dad snapped, his voice suddenly sharp. His hand dropped from my shoulder. 'Daniel says. That's all I ever hear any more.'

I flinched.

'He's not your parent, Olivia. He's just your piano teacher. Though, I'm starting to wonder if he even remembers that.'

* * *

'Tempting.' Callum shot me a playful look. 'But I'm not sure I have the patience for dealing with demanding customers all day.'

'Yeah.' I let out a tired sigh at yet another reminder of the problems with owning a café. I picked up the bucket. 'It can be a bit wearing at times.'

His expression shifted slightly, a soft curiosity replacing the amusement. 'You ever think about doing something else?'

The question caught me off guard. I hesitated, gripping the bucket handle in my hand a little tighter.

'I—' I swallowed. 'I don't know what.' It was the truth. I didn't know any more.

Callum tilted his head. 'You must have had other dreams before this.'

I glanced down at my fingers curled around the ridged plastic handle of the bucket. Heavy and unyielding, the weight of it had turned my fingertips white. It was so different from how my fingers used to dance lightly across the smooth keys of my piano. Free. Passionate. Powerful.

Callum was right, I did have dreams once. But that was a lifetime ago.

Shrugging, I gave the only answer I could. 'The café keeps me busy.'

He studied me for a second longer before nodding. 'Fair enough.' He paused. 'But busy isn't the same as happy.'

I felt my body brace against the impact of his words. I couldn't think how to reply.

Perhaps I didn't need to.

'So why keep the café if you don't love it?' he asked simply.

I blinked as I stared at him. 'It was my mum's.'

'Well, yeah, but—'

'It was my mum's,' I repeated, more firmly this time. That fact was all that mattered. She'd worked hard to create a business from nothing. 'The café's her legacy.'

'You make it sound so dramatic. It's just a café,' Callum insisted.

Just a café.

His words grated against me. It wasn't just a café. It wasn't *just* anything.
It was *everything*.

He didn't get it. How could he? How could anyone?

They didn't know what we'd been through to have even this. And Callum? I snorted. He didn't own anything solid – a home, a business – nothing tangible that was a visible symbol of hopes and dreams. He lived in the moment.

But I knew what it meant to build something, only to have it disappear from under you. And so did my parents. They'd lost the restaurant because of me.

My gaze drifted to the empty glass display cabinet on the counter. For a moment I could see Mum behind it filling the shelves with her freshly baked cakes with such care and pride.

Mum might be gone, but I wouldn't take the café from her, too.

I turned away and hurried to the kitchen to empty the bucket, grateful for the escape from Callum's questions but also strangely disappointed by the distance between us.

I lingered at the sink, listening to the soft scrap and thud as Callum set the rest of the chairs back into place in the other room. Something about his presence drew me back in.

Slipping behind the counter, I straightened the already neat display of clean cups and mugs, pretending I still had something to tidy. I wasn't ready for this moment to end. For him to say goodbye.

Callum stretched his arms over his head, then sighed dramatically. 'Well, I suppose I should let you get home.'

Disappointment settled deeper in my chest.

I forced a smile. 'Yeah, I guess so.'

But neither of us moved.

'Thank you for your help. Again.'

Callum smiled. 'You're welcome. Again.'

His smile was infectious, and I found myself grinning back at him. It felt odd and unfamiliar. It wasn't as though I never smiled. I smiled all day at customers. It was part of the job to be welcoming and friendly. Mum had insisted on it. But this felt different.

It felt real.

His gaze flicked towards the window, where the darkness outside turned the glass into a mirror, reflecting our images back at us. He turned back to me, a flicker of hesitation in his expression. 'How about dinner?'

I froze.

'Together,' Callum added, as though he felt his question needed further clarity. 'You can pick the restaurant.'

'I...' I couldn't think of a response. It felt as though my brain had short-circuited and couldn't function.

'Am I overstepping?' Callum asked, taking a tiny step back.

I shook my head. 'No, you're not. You just—'

'Surprised you?'

'Right.'

I smiled, grateful for the explanation he'd provided. It wasn't entirely inaccurate. His invitation had caught me off guard, but the thing that made me hesitate wasn't surprise. It was fear.

Fear of what it would mean to say yes. Fear of letting someone else in, of lowering my guard, even a little, and risking it all going wrong again.

But it wasn't just that. What scared me more was the part of me that *wanted* to say yes. The part that craved connection. Possibility. Hope.

I'd learned last time that wanting something was dangerous.

And not getting it was worse.

'So, is that a yes?' Callum asked, his expression hopeful.

'I—' I hesitated, my mind racing for an excuse. Not because I didn't want to. But because I *did*.

And that terrified me.

I knew what wanting something could lead to. It had a habit of ending badly.

And not just for me.

Callum studied me, his teasing demeanour softening. 'It's just dinner, Olivia.' His voice was warm, reassuring. 'No pressure.'

I swallowed hard, my heart thudding against my ribs.

Was I really going to do this?

'I...' The word lingered between us. Then, before I could overthink it, I exhaled and nodded. 'Okay.'

Callum's smile widened. 'Yeah?'

'Yeah,' I said, a nervous flutter stirring in my stomach.

For the first time in a long time, I was stepping outside the routine I'd built around myself.

And despite the fear creeping at the edges of my mind, I realised something unexpected.

I wanted to.

11

NOW

December

A chill seeped into my palm as I grasped the metal handle and pushed the heavy door open. Dry, airless heat blasted down on me from the heater above, making the shop feel more suffocating than welcoming. I hesitated in the doorway, tempted to step back into the icy air outside. Retreat to the café and pretend today was just like every other Monday morning.

But I couldn't. I needed answers.

I let the door swing closed behind me and edged further into the shop. Shelves lined with second-hand books and delicate trinkets sat alongside rails of neatly sorted clothes. Everything was bright, tidy, inviting.

At least that was the aim.

To me it was just a reminder that anything I'd owned that wasn't deemed a necessity or held financial value had ended up in a place like this when we'd left Portsmouth. We couldn't bring everything with us.

But worse still, despite my desperate hope, none of this belonged to Wave Media.

And yet, I couldn't give up. I couldn't just leave with nothing.

I scanned the shop, taking in every detail, as if somewhere among the racks of donated clothes and neatly stacked paperbacks, I might still find the proof I needed. The proof that I wasn't wrong. That I hadn't been lied to.

My gaze landed on the woman behind the counter. She was in her sixties, her silver-streaked hair tucked behind her ears, a warm, welcoming smile lighting up her face as she folded a stack of donated clothes.

I parted my lips, the question poised on the edge of my tongue. She would know. If Wave Media existed – if Callum's job was real – she was my last hope of proving it. But if she had never heard of them... then what?

Then it was over.

Then it was a lie.

'Can I help you?' the woman asked, her voice kind and open as her gaze met mine.

My throat tightened as my pulse hammered in my ears. I needed answers. But part of me – the part still praying that this was all a mistake – wanted to turn around, walk back out the door, and pretend I had never come here at all.

Because once I asked the question, I couldn't take it back.

I swallowed hard. 'I hope so,' I said, my words barely above a whisper. I cleared my throat and tried again. 'I'm looking for Wave Media.'

Her smile faltered, the lines on her forehead creasing. 'Wave Media?' she repeated hesitantly.

I nodded. 'It's a marketing agency. This is their address.'

A slow shake of her head. 'Sorry, love. Never heard of them.'

The floor felt unsteady beneath me.

I fumbled for my phone, my hands suddenly clumsy as I pulled up their website. 'It's right here,' I said, turning the screen towards her, desperate to prove her wrong.

She *had* to be wrong.

She adjusted her glasses and peered at the screen, her frown deepening.

'Could they have an office at the back? Or upstairs?' I asked quickly, my voice rising with urgency.

She chuckled, shaking her head. 'The only thing out back is a very disorganised stockroom full of donations to sort, not exactly a fancy marketing company.'

'And upstairs?' I pressed.

'Oh, that's just Mrs Garrison's flat,' she said, gesturing towards the ceiling.

'Maybe it's her business?' I suggested, grasping onto the last thread of hope.

The lady chuckled again. 'I doubt it. She must be in her eighties now. She used to be a schoolteacher, not a marketing expert.'

A cold prickle of unease crept through me. My hope that Google Maps had been out of date was completely crushed. But I wasn't ready to give up. I couldn't.

If the map wasn't out of date, then maybe Wave Media's website was. 'Perhaps it's an old address for them?'

The lady shook her head again. 'No, dear, this has always been a charity shop. At least as long as I've worked here, and that's... oh, five – no, six years now. Sorry, love.'

There was a finality to her words. It was a dead end.

Wave Media wasn't here.

'But their website...' My words trailed out.

The woman shrugged. 'A scam, maybe?' she suggested.

The words struck me like a physical blow.

A scam.

I gripped the edge of the counter, nausea churning in my stomach as my mind reeled.

Callum had lied.

The words felt like blades, sharp and piercing. I'd been betrayed again.

There was a familiarity to it. Not just the pain. But the anger that came with it. A simmering resentment for their deception.

And my naivety.

The question was where did Callum's lie end? Wave Media didn't exist, but what about everything else? Had any of that been real?

'You can barely trust anyone these days, can you?' the lady added sadly.

I nodded numbly. She was right, of course. I knew that better than anyone, and yet I'd still ended up here.

12

THEN

September

'So,' Callum said as we sat at Pizza Express. 'Who is Olivia Reed?'

My fork paused in mid-air. I stared at Callum, my mouth suddenly dry. 'How do you know my surname?'

The words came out sharp and accusatory, as though knowing my surname was somehow a violation.

I set my fork down and it clattered against the plate. Too forceful. Too loud.

I didn't like people knowing anything about me. Especially things I hadn't told them.

I valued anonymity more than anything.

An anonymity that suddenly felt at risk.

His expression shifted instantly, from playful curiosity to confusion and then concern. 'What? I, uh...' He rubbed the back of his neck. 'I might have seen some of the café's invoices in the kitchen. They had your name on them. I wasn't snooping,' he added quickly. 'They were just... there.'

I swallowed. His explanation was perfectly reasonable. He hadn't done anything wrong.

And yet I still felt exposed. He knew my name. My whole name.

The air felt thick and heavy as I wiped my clammy hands against my jeans, trying to steady my pulse.

It shouldn't have mattered. It wasn't as though my name was a secret. But hearing him say it like that, wanting to know who Olivia Reed was, sent cold dread through my body.

So many people had asked that question. People I didn't know. Strangers demanding answers as though I owed them an explanation. Kids I'd never spoken to at school whispered it in the corridors as I passed. Overnight everyone seemed to know my name.

I used to like that feeling. The sense of importance and recognition of being known. Olivia Reed, the pianist. The prodigy.

And then Olivia Reed, the *arsonist*.

My name that had once sounded impressive had been turned into a scandal.

'I'm sorry,' Callum murmured. 'I know it was none of my business, I shouldn't have been looking—'

'It's fine,' I said automatically, but my heart pounded. It wasn't fine. That one question had sent me spiralling back to a time I'd tried so hard to move on from.

But it wasn't his fault. Callum didn't know.

Silence loomed between us. I pasted a smile onto my lips. I couldn't let this ruin things. Not again. 'I feel at a disadvantage now, though,' I said, forcing a teasing tone into my voice. 'You know my full name, and where I work. But all I know about you is that you're from Portsmouth and work in marketing.'

'Fair point,' Callum conceded, his shoulders visibly relaxing. 'What do you want to know?'

'Hmm.' I tapped my finger against my chin, pretending to think. 'Let's start with an easy one. What's your surname?'

'Hayes,' he said firmly.

I nodded slowly as the name repeated in my mind. *Callum Hayes.*

It meant nothing to me. Clean. Anonymous. A blank slate.

Unlike mine.

Reed came with history. With questions. With assumptions.

Sometimes I wondered what it would be like to let it go. I was old enough now. There was nothing stopping me. No one to object.

Mum wasn't here to insist I hold on to it. And Dad... well, he'd probably welcome the chance to erase any remaining trace of me. He'd cut me out in every other way possible.

But what name would I choose?

Olivia Hayes.

The name sprang into my head so suddenly, so absurdly, I almost laughed. The first date wasn't exactly the time to be trying on someone's surname, like trying on a pair of shoes.

And yet...

It wasn't about him. Not really.

It was about the name. The sound of it. New. Unfamiliar. Unburdened. And I had to admit, it did have a nice ring to it.

I pushed the thought away quickly, hoping it hadn't shown on my face. It was just pizza...

Still, the name lingered at the edge of my thoughts like a familiar tune I couldn't shake free.

I cleared my throat, forcing my gaze back to him. 'And where do you work, Mr Callum Hayes?'

'For a marketing consultancy,' he replied.

I rolled my eyes. 'I know that much. I meant which one?'

'Oh, right. It's called, um, Wave Media,' Callum said. 'Do you know them?'

I shook my head. 'But as you have probably gathered from the frequent lulls at the café, marketing is not an area I have a lot of familiarity with.'

Callum chuckled. 'It's not everyone's cup of tea.'

I arched an eyebrow. 'Did you do that on purpose?'

'What?' he asked, looking at me innocently.

'Cup of tea?'

He still looked confused.

'We were talking about the café,' I pointed out, now regretting my failed attempt at humour.

'Ohhh.' Callum finally caught on and let out an exaggerated groan. 'Okay, so we have established marketing and puns are not your strengths.'

I shrugged, admitting defeat.

'So what do you like?'

I shifted uncomfortably. What I liked hadn't been a consideration for a long time. It was safer that way.

I'd liked music. And that simple enjoyment had led to disaster.

'Okay,' Callum said, his soft chuckle filling the silence. 'What do you do when you're not working at the café, then?'

I smiled slightly, grateful for the easier question. 'Sleep, mostly.' I chuckled. 'At least, I try,' I added ruefully.

'It was a serious question,' Callum objected.

'I am being serious,' I assured him. 'The café's open seven days a week. I don't exactly get much downtime.'

He shook his head, leaning back in his chair as if I'd just told him the sky was green. 'The café opens at eight thirty and closes at five. You've got the whole evening. You must do something besides sleep.'

I rolled my eyes. 'Do you really think my day starts the moment I open the door at eight thirty?' I laughed at his naivety. 'Where do you think all those cakes and pastries come from that we sell?'

He raised his eyebrows. 'What, you bake all that? I thought you just got it delivered pre-made.'

'Oh, I wish.' I exhaled a quiet laugh. 'Mum would never go for that.'

'Your mum?' Confusion creased Callum's brow. 'But I thought you said...'

His unfinished sentence hung between us, but it was enough. I knew why he was bewildered. Mum was gone and yet I still spoke of her in the present tense, as though she could still object to anything, still have an opinion.

Although, in a way, she did. At least in my head.

Her voice still echoed there. She was part of every decision I made. I followed her routines. Her rules. Even now. *Especially* now.

After all, wasn't that precisely why I was still doing things I hated? The baking. The long hours. The relentless pretending.

Because it had mattered to *her*.

And part of me felt like I owed it to her to keep it all going. To keep her dream alive.

It wasn't really as though I was sacrificing anything to do so. I'd let go of my own dreams eight years ago. I'd had to. Mum's were all I had left.

Then again, perhaps my reasons weren't as noble as all that. Perhaps the truth was, I just didn't know who I was without her rules to follow.

Mum's rules kept me safe.

And maybe everyone else too.

13

NOW

December

I barely remembered leaving the charity shop. The streets of Christchurch blurred around me as I walked in a daze, not fully aware of where I was going. Or for that matter even caring.

Searching for Callum had only led to more questions than answers.

Wave Media's website was sparse to the point of suspicion, and the address led to a charity shop. The entire company felt wrong.

But if it didn't exist...

Did Callum know?

The question pressed against my chest like a lead weight, crushing the air from my lungs. He'd worked for the company for over three months, or at least, that was what he claimed. Could he really have not known?

Anger bubbled inside me as I realised the most likely answer was no. It was unrealistic to think that he wouldn't have known. Which meant he'd deceived me. Lied to me.

But why?

I had nothing he'd want. No money. No connections. Just a failing café and a two-bedroom flat above it. If the goal was to live rent-free, he'd already achieved that. Why fake a job?

He knew I didn't care about his career – not really. I never pressed him for details. I knew he had debts. It wasn't as though he needed to deceive me about his financial security. I hadn't fallen in love with a job title or bank balance. I fell in love with him.

So why pretend?

Anger battled with confusion, making my head throb. Part of me screamed that his reasons didn't matter, only his actions did. But I knew better than to believe that. Everything always mattered.

Yet that certainty felt like it was a tether, pulling me back, depriving me of the ability to fully surrender and let anger consume me. I couldn't let myself hate him. Not yet.

But where did that leave me?

In limbo, I realised as my stomach hollowed.

It was like staring at a jigsaw puzzle with half the pieces missing. The gaps were too big. I couldn't see the full picture. But I needed to. Because deep down, I still hoped that if I could make the pieces fit, it would all make sense. It would be explainable. Forgivable.

That we could move on.

But I'd spent years chasing missing pieces before. Sometimes the pieces stayed missing. Sometimes that sense of living in limbo didn't end.

I reached the river, and my pace slowed. It had been Callum's favourite place. We'd often walked along the riverbank hand in hand, the silence between us comfortable and full of warmth. Now it just felt hollow and cold. Even my hand ached for the touch of his skin against mine.

I shoved my hands into my pockets and let out a deep sigh, watching as my breath formed a cloud of condensation in the air that lingered for a moment before disappearing without a trace.

But if Callum hadn't intentionally lied to me, then what did that mean?

Ever since I'd got home last night, I hadn't been able to shake the feeling that Callum wouldn't just leave. Not like that. Not without telling me.

Which meant something had happened.

The words repeated in my head as their meaning sank in deeper with each breath. *Something had happened.*

Fragments of our conversations whirled through my mind, Callum's life in Portsmouth. His best friend Rob. The scandal he'd tried to expose at their firm. The fallout. The betrayal.

What if Callum's past hadn't let him go? What if it had followed him here?

I exhaled slowly, sinking onto a bench beside the river. I knew how it felt to try to outrun the past, but to never fully be free of it. Even with the new life Mum had built for us here, I wasn't completely free. I still lived in fear. In isolation.

Did Callum too?

If Wave Media hadn't been fabricated to trick me, then did it mean Callum had been deceived too?

It seemed impossible that he could have missed something so fundamental as the company office not existing. He worked remotely, he always had, but—

I frowned. He must have worked from the office sometimes. Now that I thought about it, though, I couldn't recall a single time he'd mentioned going there. Had he ever been there? He met with clients, sure, but always at their offices. Those meetings meant trips away, cancelled plans. Even the clients never seemed to go to Wave Media's office.

Was it possible that Callum was caught up in something bigger? Something he didn't realise he was part of?

What if my own insecurities had just been distracting me? They were causing me to focus on us. On me. But what if none of this had anything to do with me?

Had Callum been pulled deeper into their corruption? Or was he running from it?

And if he left to save himself, why abandon me?

The memory of the empty nail in our bedroom flashed through my head. He'd taken the photo. *Our* photo.

Because it mattered?

Because *I* mattered?

My breathing quickened as hope soared through my body. Was it possible he was trying to save me from whatever he'd got caught up in?

I pulled my phone from my pocket and stared at it, clenched in my hand. My fingers hovered over the screen.

When Dad disappeared, I'd told myself I couldn't do anything. That I wasn't supposed to. He didn't want me to.

But this was different. This was Callum.

I jabbed at my phone screen, my hands shaking as I dialled the only number I could think of. My breath caught in my throat as I stared at the call button, hesitating.

The last time I'd made this call, it had destroyed everything.

* * *

I tore free from Daniel's grasp and staggered onto the street, my heart hammering in my chest. A deafening crash behind me made me drop to my knees, my hands instinctively covering my head as shards of glass rained down on me.

An agonising scream lodged in my throat that still burned from the smoke, each rasping breath a battle. Instinctively, I glanced back at the building, flames roaring from the broken window.

I crawled on my hands and knees, unable to summon the strength to stand. Blood dripped onto the tarmac from the pieces of glass embedded in my arms and hands. But I barely felt them. The red blistered skin on my leg overpowered everything else.

Fumbling through my pocket, I pulled out my phone. My fingers trembled so hard I could barely tap the screen. I needed help. I needed someone.

I checked behind me, frantically searching for Daniel.

I needed anyone but him.

* * *

Right now, what I needed was Callum.

'You've gotta take a few risks in life to get what you want.' Callum's voice reminded me.

He was worth the risk.

I pressed the button.

'999, what's your emergency?'

'My boyfriend's missing,' I blurted out, my words tumbling over each other. 'All his stuff has gone. He's gone. But he wouldn't just leave. Not Callum.'

14

THEN

September

The automatic doors whooshed open, granting us entry. Excitement bubbled in my chest as Callum and I stepped inside, my hand nestled snugly in his. I'd walked past the Captain's Club Hotel so many times. Sitting on the edge of the riverbank, majestic and enticing, it was impossible to overlook, yet I'd never been inside. Until tonight.

The hostess greeted us with a warm smile before leading us into the restaurant. But in that instant, my excitement dissipated. My chest tightened as the unmistakable sound of a piano sonata drifted through the air.

'I didn't realise there'd be a pianist,' I said, reluctantly lowering myself into the chair.

'I thought you'd appreciate it.'

My stomach somersaulted. 'You did?' I forced the words out, desperately fighting to make my voice sound normal as the thud of my own heartbeat resounded in my head.

He didn't know the piano had once been my life. I'd never told him.

'I figured it would be nice to have a different vibe. You spend all day in your café; you need a change occasionally.'

'Oh.' The word escaped in a gush of relief. Of course he didn't know. No one knew. Not here.

That was why my parents had moved us down here.

'That's so thoughtful,' I said, pasting a smile into place.

'What did you think I meant?' Callum asked.

The tension that had momentarily released from my shoulders was instantly back. My reaction had been too defensive. Of course he was curious now. I shrugged weakly.

Callum jerked his head towards the piano. 'Do you play?'

'No.' My denial was sharp and loud.

Too loud.

The couple at the table next to us turned their heads towards us in surprise at my outburst. I shifted my gaze cautiously to Callum, dreading the curiosity I knew I would see there.

'Did I say something wrong?' he asked, his voice full of concern.

This time, I bit back my denial. I couldn't make the same mistake again. I had to be more careful.

'No,' I repeated, ensuring my voice stayed soft and level.

Callum's eyes narrowed, and I could see it wasn't enough.

'I used to play,' I admitted quietly. 'A long time ago.'

It felt like another life. The 'before', when I was a pianist. And the 'after', when I never touched those keys again.

* * *

The metronome on top of the piano ticked relentlessly, but I barely noticed it. My fingers flew over the keys. It felt almost instinctive. My gaze was fixed on the sheet music in front of me, but more out of habit than necessity.

I lifted my hands from the keys and exhaled as the final notes faded into silence.

Daniel had said this piece was too advanced for me. I'd known he was wrong, that I would be able to play it. But I'd done more than that – I'd played it flawlessly.

I glanced to my left, where Daniel sat. I'd expected to see his typical beaming smile, full of admiration and pride at my performance. But instead, he seemed frozen in place, his eyes glossy and sad.

'Did I do something wrong?' I asked, glancing back at the sheet music. I was sure I'd hit every note perfectly, but I must have missed something.

'No,' Daniel said, his voice thick and gruff. 'It was incredible.'

'Then why do you look so sad?'

'I haven't heard that piece played like that since Eleanor—'

He stopped abruptly.

'Eleanor?' I questioned, not recognising the name.

'My wife,' he said heavily, as if the words were a weight on him.

I blinked. Of course I'd known he was married. I saw the gold band on his left hand every time he played. But he'd never mentioned her before. And I'd never imagined she was a pianist too.

I'd seen her once. She'd stood in the doorway watching me play. Our gazes had met as I finished the piece, but there was something unsettling about her expression. Like the music had affected her, but I couldn't tell if it was in a good way or a bad one. And then she'd slipped away without a word.

'I didn't know she played too,' I said quietly.

'She used to,' Daniel said wistfully. 'A long time ago.'

I wanted to ask why she stopped. But I didn't. Something about Daniel's expression, closed off and unreachable, told me it wasn't my place.

* * *

'Were you any good?'

I swallowed. 'Not bad.'

I stifled a rueful laugh. As a child, Mum had worried I'd become conceited and big-headed about my success. It turned out she need not have worried. Not only had my promising career ended before it had even begun, but my ability, which had once been called magnificent by the local papers, I now shrugged off as simply *not bad*.

'Knowing you and how modest you are, that means you were good,' Callum interjected.

I blinked as I stared at him in surprise.

'I'm right, aren't I? I can see it in your face.'

I tried to settle my features into a neutral expression, but it felt forced and fake. I attempted a dismissive shrug.

'Yeah, that's what I thought,' Callum responded with a laugh. 'So, if you were so good, why did you stop playing?'

Why?

It was such a tiny word, but to me, it felt so huge. I'd carried the weight of that *why* with me ever since the last moments my fingers had danced across the keys.

'My parents needed help getting the café up and running when we moved here. It became the focus. They needed all the help they could get.' I paused. It felt wrong to make it all about them. Giving up had never really been discussed when we moved here, but then, neither had continuing. 'There wasn't really time or money for a hobby.'

It was the first time I'd ever reduced my playing to being merely a *hobby*. It had been my passion, my life, my future. But it had also been my undoing.

'So you sacrificed for their business venture?'

I cringed. 'It wasn't like that.' I couldn't let him blame my parents. 'But the café was their priority. It was their livelihood. Moving here meant they had to start from scratch and build it up from nothing.'

'So why did they move here?'

The answer to that was simple. There had never been any question about why we'd walked – or, more accurately, *run* – away from the lives we'd loved in Portsmouth.

'Because of me.'

15

NOW

December

'We'll need you to come to the police station to make an official report,' the police officer said.

I grimaced, thankful that it was a phone call and she couldn't see my body recoil at the request. I hadn't set foot in a police station since leaving Portsmouth.

I'd promised myself I never would again.

'Okay,' I said, surprised by how normal my voice sounded, despite my pulse thundering in my ears. My discomfort was irrelevant. The only thing that mattered now was Callum. And if going to the police station would help bring him back, so be it.

'Can you come in at 10 a.m. tomorrow?'

'Tomorrow?' I echoed, clutching the bench. Tomorrow felt like a lifetime away. I couldn't wait that long. *Callum* couldn't wait that long. 'But he's been gone for hours. Can't I come in now?'

'I'm sorry. We have no one available any sooner, I'm afraid.' Her tone was kind but firm.

I wanted to push back, to argue, to demand she find someone. Anyone.

But I didn't.

My shoulders sagged. 'Okay,' I said despondently. What choice did I have?

'It would be helpful if you could bring a recent photo of Callum with you.'

I nodded, even though she couldn't see me. 'Yeah, of course.'

Her voice continued, soft but professional. Occasional words seeped into my brain – an adult, no immediate concern, no known vulnerabilities.

'But Wave Media...' I interjected.

There was a pause on the other end of the line, followed by the gentle rustle of paper. I could almost picture the officer flipping back through her notes.

'Right, his employer,' she said finally.

'It's not a real company,' I reminded her. 'I told you; I've just been to their address. It's a charity shop.'

'That is certainly odd,' she admitted, her voice still calm and even. 'But there could be several potential explanations.'

'Like what?' I demanded. 'What reasonable explanation could there be for a fake company?'

'It could be an error on the website. Or Callum may have fabricated—'

'You think Callum lied to me?' I snapped. 'That he made up a job? A company? For what purpose?'

My defensiveness was instinctual. It wasn't as though her suggestion that Callum had lied was a shock. That question had already seeped into my brain. But a tiny niggly silent doubt was so different to hearing it said aloud by someone else. That made it more real. More disturbing. And my entire being rebelled against it.

Callum wasn't here to defend himself. So I had to.

'These are all valid and important questions,' the officer assured me evenly. 'And they warrant further investigation. But at this stage, they don't necessarily indicate a reason for concern.'

A reason for concern.

Those four words felt like a slap. Callum's disappearance had been dismissed so easily. *He'd* been dismissed so easily.

I knew how that felt.

* * *

'You're in shock,' Mum said as she sat beside my hospital bed.

I shook my head and winced as the nasal cannula tugged at the skin beneath my nose.

'Mr Sinclair saved you. He saved your life,' Mum repeated as though that act proved I was wrong.

To everyone else, the two things felt mutually exclusive.

No one could dispute he'd saved my life. But I couldn't prove he'd tried to kill me in the first place.

'You should be thanking him. Celebrating his heroism. He charged into a fire for you. He saved you. And yet you...' Mum shook her head, unable to define my behaviour.

I was beyond comprehension.

And it wasn't the first time.

* * *

I wrapped my free arm across my body, trying to fend off the penetrating cold that had seeped into my bones. 'Everything about this feels wr-wrong,' I said, my voice breaking.

'I understand your concern,' she said, her tone softening. 'But until we have more concrete information, we can't escalate the case. Tomorrow we'll fill in a missing person's report. For now, the best thing you can do is gather anything useful – documents, phone numbers, a photo.'

The photo.

My thoughts drifted back to the empty nail on our bedroom wall, but I didn't say anything. If Wave Media hadn't been enough to convince them, a missing photo certainly wouldn't.

Her reassurances were meaningless to me. I would only be satisfied when I could see Callum was safe with my own eyes.

As I hung up, the nervous energy that had propelled me through the last few hours suddenly drained away, and I slumped back against the bench, the wood cold and damp beneath me.

But I couldn't stop now. I had to keep going.

For Callum.

The police officer had asked for a photo. It was something small, but it was a start.

My hands trembled as I unlocked my phone and scrolled through my camera roll. Photo after photo of coffee cups and cakes filled the screen, feeble attempts at capturing 'artistic' shots for the café's social media page. Callum had often teased me about my poor photography skills, promising to help me overhaul the account to make it more polished and professional. But he'd never got around to it.

I hadn't pressed him on it. He did enough to help me with the café as it was.

I kept scrolling. Interspersed between cups of coffee, there were a few photos of us. I smiled as I paused on the first one. Callum's arm was wrapped around me as he nuzzled my neck, his face hidden by my hair. I remembered that day. That moment. It felt so precious. And yet right now, that photo was unhelpful.

I moved to the next, taken when he was hanging Christmas decorations for me at the cafe. I'd tried to catch him off guard, but somehow he'd ducked behind the Christmas tree just as I took the photo.

Scrolling on, there was one where I caught his gorgeous grin, but the rest of his face was obscured as he raised his hand, blocking the camera.

Nothing was usable.

I frowned slightly. Was it just a coincidence?

Was he being playful? Or intentionally hiding?

Then again, it wasn't all his fault. I didn't take many photos to begin with. I'd never been a fan of selfies. I'd learned long ago to stay in the background, out of sight.

After Portsmouth, I didn't want to be seen. Being visible had once meant praise, applause. Later, it meant judgement. Headlines. Whispers.

I learned to erase myself before anyone else could do it for me.

I knew what had caused my aversion to being photographed. But what had caused Callum's?

16

THEN

September

'What do you mean, they moved because of you?' Callum leaned closer to me, his curiosity practically tangible.

Panic surged through me, and I fought to keep my body from shaking. What had possessed me to admit that aloud? Especially to Callum.

I'd carried the guilt alone all these years. It was behind me now. Dad had left. Mum had gone. There was no one left to resent me. To judge me.

Unless I told them about the destruction I'd caused.

'I was going through a tough time,' I replied vaguely.

'Tough enough to cause your parents to shut down their business and uproot your life?' Callum's tone held a mix of confusion and disbelief.

It didn't compute to him. How could a kid of fourteen years old have that kind of impact?

'I'd never really fitted in,' I admitted quietly. 'I was obsessed with becoming a pianist. At least that's what Dad said.'

'Ah,' Callum murmured. 'Let me guess, that kind of passion made you unpopular at school?'

'Kids can be cruel,' I replied with a shrug. Then again, I added silently, so could adults. 'They thought I was boring and weird.'

* * *

'Hey, Mozart!'

I kept my gaze down and clutched my music folder to my chest as I quickened my pace across the school playground.

'What's your hurry?' the voice called after me. 'Afraid to keep your precious piano waiting?'

Laughter erupted around me, but I tried to block it out. Ignore them, and they'll get bored eventually. That was what Mum kept telling me. But if anything, the older I got, the more they teased.

A sudden movement to my left caught my attention, but before I could react, a football slammed into my side. I stumbled sideways from the impact, my grip loosening. My folder slipped from my hands, and sheet music scattered across the wet concrete.

The laughter intensified, now accompanied by slow, mocking applause.

I dropped to my knees, scrambling to salvage the pages as tears burned behind my eyes. I gritted my teeth, determined not to let them see me cry.

A group of boys from my class rushed forward, but I knew they weren't coming to help. My fingers darted between their feet as they kicked at the pages, tearing them, grinding them into the mud.

'Olivia!'

Silence fell across the playground as Dad's voice cut through the noise.

The boys scattered instantly.

I let out a shaky breath, snatching up the last of the crumpled pages before scrambling to my feet.

Dad hurried towards me. I peered at him through bleary eyes. For a fleeting moment I was afraid he'd make a scene. Yell at the kids, storm after them, demand to know their names and threaten to call their parents. Something. Anything.

And yet, at the same time, part of me was just as afraid that he wouldn't.

As he reached me, his gaze met mine. There was no outrage in his expression. No anger. Just pity.

'Olivia,' he said, shaking his head wearily. 'Why do you make it so easy for them?'

My throat tightened. 'W-what?'

His gaze flicked to the ruined sheet music in my hands, then back to me.

'You make yourself too easy a target. You're not a little kid any more. This is secondary school. If you just tried a little harder to fit in—'

'Maybe I don't want to fit in with them,' I interrupted. My lower lip quivered, but I held my ground.

He exhaled heavily. 'It would be nice if you fitted in somewhere, that's all.' He jerked his head towards the pages in my hand. 'And that isn't the way to do it.'

* * *

Callum nodded. 'Secondary school isn't the place to stand out as different,' he said with understanding.

'I should have tried harder to fit in. To make things easier for my parents.' I shrugged helplessly.

'Why do you do that?' Callum asked.

My brow furrowed. 'Do what?'

'Take responsibility for things that aren't your fault.'

'But I should have—'

'Why?' Callum cut me off. 'Why should you have done anything?'

I floundered for the words to explain it. It was my responsibility. I knew it was, without question, and yet I couldn't explain why.

'You're not responsible for everything that goes wrong, every mistake someone else makes, every disappointment they feel.'

'Well, no, of course not,' I scoffed. When he said it like that, it sounded so stupid. And yet, something inside me felt off. Logically, his words were right. So why did they feel so wrong?

'Did you stand out as different at secondary school too?' I asked, shifting the conversation away from me. 'It sounded like you were speaking from experience.'

Callum grimaced. 'Let's just say you weren't the only one who had career aspirations at a young age.'

'You were passionate about marketing when you were a kid?' The idea stunned me. It felt like an unusual career choice for someone so young. Football stars, pop icons, or social media influencers were the more typical aspirations when I'd been at school.

'Not marketing,' Callum admitted. 'Writing.'

'You mean, like a novelist?'

He smiled faintly but said nothing, his gaze drifting towards the river. 'There's something invigorating about capturing a story on paper, digging into the details, the people, the questions,' he said finally. 'It's like peeling back the layers until everything starts to take shape.'

There was a longing to his words. More than just passion, it was a need. As though writing was part of him.

I knew that feeling.

But I also knew where it could lead. And how dangerous it could be.

'How did you go from novelist to marketing consultant?'

'Necessity, I guess,' Callum replied. 'It was a stepping stone, but...'

'Stepping stones don't always lead where you expect them to,' I finished for him.

He turned and as his gaze met mine, a charge of electricity tingled through my body, subtle but undeniable. As though, somehow, we were connected. A silent understanding that we had both ended up in lives we hadn't planned. And in the process, we'd each lost something. Some part of ourselves.

'You've never mentioned your dad before,' Callum said suddenly.

I froze. The mere mention of Dad was like a sharp punch. He was someone I tried hard not to think about. Not that I always succeeded, but avoiding talking about him was easier. I knew how to end conversations.

'He left us. He chose not to be part of our lives. So why would I want to waste my time talking about him?'

'I'm sorry,' Callum said quickly.

I tried not to smile. It felt wrong to relish making someone feel remorseful simply for mentioning Dad. But I'd learned it was a necessity. It was the most effective way to ensure the end of that conversation.

And that was essential.

'But...' Callum tipped his head to the side, studying me inquisitively.

My stomach flip-flopped. That wasn't the expression of someone who was going to let the topic drop.

'Why did he leave?'

I frowned. Callum's tone was soft and concerned, as though Dad's reasoning mattered. Of course it did. But that reasoning was precisely the part I wanted to avoid.

Callum's gaze bore into me, curious and unrelenting. He wasn't going to be deterred. He wanted an answer. An explanation.

I shrugged dismissively. 'Life here in Christchurch wasn't what he'd hoped for.'

I felt the tension in my body ease slightly as I silently congratulated myself on my carefully balanced reply. There was a skill to being truthful and yet evasive at the same time. It was a skill I'd had a lot of practice in over the years.

'How so?'

I gritted my teeth, fighting to hide my frustration at his endless questions. It wasn't his fault. He was just trying to get to know me. To know my life. He didn't realise that was the one thing I didn't want him to do.

'The restaurant was everything to Dad,' I said sadly as the past washed over me.

'What restaurant?'

My breath caught in my chest. I hadn't intended to mention the restaurant. Mum had told me so often not to talk about it. Not to share any of the details of our lives before Christchurch.

We couldn't risk the same thing happening here as it had there.

'Liv?'

Something inside me soared at the sound of the shortened version of my name slipping from his lips with just warmth and care. It was the first time he'd ever called me that. And yet, within the same heartbeat, that flicker of excitement was crushed beneath a wave of panic.

I swallowed. It was too late now. I couldn't take the words back. All I could do was downplay their significance and hope Callum would let it drop.

'My parents used to own a restaurant. They started it together when they first got married.'

Memories of The Reeds Fishbar flickered through my mind, the old-fashioned mix of dark wood and gleaming brass, softened by Mum's delicate touches of crisp white tablecloths and deep blue candle holders. But it was the tall picture windows that truly transformed it, flooding the space with light and a sense of warmth.

'What happened to it?'

The question jarred against me, paranoia sending my thoughts into overdrive. How did he know something had happened to it?

'I mean, it's a bit of a switch, isn't it? To go from a restaurant to a café?'

I let out a breath. 'Yeah, I guess so.' I shrugged feebly. 'But you know what it's like in the hospitality industry. Restaurants fail all the time.'

As I said it, I wondered if Callum did know. He worked in marketing, but did that mean he dealt with restaurant marketing? Did he work with hospitality businesses?

'Ah.' Callum nodded. 'So the café was a second chance.'

'Hence the name,' I said with a slight smile. 'Second Cup Café had been Mum's idea. A kind of secret nod to our new lives here.'

'That's sweet,' Callum said, nodding again as though he understood, but he couldn't. Not fully.

Our move here, the café, none of it was about a second chance for a business.

It was a second chance for me.

'So that's why they moved, not because of you?'

'Well, er, I...'

'I couldn't understand why they would completely uproot everything, rather than just sending you to a different school.'

'Mmm,' I murmured. How could I explain that the restaurant failed because of me? Because everyone was scared to dine at a restaurant owned by the parents of an arsonist?

'And the piano?'

'Wasn't part of our new lives.'

'But it was your dream. Your identity.'

The words resonated within me. No one else had ever understood that before, only Daniel. Playing the piano wasn't just something I did, it was who I was. It was part of me.

Until it wasn't.

'A lot of things had to be left behind in Portsmouth. Anything of value was sold and anything that was worthless...' I shrugged.

'But dreams are never worthless,' Callum said earnestly.

'Mine were,' I replied flatly.

Callum looked like he wanted to disagree. To tell me I was wrong. But something stopped him. Maybe he could see from my expression that it was futile. Or maybe deep down he knew I was right.

I cleared my throat. 'Starting from scratch here was harder than any of us had anticipated. The only place my parents could afford was the café. It was supposed to be temporary, just something to tide us over until they could afford to refurbish and turn the place into a restaurant. But the café never really took off.'

'So your dad just left?'

I nodded. 'Running a failing café after years of owning a successful restaurant was hard on him.'

'It must have been hard on all of you. But abandoning your family because of a struggling business doesn't make sense.'

I didn't respond. I couldn't.

There was so much more behind Dad's departure. And it had nothing to do with the café.

'Why did the restaurant fail, anyway?'

I forced my shoulders to rise and fall, but they were too tense for it to form a nonchalant shrug. 'Restaurants fail all the time.'

'Yeah, I get that. Especially new businesses. But yours was established. And you said it yourself, it was successful. So how did it go from that to you guys losing everything and ending up here?'

'Not enough customers to keep it afloat,' I replied cautiously. 'I guess my parents needed someone like you around back then.'

Callum blinked. 'Me? Why me?'

'With your marketing skills,' I said with a frown.

'Oh. Yeah, of course,' Callum said with a feeble laugh. 'Marketing is key.'

'Mmm,' I murmured as I studied him. Was it my imagination or had his confusion lasted just a second too long? Almost as though he didn't really understand what marketing had to do with him.

'But didn't you have repeat customers? If they started when they got married, then they must have been known in the area.'

'I was a kid,' I said lamely. As though my teenage years made me ignorant of the grown-up matters of business.

'You said you were fourteen,' Callum reminded me. 'Old enough to understand what was happening.'

I inhaled sharply. Why was he pressing this? Surely he had to realise how uncomfortable talking about the past made me. So why did he refuse to let it go?

Resentment bubbled inside me. He seemed so thoughtful. So kind. But this wasn't kind. It was intrusive. He was picking at a scab that hadn't healed. One that should've been left alone.

I gritted my teeth. I didn't owe him an explanation. I didn't owe him anything. 'It's complicated,' I said flatly, hoping that would dissuade him.

But in truth to Dad, his reasoning had never been complicated. He saw it as simple and obvious.

There was one overarching reason for everything: the restaurant's failure, the move, his departure.

Me.

Not that I could share that with Callum. Especially now, when it was clear his inquisitive nature wouldn't be able to let it go at that. He'd want details. Reasons. He'd want to know what I'd done that was so unforgivable my own father couldn't bear to be around me.

And the answer would make Callum leave too.

17

NOW

December

I paced the living room, my mind racing. I had done exactly what the police officer on the phone had suggested. I'd returned home, left my phone on, the volume turned up, waiting for any news or sign of Callum. But all it had achieved so far was a mounting sense of helplessness.

This wasn't working.

I checked the time on my phone: 10:30 a.m. I inhaled slowly. On a normal day I'd already have been at the café for hours. Finally catching my breath after an early start of preparation and the morning chaos, reluctantly bracing myself for the lunch rush. But today there was something appealing about the place I usually despised. There was a rhythm to it. A familiarity.

Right now, maybe that was exactly what I needed. Even the curt barked orders from hurried customers was preferable to the unbearable silence of the flat. At least amidst the lunch rush there was no time to think. No time to feel.

The bell above the door jingled as I stepped inside. The air was heavy with the earthy scent of coffee. Normally it felt suffocating. I'd never liked coffee, not even before it became the scent of my everyday life. But today, I welcomed it.

Here, everything was just as it had been. The spotlessly mopped floor. The pristine tables. Rows of neatly stacked cups lined up above the coffee machine as though they'd been silently waiting for my return. Everything in its place. Unchanged. Untouched.

The flat felt wrong with every trace of Callum gone. The emptiness was practically tangible and unescapable. But here I could pretend that things were okay. That *I* was okay.

I flipped the sign to open, more out of habit than expectation of a sudden flurry of customers. I'd already missed the morning commuters and knew the ebb and flow of the place well enough not to expect many customers now until almost twelve. But at least here there were tasks to be done.

I tied my apron, washed my hands, and started emptying the dishwasher that I'd left to run last night. It felt like a lifetime ago now. I'd followed the same evening ritual, completely unaware that my life beyond the café walls had changed. That I was alone.

I shook my head. I couldn't allow my thoughts to go there. It was a downwards spiral to focus on the things outside of my control. Outside of the routine.

As much as I'd always hated the café, the routine was one thing I'd been grateful for. Like a well-rehearsed sonata, there was a kind of beauty to the flow of it.

Mum's rules were rigid and restrictive, but they were also comforting. A structured melody I knew by heart. She'd drilled them into me with the same precision Daniel had demanded of every note.

Before he'd abandoned me.

* * *

Daniel stared at me, a pained expression contorting his face. 'I don't understand why you're making these accusations.'

'I know what I smelt. What I saw.'

'Why would I set fire to my piano?'

'Why would I?' I countered defiantly.

Mum and Dad stood beside us, their heads turning back and forth as though they were watching a tennis match, waiting to see who would win.

Daniel let out a weary sigh. 'This is all my fault.' A surge of triumph rushed through me, and for the first time since the smoke had engulfed me, I felt like I could breathe again.

He turned to Dad. '*I know you had concerns that I was pushing Olivia too hard. Filling her head with unrealistic dreams. It was never my intention. I honestly believed she had something special. But maybe you were right. Maybe I was blinded by my own aspirations for her that I couldn't see the pressure was too much for her.*'

'What?' I shook my head. 'No, that's not true.'

'*Raw talent isn't enough,*' Daniel continued. '*It takes grit and strength of character to handle the constant criticism that comes with striving for perfection.*'

Tension seeped into my body as his words crushed me like a vice. 'I am strong enough,' I said, fighting to find my voice.

Why was he saying this? He'd always believed in me. Believed in my future.

But if he'd made a mistake...

'*Perhaps I handled it wrong. I should have been less blunt. But it wouldn't have been right to keep giving her false hope. I'd have been setting her up for failure.*'

False hope.

Failure.

The words repeated on a loop in my head.

'*But I hadn't realised the extent of her obsession. Not just for the piano*' – Daniel lowered his gaze to the floor – '*but also for me,*' he added so quietly I had to strain my ears to hear.

I staggered backwards, his accusation, quiet but wounding, stinging like a slap. 'No,' I gasped. 'That's not true. I'm not obsessed.'

The words seared my throat. The mere act of having to defend myself from such a hurtful claim was excruciating.

Daniel was my friend. My only friend. I'd trusted him. Believed in him. Just like he'd believed in me.

At least I'd thought he had.

But that wasn't obsession. That was kindred spirits.

We shared something. A connection. But it wasn't about him. It was about the music.

Music set us apart from everybody else. And in turn it united us. A quiet little clique that no one else understood. No one else was meant to.

'What happened?' Dad asked.

Daniel inhaled slowly. 'Olivia took it badly when I told her.'

I blinked. 'Told me what?'

Daniel lifted his chin, his gaze fixed on me. 'That I couldn't teach you any more.'

* * *

I added the clean cups to the carefully stacked rows above the coffee machine.
I didn't even need to count to know the precise number to put there to ensure
the pile didn't topple. My hands moved automatically, trained by years of
muscle memory, just as they once had moved across the piano keyboard.

But even as I lost myself in the routine, my head was full of music I hadn't
played in years.

I pushed the memories back down. I wasn't that girl any more.

18

THEN

September

'You look awful,' Maddie said the moment I slid into the booth across from her.

'Thanks,' I muttered, slumping against the worn leather as Lucy shuffled over to make room.

'She means that we're worried about you. You're working too hard and look tired,' Lucy added, scowling at Maddie.

'I *am* tired,' I admitted, wrapping my fingers around the glass of white wine they'd already ordered for me. 'It's just temporary.'

Maddie scoffed. 'Yeah, right.'

Lucy elbowed her.

'Oww,' Maddie objected, shuffling away from Lucy.

'What Maddie is trying to say – diplomatically, obviously – is that you've been saying that for six months and things don't seem to be improving. At this point, "temporary" is running the risk of becoming permanent.'

Maddie folded her arms across her chest. 'I can speak for myself you know.'

Lucy arched an eyebrow, an amused smile playing on her lips. 'That's what I'm afraid of.'

I laughed in spite of my exhaustion.

'You never take a day off, Liv,' Lucy said, growing serious again. 'You're working yourself into the ground.'

I kept my gaze down as I took a sip of wine. I couldn't deny they were right. 'It's just me now,' I murmured quietly. 'Ever since Mum died, everything's fallen on me. We were barely staying afloat before. Now it feels like the whole thing could sink any minute.' I let out a weary sigh. 'Without her, and her superior baking skills, we've lost even more customers. I don't know how we will manage if we lose any more.'

'We?' Lucy asked gently, arching a brow. 'It's your café now, Liv.'

I swallowed. It was so hard not to still think of the café as Mum's. It had always been hers.

'You need more fun in your life,' Lucy said. 'You need to get out more. Have a life outside of the café.'

'I'm out right now,' I pointed out, gesturing at the pub.

Lucy rolled her eyes. 'Yeah, but we don't really count.'

'Excuse me?' Maddie objected dramatically. 'Did you just say we don't count?'

Lucy grinned. 'Not like that. I just mean, we've been your people since school. You need more than just us in your life.'

'Yeah, fair enough,' Maddie conceded.

I gave a half smile. 'You two have been worried about me since we met.'

'Of course,' Maddie said, her eyes wide.

I waited for her typical bluntness to point out how sad and lonely I'd looked as a new student joining partway through Year 10, and how they'd taken pity on me.

'I knew right from the beginning we were going to be tight.' There was such affection in her voice.

I blinked.

'Wow,' Lucy said, staring at Maddie. 'That was so sweet and un-Maddie like.'

Maddie looked indignant for a second, before she laughed. 'Yeah, felt weird saying it.'

'You're not wrong,' I admitted, feeling the warmth of the wine, and of being seen. 'But lately... it's been different.'

Their heads both snapped towards me.

'What do you mean?' Lucy asked, narrowing her eyes.

Maddie leaned forward. 'Oh my God. You've met someone.'

Heat crept up my neck.

'You *have*.' Maddie was practically bouncing.

Lucy beamed as she leaned closer. 'Okay, we need details. What's his name? What's he like? How serious is it?'

I laughed, cheeks burning. 'I don't even know what it is yet. But...' I licked my lips. 'I think I really like him.'

'Well,' Lucy said, triumphantly raising her glass. 'Then we're officially forcing you to take a day off.'

'I can't just close the café.'

'So hire someone,' Lucy said with a shrug, as though it was that easy. 'A student. Pay them minimum wage.'

'*I* don't make minimum wage.'

'Oh, I have the perfect solution,' Maddie said, waving her hand excitedly. 'My younger brother. He's seventeen. Good with people and desperate for cash.'

I looked at her flatly. 'This is the same brother who set fire to the toaster trying to make cheese on toast?'

Maddie shrugged. 'That was ages ago.'

'It was last week,' Lucy corrected.

'Was it?' Maddie asked, feigning ignorance. 'Okay, so maybe don't let him loose near kitchen appliances unsupervised.'

I frowned. 'It's a café, Maddie.'

She shrugged. 'Think about it, that's all I'm asking.'

Lucy and I glanced at each other, desperately trying not to laugh. 'Sure,' I said, 'I'll think about it.'

'And in the meantime, we'll do it,' Lucy said. 'We'll cover one day at the weekend. Once a month. Maddie and me. Like old times.'

'Hey, what's this "we" business?' Maddie objected.

'Oh, come on, you know you loved working in the café when we were at college.'

Maddie's eyes narrowed. 'I seem to recall you volunteering me then, too.'

I tipped my head to the side, my wine glass paused in front of my lips. 'What do you mean?'

The girls exchanged a look. Panicked. Guilty.

'What's going on?' I demanded, setting my glass down on the table.

'Lucy may have persuaded your mum to let us work in the café.'

'Because you wanted part-time jobs, and it meant we all got to work together,' I said, not understanding what the big deal was.

'It was kind of more voluntary...' Lucy mumbled.

'What?'

'I mean, your mum paid us what she could, when she could, but we weren't doing it for the money,' Lucy added quickly.

'When is a job not about the money?'

'When it's about spending time with a friend,' Maddie said with a slight shrug. 'While we were at college you were working in the café, all day, every day. Weekends too. And when you weren't working, you were shattered. You didn't have the energy to hang out in the evenings. So we figured the best way to hang out with you was to be where you were.'

I blinked. 'You... But...' I couldn't form words. They'd given up their free time to work for nothing.

Nothing except time with me.

'That's insane,' I said, staring at them.

Maddie and Lucy grinned at each other. 'Yep,' they said in unison.

I shook my head, my mouth opening and closing. 'I'm so sorry,' I managed finally.

'What for?' Maddie asked.

I glanced back and forth from one to the other. They both looked confused. But that didn't make sense. My apology was years late, but they didn't even seem to know what it was for.

'For making you do that. For wasting your time in the café. For—'

'Hold on, you didn't make us do anything,' Lucy interrupted.

My gaze darted to Maddie, bracing for her contradiction.

But she nodded. 'Lucy's right,' Maddie agreed. 'First of all, it was her idea, not yours. And secondly, no one can make me do anything I don't want to do.' She stuck her tongue out at Lucy. 'Not even her.'

Lucy laughed. 'It's true. Believe me, Maddie is impossible to persuade to do anything she's not totally on board with.'

'But...' My voice trailed off. I couldn't process what I was hearing. Or more importantly, what I wasn't hearing. No regret. No resentment. No sense of a debt that I couldn't even begin to repay.

I blinked again, adjusting my focus as I studied them. They'd been part of my life for years, but it felt like I was seeing them properly for the first time.

Had I ever truly known them?

Had I let myself?

Tears welled in my eyes. All these years I'd felt alone and barely tolerated, when maybe the opposite had been true all along.

'So, what do you say? It'll be like old times. We can work one Sunday a month. You get a day off. Maddie and I get to hang out together.'

Maddie nodded. 'That's not a bad plan, actually. It's autumn. No tourists. Short Sunday hours. No deliveries.'

'But...' I glanced back and forth from one to the other. Their excitement, their concern, even their presence in my life was inexplicable. And yet somehow, it felt right.

'Come on,' Lucy urged. 'Say yes, you know you want to.'

My lips quivered, the starts of a smile already forming. 'Okay,' I conceded. 'One Sunday, as a trial.'

They cheered.

My heart soared. For the first time, I truly felt like I was part of the group. A friend.

I swallowed. Except...

Friends didn't lie to each other.

'Now,' Maddie said, her eyes gleaming. 'I want to know more about this new guy...'

19

NOW

December

I shuffled in my seat, impatience prickling my skin as PC Monroe bent over his paperwork, his pen scratching against the page. Callum was missing, yet all he seemed to care about was filling in a form.

'*It's procedure,*' Mum's voice whispered in my head, calm and reasonable. '*The police are just doing their job.*'

But it wasn't enough. Not then. Not now.

'Miss Reed?' PC Monroe's voice snapped me back to the present.

I blinked, trying to shake myself free of the past, but it clung to me, never really relenting. 'Sorry,' I said quickly, deluding myself into thinking I could focus on the present.

'I asked if you could provide contact details for Callum's family, friends, or colleagues? Anyone who might know where he is?'

'No,' I replied, trying to bite back my frustration. 'I told you Callum doesn't speak to his family.'

The pen paused for a fraction of a second before continuing. 'And his friends?'

I hesitated. This was it. The time to explain everything I knew about Rob and what happened in Portsmouth. That combined with Wave Media's fake address would surely make the police take Callum's disappearance seriously.

But what if their investigation made things worse for him, like it had for me?

'Miss Reed?'

'I... I don't know,' I admitted reluctantly. 'Callum hasn't been here very long, and he works from home, so I don't think he meets a lot of people to make new friends. Any free time he has, he spends with me.'

'No school friends? Mates from college or uni?'

I swallowed. 'There was Rob. I... I don't know his last name,' I stammered. Part of me felt like I was telling him too much, but at the same time, I wasn't sure if I was telling him enough. 'Rob was Callum's best mate,' I added, but I clamped my mouth closed before I could say more.

Right now, I wasn't sure what Callum was involved in. Working for a fake company didn't look good for him. And whilst I wanted the police to find him, I didn't want them to arrest him on some misunderstanding, or something his old firm had framed him for.

Perhaps I shouldn't have come to them in the first place. I knew how their involvement could spiral out of control.

But what other choice did I have? If Callum was in danger, he needed help. And I was out of ideas on how to help someone I couldn't even find.

'Oh, he's still in touch with Ace, Rob's ex-girlfriend. I've seen texts from her on his phone.'

'Ace?'

My shoulders dropped as I realised how unhelpful that news was. 'Sorry, I don't know her real name.'

PC Monroe nodded and scribbled more notes. 'Anyone else?'

Another pause. 'He never mentioned anyone. Maybe he lost touch after moving here.'

PC Monroe nodded thoughtfully, jotting something down. 'From Portsmouth, right?' he confirmed, glancing at his notes.

'Yes.'

'And how long has he been in Christchurch?'

'Just over three months.'

'So, you've been dating since he arrived?'

'Pretty much.'

'And you've never visited anyone in Portsmouth together?'

I stiffened. 'No. I'd never go back there.'

His head snapped up, his gaze sharp.

'Back?'

I cursed myself inwardly, my pulse quickening. The police station had rattled me. I was usually more careful than this.

'Just bad memories there, that's all,' I said, hoping my dismissal sounded light and breezy, as though my loathing of Portsmouth was irrelevant. And it was, at least in respect to Callum.

PC Monroe studied me for a moment longer than I liked before finally nodding, though the wary crease in his brow lingered.

I knew from experience that to the police, everything was relevant. Everything was a thread to pull.

'What about work? You told the officer on your initial call that you had concerns about the company.'

I nodded. 'Wave Media, it's a marketing agency. But...'

My vision narrowed, darkness creeping in at the edges as I thought about the charity shop. I drew a slow breath. I couldn't afford to panic. 'I tried to contact their office. I even went to the address listed on their website, but it doesn't exist,' I said, struggling to keep my voice from shaking.

PC Monroe's pen hovered mid-air, as though waiting for me to continue.

'Callum worked remotely. I'm not even sure if he ever visited the office, so he might not know...' I finished lamely.

'Hmm,' PC Monroe murmured, sounding unconvinced.

I couldn't blame him. It felt preposterous that Callum wouldn't know the company he worked for didn't actually exist.

PC Monroe's gaze locked on me, as though he was assessing every detail. 'How would you describe your relationship?'

'Good,' I answered firmly. 'We're good.'

His stare bore into me and I shuffled, feeling as though my reply wasn't enough.

'He makes me happy.'

'Happy' was a description that hadn't applied to me in so long I'd given up on the idea of it even being a possibility. Until Callum.

'And him?'

I drew back in the chair. It felt like there was an implication to his question. Just because I was happy with the relationship didn't mean Callum was.

'He's happy too,' I assured him, aware of the terseness of my tone.

I knew that loving someone didn't guarantee they'd love you back. Or that needing them would make them stay.

'So there's no reason you can think of why he might leave?'

His question was like a wave of icy water, bringing the past back.

'It's because of me, isn't it? Dad left us because of me.'

Mum turned her head, unable to look at me. Her silence answered for her.

I cleared my throat. It wasn't the same. Callum wasn't like Dad. He loved me.

Though I'd thought that about Dad once too.

'No,' I replied firmly. 'He had no reason to leave.' But despite the conviction of my tone, the words felt fragile when I said them out loud.

There were things from my past that Callum didn't know. Or at least, I hoped he didn't. But his curiosity had been growing. He'd been asking more and more questions. But worst of all, he'd been talking to people.

People he shouldn't be talking to...

'Did you bring a photo with you?'

'I... er...' I swallowed. 'I couldn't find one.'

This time, PC Monroe didn't even try to conceal his surprise.

'Callum's kind of camera shy,' I explained feebly. 'He hates having his photo taken.'

'Hmm...'

'We *did* have a photo of us. On the wall, but...' I nibbled my lip. 'He took that too.'

'I see.'

But his tone implied he didn't.

I knew that tone. A mixture of pity and contempt.

* * *

The walls felt too close. There were no windows. No natural light. Just the relentless buzz of the bright fluorescent ceiling light.

My throat tightened as I stared at the door. The one and only door.

'You're free to leave at any time,' PC Rourke reminded me, as though sensing my distress at being in the closed-in space.

I swallowed.

It wasn't the same. I wasn't trapped. Not really. Not like I had been in the fire. But somehow my body didn't seem to be able to tell the difference.

'When we spoke to you at the hospital, you claimed your piano teacher, a Mr Daniel Sinclair, had started the fire,' PC Rourke said gently.

I nodded.

'Did you see him start it?' PC Ellison asked, from beside his colleague.

I glanced at Dad sitting next to me, his back stiff and straight. 'No,' I admitted.

'You were in the music room in Daniel's house alone at the time, is that right?'

I nodded again. 'He was outside. He told me to go in and start practising.'

'But if Daniel was outside, how could he have started the fire?'

'I don't know, exactly,' I replied grudgingly. I didn't like PC Ellison. I didn't like his questions or the way he looked at me as though he was studying every movement, every expression.

'You were the only person in the music room when the fire broke out,' PC Ellison said.

'But the room smelt of vanilla and petrol when I walked in.'

'Ah yes, vanilla,' PC Ellison murmured. 'From the vanilla candles you said you saw in the room?'

I nodded as I edged forwards in my chair. 'Yes, exactly. The house always smelt of them.'

'Sinclair should never have lit candles around a child. It was inevitable that one would get knocked over at some point,' Dad said, folding his arms across his chest.

A child.

That was how he still saw me. Young and immature.

'I didn't knock a candle over,' I protested.

Dad scowled at me. I knew he was trying to silence me.

But I didn't want to be silenced. I wouldn't let them blame me for this. I wasn't some clumsy little kid that had carelessly started a fire.

'And what about the petrol?' I demanded. 'I know I smelt that too.'

PC Ellison nodded in agreement. 'The Fire Investigation Officer had determined the presence of an accelerant.'

'What are you saying?' Dad asked, suddenly shifting forwards. 'That it wasn't an accident?'

'The fire is being treated as arson,' PC Rourke replied.

I nodded enthusiastically. This was good. They weren't just going to write this off as my mistake. They would investigate Daniel. They would prove he'd done it. They would figure out why.

'I understand that Daniel had told you he couldn't teach you any more,' PC Ellison said.

'That's not true,' I objected.

'So he didn't say that?'

I hesitated. 'Well, sort of,' I admitted reluctantly. 'But it wasn't the way you think,' I added quickly.

'Really?' PC Ellison exchanged a bewildered look with his colleague. 'Your piano teacher told you he couldn't teach you any more. The meaning seems pretty clear to me.'

'But he wasn't being serious. It was a joke. He said I'd advanced so much that I was surpassing him and would need a more advanced teacher soon.'

'Daniel Sinclair is a concert pianist who trained at the Royal Academy of Music,' PC Ellison pointed out. 'Yet a fourteen-year-old who attends a regular secondary school has supposedly surpassed him.'

His statement hung like a question. He didn't believe me.

'It must have been hard to hear,' PC Rourke said, his voice full of sympathy as though he was on my side.

But he wasn't. No one was.

'To have sacrificed so much chasing your ambition only to learn it wasn't good enough. That you weren't good enough.'

My skin bristled. 'I am good enough.'

PC Rourke and PC Ellison exchanged a look. They thought I was delusional. That I couldn't accept my own limitations.

My failure.

* * *

'Is there anything else you can think of? Any reason to be concerned?'

PC Monroe's question made my stomach plummet. I clasped my hands together in my lap, my grip tightening.

'I know it's unsettling,' PC Monroe said gently, his tone softening. 'But anything you can tell us about his life and his state of mind could help.'

I nodded slowly, swallowing against the lump in my throat. 'I understand.'

I truly did. I knew how these things worked, how they had to consider every angle. Every possibility. Especially foul play.

But I also knew where that road could lead.

'No,' I said finally. 'There's nothing specific I can think of. It's just...' I faltered. 'It's just completely out of character for Callum. That's what worries me.'

PC Monroe nodded. 'Okay then. Based on the circumstances you've described, together with a number of other factors including his age, the fact he appears to have left voluntarily and is not believed to have any specific medical or other vulnerabilities, my risk assessment has graded Callum as low risk at this time. The risk will be periodically reviewed and may change in light of additional information received by the police.'

'Low risk,' I echoed hollowly. 'Does that mean you're not going to do anything?'

'We'll monitor the situation and make some follow-up checks, but we have to prioritise cases based on their risk.'

I stared at him blankly. He didn't think Callum was important enough to be a priority.

'If you have a specific concern, a reason to believe he's in danger from himself or someone else, I will escalate his case,' PC Monroe added.

I hesitated. I wanted to say yes, to beg him to escalate it, to make Callum a priority, but I couldn't. I didn't know anything concrete. My belief in Callum wasn't enough. My opinion hadn't counted to the police before. Why would it now?

Working for a company with a fake address didn't look good for Callum. Perhaps I shouldn't have told PC Monroe that. I took a shaky breath. What if he thought I knew more? What if he thought I was lying?

Again?

'We'll investigate Wave Media and try to locate any friends he might have spoken to,' PC Monroe said, standing and gesturing towards the door. 'If something comes up that raises concern, we'll escalate the case. In the meantime, go home and keep your phone on in case he calls.'

I nodded and stood up slowly, my legs heavy and uncooperative.

'We have your number and will contact you with any updates or further questions. Please notify us if Callum gets in touch or if you think of any additional information.'

I stepped through the doorway feeling even more lost than when I'd arrived. As frustrating as it had been to simply sit and fill in a form instead of actively searching for Callum, at least it had been something. Now...

'You think he's just left me?' I said flatly.

The words left a bitter taste in my mouth. Voicing the fear that echoed in my brain felt like a betrayal to Callum. To our relationship.

My throat constricted. And yet the words were familiar.

Leaving was a pattern all the people in my life followed eventually. Now it was Callum's turn.

But why?

The others made sense. Dad's disappearance. Mum's disconnection. But Callum?

'He did take his clothes,' PC Monroe replied, as though that said everything. Perhaps, to him, it did.

I understood his reasoning; it was logical. But sometimes life wasn't logical. People weren't logical.

20

THEN

September

'Thanks for picking up dinner,' I said as I greeted Callum at the top of the stairs to the flat.

'No worries,' he replied, kissing my lips lightly before following me inside. The scent of Chinese food drifted in with him, filling the small open-plan living room.

'I really didn't have the energy to cook tonight,' I admitted as I grabbed a couple of glasses for the wine he'd brought with him.

'Don't worry about it,' Callum said brightly. 'I'm always happy for an excuse for a takeaway. It makes me feel less guilty about failing to keep my healthy eating goals.'

I cringed as I placed the wine glasses on the coffee table. 'Now I feel even more guilty.'

Callum laughed as he set the paper bag of food and bottle of wine beside them before turning to me with a mischievous grin. 'So, do I get a tour before we eat?'

It was my turn to laugh. 'Sure, but it'll be a short one. There's not much to show you.'

I guided him through the living room and jerked my head towards the tiny kitchen. 'It's a bit small compared to the café's kitchen.'

'It's practical,' Callum said diplomatically.

'And over here's my bedroom.' I signalled towards the open door.

Callum leaned against the door frame, his gaze drifting lazily around the room. 'Nice,' he said. 'And through here?' he asked, indicating a closed door.

'That's Mum's room,' I said, my mouth suddenly dry.

Callum's head jerked back, and he studied me silently, sorrow evident in his eyes. 'I'm sorry,' he said gruffly. 'I didn't mean to—'

'It's fine,' I assured him quickly. 'It's just...' I scrunched my nose. 'It's still weird being here without her.'

He nodded. 'Yeah, it must be. I didn't realise you worked *and* lived together.'

I shrugged. 'Everything we earned went back into keeping the café afloat. It made sense for me to keep living here. I kept thinking I'd get a place of my own when business picked up.' I shrugged limply. 'I guess there's no hurry now.'

'It's convenient, though. At least you don't have to worry about a commute,' Callum joked, trying to lighten the mood.

I laughed. 'I'm just glad the flat has a private exterior entrance. It makes pretending I have a life outside the café slightly easier.'

Callum chuckled. 'Yeah, it must be weird, living and working in the same building.'

'I've done it for so long, I guess I'm used to it. A trip to the supermarket is about as exciting as it gets for me these days.'

'It must be tough, running the café alone.'

I nodded. 'It was always a lot of work, but at least when there were two of us we could take a break from time to time.'

'What about your dad?'

I frowned. 'What about him?'

'Could he help you out?'

I snorted. 'I'd have to find him first.'

'Haven't you had any contact with him since he left?'

I shook my head.

'Did you try reaching out to him?'

My eyes widened in surprise. 'Why?'

'For closure,' Callum said, as though it was something critical that would suddenly make everything okay.

'He packed everything he owned and left without even saying goodbye or leaving a note. I think that's pretty definitive closure.'

'Is it?' Callum asked, looking dubious. 'I mean, I get that from his side, it is. He left on his terms, in his way. One that avoided actually having to face the consequences of his actions or see you face to face. But what about you? What do you want?'

'That doesn't matter,' I replied with a shrug.

'Of course it matters,' Callum assured me, reaching for my hand. 'You matter.'

I swallowed and turned away. He was wrong. If what I'd wanted, what I'd *needed*, mattered, then none of it would have happened. I wouldn't have even been in Christchurch. I would have been at music school.

My gaze drifted back to Mum's door. It had been six months, and I still hadn't opened it. At some point, I needed to go in and clear her things out – dust, vacuum, at least open a window. But I couldn't. Not yet.

'I still keep thinking she'll walk out of that room any second,' I admitted.

Callum pulled me to him, wrapping his arms around me. 'It gets easier. It just takes time.'

'Sounds like you're speaking from experience,' I murmured as I peered up at him.

'Similar, but different,' Callum said, nodding slightly. 'I lost my grandfather just over a year ago.'

There was a slight wobble to his voice as he spoke, and instinctively I held him tighter. 'I'm sorry. I didn't mean to bring back painful memories,' I said.

Callum shook his head. 'You didn't. They're good memories. My grandfather was quite a character. Full of life and energy, even in his nineties. He was the one person in my family who really got me. Who accepted me.'

'That must have been special,' I said, fighting the wave of envy that flooded through my veins. How different life would have been if someone had accepted me for who I was. My differences had stood me apart from the beginning. If they hadn't, maybe people wouldn't have been so quick to judge.

Maybe then someone would have believed me.

I thought I'd had Daniel in my corner. That I could count on him to stand up for me.

Until he turned on me too.

My breath caught, shallow and sharp. I still couldn't understand why he'd done that. Not him.

He'd been the one person who'd believed in me. Believed in my potential.

So what had changed? How did we go from him being my biggest supporter to the man who destroyed not only my career, but my life?

'The rest of my family, however...' Callum inhaled deeply as he pulled away. 'They'll never forgive me.'

He dropped down on the sofa and started unpacking takeaway containers from the paper bag. I stared at him, unable to move.

'Forgive you for what?' I asked hesitantly as my body tensed.

I knew how it felt to be condemned by your family. But I also knew what it took for that to happen.

'For following my own path,' he replied. 'For not pursuing their goals, their plans for me.' He shrugged. 'For making my own decisions. My own life.'

'Oh.' The word escaped in a gush of relief as I sank down on the sofa beside him. He hadn't done anything wrong.

'They expected me to follow in their footsteps, become a solicitor and take over the family firm one day.'

There was a familiarity to his words. I could imagine the conversations he'd had, fraught with tension and resentment. I'd been there myself. Unlike Callum, though, I'd conceded. I'd given up on my dreams.

After the fire, I didn't have any other option.

Callum, however, had stood up to his family. He'd fought for what he wanted. I admired him for that. But more than that, I was jealous. Jealous that he'd done what I couldn't.

'It must have been hard to stand your ground and go against your family.'

'I had my grandfather's support,' Callum said. 'He didn't care that I didn't want to be a lawyer. He just wanted me to be happy. He said knowing what you wanted and going after it showed more character than just toeing the line and following other people's expectations.'

I shuffled uncomfortably. 'I'm glad you had him,' I said honestly, though I couldn't help but feel jealous again, that no one in my family had supported my ambition in the same way. Mum had tried, at least in the beginning. But even she had lacked conviction.

* * *

'I hope this means you've already finished your homework.' Dad's voice boomed from the kitchen, disrupting my rhythm as my fingers stumbled over the keys.

'I'll do it in a minute,' I assured him, trying to regain my focus.

'It's always that damn piano ahead of everything else.' Dad's frustration didn't ease.

'She enjoys it.' Mum's voice was calm and soothing, and I had to play more softly to hear her above the music.

'She'd enjoy other things if she gave them a chance,' Dad retorted.

'Cooking is your passion. Music is hers.'

'She's fourteen. She doesn't know anything about passion. It's a hobby. One she's good at, I'll grant you that, but a hobby nonetheless.'

I bristled at his words, my attempts to continue playing completely abandoned as I crept closer to the door. How could Dad dismiss it as though it was insignificant?

'Daniel says she has a good chance of getting into the Royal Academy of Music, and from there, she could go anywhere.'

Dad scoffed. 'Daniel went there himself, and where did it get him?'

Mum didn't reply. Her silence felt like a betrayal.

'I want more for our daughter than a lifetime of disappointment and failure.'

'You don't know that she'll fail. You can't write her off. You can't write her dreams off. Not without at least letting her try.'

'I'm not writing them off. I'm just pointing out that investing everything into one goal is crazy.'

'We invested everything into buying this restaurant.'

'We weren't fourteen years old.'

Mum chuckled. 'Your mum still thought we were crazy.'

Dad sighed. 'You're missing the point.'

'Am I?' Mum asked. 'It's a child's job to follow their dreams, and it's a parent's job to worry. That doesn't make Olivia wrong and us right.'

'You don't really believe she'll make it, do you?'

I flinched. The bluntness of his question stung. I'd known he had doubts, but I'd always told myself that it was just because he was my dad. Of course he'd be worried about me. Protective. Cautious.

But the certainty in his tone told me it was more than just fatherly concern. He didn't believe in me. He didn't believe I had what it took to make it. To be a success.

To even try.

I swallowed.

'I believe in letting her try and being there to support her whatever happens.'

I drew back from the door frame, my breath catching in my throat. Dad was right. Mum didn't believe I'd make it either. She wanted me to have the opportunity to try.

But she still thought I'd fail.

Tears welled in my eyes as I fought for air. Dad's vocal disbelief in me hurt, but Mum's silence was shattering.

She was the one I'd thought I could count on. The one who would always defend me. Always fight for me.

But she hadn't.

'I want more for our girl than to end up like Daniel – a washed-up musician with a failed marriage and a kid who barely speaks to him.'

A kid.

I frowned. I didn't know Daniel had a kid. He'd never mentioned one. But then, he hadn't mentioned that his marriage had failed either. Neither detail was any of my business. They certainly weren't relevant to my lessons.

'Daniel's home life has nothing to do with Olivia's future.'

'Doesn't it? You've heard the rumours, same as I have. His wife left because she couldn't deal with his obsession any longer – supporting him financially and emotionally through every failure while he became more focused on succeeding than on his marriage.'

'We don't know if any of that is actually true.'

'We know she left him, didn't she? No wonder that poor kid barely speaks when she and Daniel come into the restaurant.'

* * *

'My grandad was something special,' Callum said, his gaze drifting somewhere in the distance. 'I still can't believe he's gone. All I have left of him is *The Elusive*.'

'The what?' I blinked, wondering what I'd missed when I'd allowed the past to distract me.

Callum smiled as he turned to face me. '*The Elusive*. It was my grandfather's boat. It's an IP24.'

'Oh, wow,' I said, as though I had any idea what that meant.

Callum chucked softly. 'She's an Island Plastics motorsailer, just under twenty-four feet. I know there are flashier boats, but she's solid and dependable. Living on board is a little cramped but it's actually kind of nice. Simple. No clutter. Just what matters.'

'You've *lived* on a boat?'

'Err...' Callum swallowed. 'I did. For a while.' He rubbed the back of his neck. 'After everything happened in Portsmouth, finances got a bit tight.'

I tried to picture it, Callum living on a boat, cooking dinner on a tiny hob, falling asleep to the sway of the current. The image was both calming and lonely.

'I'd love to see her sometime,' I said wistfully, drawn to the idea of being able to just sail off whenever and wherever you wanted.

His expression shifted. For the briefest second, I saw something flash across his face. Something sharp and sudden. Panic.

It vanished almost instantly.

'Her berth is in Portsmouth,' he said quickly.

'Hmm,' I murmured, sensing the wall he'd just put up.

A twinge of tightness caught in my chest as disappointment caught me off guard. He barely knew me. It wasn't a big deal if he felt the need to shut me out of things that were too personal to him.

After all, hadn't I been doing the same thing to Lucy and Maddie for years?

I swallowed. Was this how it felt to them too?

'Dad was furious when he discovered he'd left it to me. That was the final straw for him, I guess.'

'What do you mean?'

'He's not spoken to me since the funeral. None of my family has. As far as they're concerned, I don't exist. Not unless I go back to uni and get a postgraduate diploma in law.'

'Will you?'

Callum snorted. 'No.'

The tension in my shoulders eased as I leaned back against the sofa. I was glad he was stronger than I'd been. I'd discovered that following what your parents wanted didn't necessarily mean they wouldn't abandon you.

'If they can't accept me as I am, then they don't deserve to be in my life,' Callum said firmly. But I could still hear the pain in his voice.

'You're right,' I assured him. 'They don't.'

But I knew how much it hurt to be let down by the people you should have been able to count on.

There was more than one way for a parent to abandon a child. I knew that. Even if they were physically present, it didn't necessarily mean they were really there.

Dad had walked out. And Mum had stayed. And yet, the truth was, I hadn't really had either of them.

It was surprising how much that still hurt. I'd lived and breathed that truth for years. Yet it had never stopped me from hoping it would change.

Not that it could now.

Callum nodded slowly, lost in his own thoughts for a few moments, then suddenly turned back to face me, a mischievous glint in his eyes.

'So, what did you think I'd done?'

'Huh?' I grunted, confused by the sudden shift in conversation.

'When I told you my parents couldn't forgive me, for a second you looked really spooked, like I was about to confess to a crime or something.'

I laughed nervously. 'Did I?'

'Yeah, you did. What would you have done if I actually had confessed?'

I swallowed. 'I guess it would have depended on what you'd done.'

Callum tipped his head to the left. 'Would that really make a difference?'

There was a time when I would have said no, without hesitation. When the line between right and wrong, innocent and guilty, had been clear. But now?

'I'm not sure,' I admitted honestly.

Now it was Callum's turn to draw back from me. 'You think some crimes are excusable?'

I frowned as my thoughts drifted to another time, another place. 'I think there's a difference between excusable and understandable.'

Silence stretched between us. For the first time, Callum didn't have a response.

21

NOW

December

I worked in silence, methodically topping up the sugar jars, refilling the napkin holders, aligning the takeaway cups into neat stacks. Over the last two days the café had become a place to retreat to. After every encounter with the police, I found myself drawn back here. I told myself I didn't have a choice. I couldn't afford to keep the café closed all day. But I knew that was only part of the truth.

It was Mum's space. Even now it was filled with her presence. Her routines. Her rules. I'd spent so long feeling resentful of it, of her, that I overlooked what it truly was. Isolation. Protection. Safety.

Loud, upbeat music resounded as my phone vibrated in my pocket. For almost forty-eight hours, I'd been *willing* it to ring. And now...

My heart hammered as the ringtone sliced through the steady hum of the café. Hands trembling, I yanked my phone from my pocket, my breath catching as my gaze dropped to the screen.

Unknown number.

Callum?

It could be. It *had* to be.

Maybe he'd lost his phone. Maybe he'd had to change his number. A dozen hopeful explanations flitted through my mind as I fumbled to answer, pressing the phone tightly to my ear. 'Hello?'

'Miss Reed?' a male voice asked.

'Y-yes.'

'This is PC Monroe.'

My fingers tightened around the phone. 'Have you found him? Have you found Callum?' My words tumbled out, my stomach twisting in a nauseating mix of hope and dread.

'No, I'm afraid not,' PC Monroe said, his voice measured. 'I'm actually calling to clarify some discrepancies in the missing persons report you filed.'

'Oh.' I steadied myself against the counter, needing its support. I'd told the police about Wave Media – about the basic website, the charity shop – but part of me had clung to the hope that it was just a mistake. An outdated listing. A typo. That somewhere, someone could confirm it was real.

But if the police were calling *me* to double-check...

I let out a weary sigh. Maybe it really didn't exist. And if it didn't, what did that say about Callum?

Did he know?

Was he in on it?

Had he lied to me too?

'Can you confirm Callum's full name, please?'

PC Monroe's request threw me, and I frowned. '*His* name?' Why was he questioning Callum's name, and not the company's name?

'Yes,' PC Monroe confirmed. 'The name and date of birth you provided don't match any records.'

My stomach twisted. 'I don't understand.'

'Let's check there's not been a mistake made on the form,' PC Monroe said calmly.

My mind reeled as I repeated Callum's full name and birth date.

'Hmm,' PC Monroe murmured before falling silent for a beat. 'That's what I have in the report. But no records are coming up for those details in our searches. The details you've provided just don't tally up.'

The café suddenly felt smaller, as though the walls were closing in on me.

I'd been here before. The doubt. The questions. The judgement...

* * *

'Talk us through it again,' PC Rourke said as he leaned on the table between us. 'The details you've given don't tie up with the statement Daniel has made.'

'Because he's lying,' I said, willing him to believe me. To finally see that just because he was the adult, it didn't make Daniel right and me wrong.

'How did the fire start?' PC Ellison asked, ignoring my accusation.

'I told you, I don't know,' I replied. 'There was a whooshing sound behind me and when I turned, flames were already sweeping across the carpet from the door to the piano.'

* * *

'I'm sure I've got it right,' I said, though my voice wobbled slightly, and I gripped the edge of the counter. 'At least... I think that's what he told me.' I swallowed. 'Maybe I misheard him, or maybe I've remembered it incorrectly.'

'Are there any additional details that could help me track down his records?' PC Monroe's voice remained friendly, but there was a stiffness to it now.

'I, er, I can't think of anything. Callum doesn't really talk about himself that much,' I replied, realising the truth of my words as I spoke.

'I understand,' PC Monroe replied, but his tone implied the opposite.

How could he, when I didn't even understand it myself? Callum had been living in my home for two months, and yet I didn't even know his correct date of birth or where he worked. Was I so caught up in my own life that I hadn't paid enough attention to his? Could I have really got it all so wrong?

After all, I had before. I'd misjudged things. Misjudged people. And as a result, I'd got myself caught up in a situation I couldn't get out of.

Had I done it again? Made another mistake?

And if I had, what would I do this time?

Or—

I paused, not wanting to finish that thought. But it refused to stay dormant, refused to be silenced.

What if he'd lied?

Like Daniel had.

And if that was true, then maybe I hadn't really learned anything at all.

'Miss Reed, given these discrepancies, it would be helpful to discuss this in person. If you would be willing to come to the station, we can talk about this in more detail.'

If you would be willing...

My stomach tightened. I knew what that meant. They were just words inserted into the request to make it sound like a choice.

I'd been here before.

I took a breath. No, this wasn't the same.

This wasn't about me.

This was about Callum.

22

THEN

October

'Hey,' I said as Callum walked towards the counter.

'Hi, Liv,' he replied with a weak smile. He dropped a bag at his feet before reaching to give me a hug.

'What's this?' I asked, craning my neck, my gaze locked on the large duffel bag. 'Are you going somewhere?'

I tried to make my question sound light and jokey, but my throat felt tight.

Callum didn't answer, and as I looked up, my eyes met his. My stomach somersaulted. He was leaving.

I took a step back as a wave of panic crashed over me. He couldn't. Not him too.

'I need to go back to Portsmouth. I have some stuff I've gotta deal with.' He let out a long deep breath. 'It's just for a little while.'

'When will you be back?'

'I'm not sure,' he said quietly.

A wave of nausea crept in. People who were coming back had a plan. A timeline.

'I'm gonna crash on a mate's sofa while I sort myself out.'

I fought to keep my breathing steady as my vision blurred. He was ending things.

We were over.

'I really thought I could make it work but...' He puffed his cheeks out. 'It's time I faced it. I have to sell her.'

I blinked. 'W-what?'

'The boat. I've been putting off selling it, thinking I'd find a way to keep her.' He shook his head. 'Between the berthing fees and maintenance, it's just not feasible.'

'You're going back to Portsmouth to sell your boat?' I said slowly, his words sinking into my brain through my panic.

'Yeah.' Callum ran his hand through his hair. 'I don't know how long it will take. I need to clean her up a bit, fix a few things, if I'm going stand a chance of getting a decent price for her.'

Relief flooded through me.

This wasn't about us. About me. It was financial.

He wasn't leaving me.

And yet, the weight pressing against my chest didn't shift.

'It's your grandfather's boat.'

Callum shook his head. 'I know, I feel like I'm letting him down.'

'Isn't there anything else you can do?' My pulse quickened at the thought of him selling something that meant so much to him.

The way Dad had sold my piano.

The memory hit me like a punch to my stomach. He hadn't asked. He hadn't even told me. One day it was just gone. The one thing that had meant everything to me. That had truly been mine. And he took it from me.

I couldn't let that happen to Callum.

Anger surged through me, vibrating my body with tremors that I couldn't contain. Not that I wanted to. I felt alive. Powerful. As though pure hatred was strength.

'You can't sell it,' I said, channelling that anger into determination.

'I don't want to,' he said, his eyes pleading as if he needed me to understand. 'I don't have a choice.'

'There's always a choice.'

'The job.' Callum shook his head. 'It isn't going well.'

I frowned. 'But you said it was your chance to get your career back on track.'

'It is, but...' Callum reached for my hands. 'I'm starting at the bottom again.'

'You'll work your way back up. You just need to give it some time,' I assured him.

'I know, but in the meantime, I've got to cut back. And the boat...' He shrugged heavily. 'I can't give it more time. I can't afford to.'

I pulled my hands free from his. 'No,' I said firmly, shaking my head. 'I can't let you sell your grandfather's boat. It means too much to you. You'll never forgive yourself when it's gone.'

'Liv, I appreciate what you're saying, I really do, but I just can't afford it any more. Between the fees for the berth at Ocean Haven Marina back home and the debts I'm still paying off, there's nothing left. I can't even afford to keep living in the Airbnb.'

'An Airbnb?' I interrupted, frowning. My frown deepened. 'You're staying in an Airbnb?'

Callum glanced over his shoulder at the bag on the floor. 'I was. I thought it would just be—' His gaze shifted back to me. 'I thought it would just be temporary until I got back on my feet. But—' He exhaled. 'The truth is, I'm in over my head, and I can't do it on my own any more.'

I stepped forward and stroked his arm. 'It's going to be okay,' I assured him. 'You're not alone.'

'I know.' He nodded slowly. 'I called my parents.'

I froze. 'After the way they treated you?'

'They gave me another option. They offered to help me out. It would mean I could keep The Elusive,' Callum said quietly.

I blinked, stunned that his parents had actually come through for him. 'That's amazing, I thought they refused to speak to you unless you became a lawyer.'

Callum's jaw tightened. 'They did.'

My stomach dropped. 'No. Don't tell me that you're actually thinking about giving in?'

'They'll cover my bills, rent an apartment for me, and put me through law school.'

'But you don't want to go to law school.'

Callum shrugged. 'Sometimes what you want doesn't matter.'

I shook my head. 'It always matters,' I assured him earnestly. 'Otherwise, you'll end up like me.'

Callum's eyes widened as my declaration hung in the air between us.

'You aren't happy here?' he asked, his gaze flitting around the empty café.

I swallowed. 'You were right. It was never my dream. It was—' I paused, searching for the right word. 'A necessity.'

'Then you understand.'

I took a deep breath. 'I understand what giving up on yourself really means. What it costs. And I want more than that for you. I want *better* than that for you.'

Callum kissed my cheek. 'I appreciate that, I really do. But I only have two choices. Sell the boat or take my parents' help. I don't have anyone else I can turn to.'

'You have me.'

Callum hugged me tightly. 'I know I do, but you can't help me with this.'

'Move in with me.'

The words were out of my mouth before I even had time to think them through.

Callum pulled back, and we stared at one another in stunned silence.

'Did you just say "move in with me"? Liv, I can't ask you to—'

'You didn't ask me for anything. I'm asking you.'

'But we've only been dating for a month. That's not enough time for us to be moving in together.'

'You're right,' I said firmly. 'So maybe we don't move in as boyfriend and girlfriend. Maybe we just move in as friends. Maybe it's just one friend helping out another.'

'Are you sure?'

'I have a spare room. You could have your own space.'

'You mean your mum's room,' Callum said slowly.

I hesitated. Of course he was right. There was no other room. But somehow the confirmation wouldn't come.

I hadn't thought my offer through before I spoke. I hadn't thought about what him moving in meant. I hadn't thought about what I would have to give up.

But what was the alternative?

Mum hadn't stopped Dad from taking my piano. She'd let him take the one thing that mattered. Maybe this was a way to offset that. Giving up something of hers, so Callum could keep something that mattered to him.

And maybe I could keep Callum.

I nodded finally. 'Yes.'

'But I can't take her room. That's her space. You said it yourself, you're not ready to empty it yet. Which means you're not ready for somebody else to move in there.'

I shook my head. 'I wasn't ready before.' I swallowed. 'But maybe it's time now.'

Maybe...

The word repeated in my head, like a question.

The nausea churning in the pit of my stomach told me the answer. I wasn't ready. And yet, I knew I was still going to do it.

'You'd really do that for me?' Callum's voice was thick with emotion.

I forced a smile. 'I'd do it for us.'

* * *

I stood in the middle of Mum's bedroom, my gaze drifting around the dimly lit space. Sunlight crept through the partially drawn curtains, casting long shadows across the room.

It had taken all my willpower just to open the door. To step inside. But now that I had, I couldn't help but wonder how I was supposed to do the next part.

How could I sort through her things? How could I just throw them away?

It felt impossible. It felt *wrong*.

My gaze shifted to the dressing table. For a moment I saw her sitting on the faded pink plush stool, brushing her hair in long strokes.

* * *

Mum's eyes met mine in the mirror, worry lines creasing her skin. 'You know you have an early start tomorrow. I need you in the café.'

'I'll be there, I promise,' I assured her, tugging on my jacket.

'It's too late to be going out now,' Mum said, without even checking her watch.

'It's only 9 p.m. And I'll just stay for an hour.'

'Then there's barely any point in even going, is there?' Mum asked with satisfaction.

'Lucy and Maddie invited me. I never go. They won't keep inviting me if I always say no.'

Mum pivoted on the stool and looked at me dead on. 'It's not a good idea.'

'I thought you liked them.'

'I do.' She paused. 'But this isn't about them.'

I inhaled sharply, knowing what her words meant. It was about me.

It always was.

'There'll be drinking.'

'Of course, it's a birthday party at a pub,' I replied openly.

'Alcohol makes people make bad decisions. And you...' Mum's lips twisted in a thin line. 'You don't always make the best decisions as it is.'

I bristled as I dug my fingernails into my palms to keep me from responding. It wasn't worth it. We'd had that argument too many times to hope for a different outcome this time.

'I'll have a Diet Coke, just like I always do,' I assured her, keeping my tone deliberately light to conceal my resentment.

Mum sighed wearily. 'It's a mother's job to protect her daughter. Even...' Her voice wavered. 'Even from herself.'

* * *

I flinched at the memory.

Mum hadn't intended to be unkind. She was trying to do what she thought was best.

Even if it hurt me.

'Are you okay?' Callum's voice was soft as he edged into the doorway.

I nodded. A silent lie.

'It still doesn't seem real that she's gone.' My gaze drifted back to the stool. 'I was just thinking about Mum, remembering her sitting there and—' I stopped abruptly.

'Tell me,' Callum urged.

I tore my gaze away. He didn't need to know about Mum's concerns. Her doubts.

'It still feels like she could come dashing out of this room, bursting with excitement about a new idea, a new recipe, something that would change everything and rejuvenate the café.'

I smiled ruefully. That had always been the hope that underpinned our entire existence: that if we just held on long enough, something would turn it all around.

'I think deep down, we both knew it wouldn't really work. But neither of us said it.'

'Why not?' Callum asked gently.

'Perhaps we were in denial about how bad things were.' I shrugged. 'Or perhaps we just chose to be.'

Callum frowned. 'But if you'd talked about how bad things were...' He let his words trail away.

I knew what he was implying. If we'd talked. If we'd faced the truth together. We could have closed the café. Found another way. Another life.

But maybe that was precisely why we didn't. We'd already started over. And it had cost us everything.

I sighed softly. 'Perhaps we were both afraid that if one of us cracked, neither of us would be able to hold it together.'

I couldn't let that happen. I *wouldn't* let that happen. I was the reason we'd ended up in this mess. I couldn't break again.

'Mum lost everything because of me. Her friends. The restaurant. Her life in Portsmouth. Even Dad. But more than any of that, she had lost *herself*. Her identity. Her sense of self.'

'But it was their decision to close the restaurant and leave Portsmouth,' Callum said with a certainty that showed how little he truly knew about my past. 'You were just a kid, it's not like you had any real influence on their decisions.'

I swallowed. I'd had influence. More than he could ever imagine. 'Mum wasn't the same after we moved,' I said, sidestepping his train of thought. 'She used to believe in things with such conviction.'

She used to believe in *me*, I added silently. To an extent, at least...

Unlike Dad, though, at least she stayed. Maybe it was duty, maybe it was responsibility. Maybe, as a mother, she still felt a need to protect me. But it was different. The love she had for me in those last few years was heavy, resentful, obligatory. As though she had never forgiven me.

And now, she never would.

Maybe that was what made it so much harder to let go. Not just because I missed her. Not just because she was my mum. But because, despite the strained, distant existence we had shared, I still loved her. I still wanted to fix things. I still wanted to bring back what we'd once had.

But some things were irreparable.

I opened the wardrobe. The soft scent of lavender filled my nostrils, making my eyes burn with unshed tears. It was her favourite scent.

'Liv?' Callum spoke beside me.

I turned to him, tried to smile, to pull myself together, to be okay. But I couldn't. I wasn't okay. I hadn't been for a long time. And now... I exhaled slowly. Being in this room, Mum's room, made it impossible to pretend.

'We should open the curtains. Let in some light,' I said, but I didn't move.

'Are you sure?' Callum asked.

I nodded. As hard as this was, it was time.

He reached for my hand and squeezed it tightly. 'I'm with you.'

Three simple words. But they washed over me like warm sunlight. He was with me. I wasn't alone.

I took a deep breath, gently pulling my hand away before walking to the window. I pulled the curtains back and pushed the window wide open, inhaling the cool autumnal air.

'It's time for a fresh start.' My body trembled at the thought of moving forward, but my words were firm and certain. 'I've spent enough of my life living in the past.'

* * *

Callum nodded to a pile of folded clothes. 'Are you sure you don't want to keep anything?'

I shook my head. I didn't need Mum's clothes to remember her. She was with me every day at the café. In her recipes. Her rules.

Her belongings were a reminder of how much she had already given up because of me. So many of our things, her things, had already been sold or donated, there was a kind of inevitability in donating what remained.

'What about this?' Callum's voice broke through my thoughts. He pulled a thick black binder from the back of the wardrobe.

I shrugged. 'No idea. What is it?'

He handed it to me. I opened it, turning to the first page, and a tiny gasp escaped from my lips.

'Liv?'

I turned another page. I froze as I stared at a collection of recital programmes. My fingers traced the edges, my pulse quickening.

'What is it?' Callum asked, edging closer and peering over my shoulder.

I tried to speak, but the words wouldn't come.

I turned another page. And then another.

Photos. Programmes. Performance schedules.

'It's my life,' I whispered.

All the things we had left behind in Portsmouth. The music, the recitals, the competitions. The life I thought had been erased was right in front of me, in this folder.

'I d-didn't know Mum had made this,' I stammered.

Why hadn't she shown it to me when I was younger? I could have helped her compile the photos and programmes. Shared those moments with her. Celebrated them together.

But then perhaps the bigger question was why had she kept it? Maybe, deep down, she had never really let go either.

Callum turned a page, studying it carefully. 'I thought they resented you for all of this?'

'They did,' I murmured. They lost everything because of me.

But they never seemed to care that *I* had everything, too.

At least, I'd thought they hadn't.

23

NOW

December

I stayed frozen in place behind the counter long after the call had ended, with PC Monroe's words playing on a loop.

No records of Callum Hayes.

No company called Wave Media registered.

If I'd be willing to go to the station...

The café that had felt comforting in its normality only moments earlier suddenly felt alien to me. Nothing fit. Nothing made sense.

How could there be no record of Callum Hayes?

It wasn't possible. It had to be a mistake. A clerical error. A glitch. They must have overlooked something.

Or had I?

Could I have really made a mistake and given PC Monroe incorrect information? Had I not paid enough attention to the person who mattered most in my life? If I couldn't even get Callum's name or date of birth right, what else had I missed?

My breathing quickened.

It felt too familiar. The things I thought I knew with absolute certainty were being questioned again. And with each question, that certainty grew murkier, more distorted.

Panic swelled within me as my vision blurred. I pressed my hand to my head, willing it to stop. But that gnawing sense that I'd missed something important was like a rising wave of déjà vu. I'd been here before.

Last time, I'd been fourteen. Just a kid. Easy to dismiss.

But this time...

The police didn't know Callum. To them, he was just a name on a form, one that didn't fit neatly into their structured little systems. But that didn't diminish his importance. Not to me.

I'd had no one in my corner. No one fighting for me. But Callum did. He had me. I wouldn't let them dismiss him. If the police couldn't figure out where he was, then I would. I had to.

I grabbed a napkin from the dispenser on the counter and pulled a pen from my pocket.

Callum, I scrawled at the top of the napkin, followed by his date of birth. Or at least the date I thought it was.

I paused, tapping the end of the pen against my lips as I studied the shaky writing. Then I drew a line down the centre. On the left I wrote:

Past:
Portsmouth
Family of solicitors
Rob
Marketing consultant
Marketing firm corruption – false?

On the right:

Arrived in Christchurch almost 4 months ago
Wave Media – doesn't exist?
In debt – couldn't afford to stay at Airbnb

The words looked small and uncertain. Fragmented details of a person I thought I knew. The sum of a life reduced to one flimsy napkin.

And it wasn't enough.

Did that fact mean something by itself? Was it a sign that I didn't know enough about the man I loved?

But how much could Callum have written about me? Café owner. Lives above café. No family. No outside interests. Limited friends.

My life had shrunk by necessity and design. The parts Callum didn't know would have needed many more napkins.

Could the same be true of him?

I'd told myself that our pasts didn't matter. The details of who I was before he met me were irrelevant to who I was now. Except it wasn't true. The things that had happened before – the ones I never talked about – were exactly *why* I was here, stuck in this café, clinging to routine like it might keep me safe.

So what details from his past didn't I know?

Had he simply not thought to share them? Had I never asked? Or had he intentionally withheld them?

Just like I had.

Or worse, had he lied.

I'd never done that to him. Not outright lied. I'd skirted around the truth. Omitted details that were in the past. Not to hurt him. But to protect myself.

Was that what he was trying to do, too? Protect himself?

But from what?

I let out a weary sigh. Whatever his reasons, there was one key difference between us. He knew who I was. He knew my name. Could I say the same thing about him?

Were the police unable to find any record of him because I'd made a mistake with his date of birth? Or because I'd given them the wrong name?

The name he'd told me.

There was no way I could have made a mistake about that. Digits could be transposed, dates could be forgotten, but a name? *His* name? I shook my head.

But why wouldn't he tell me his real name?

I let out a weary sigh. I was getting distracted. The details could all be ironed out once I found him.

If I found him...

I set the pen down beside the napkin, a wave of inadequacy crashing over me. I was failing him. I knew it. But what could I do with so little?

The police had more resources. More experience. If they couldn't figure out where Callum was, or even *who* he was, what chance did I have?

My certainty that he wouldn't just leave me was starting to waver. Given everything I didn't know about him, how could I truly be sure of anything? One thing I'd learnt from the past was nothing was impossible.

But I couldn't allow myself to lose faith. Not now. Because if I did, how would I keep going?

I'd barely managed it last time. But I'd had Mum then. She'd needed me to be strong. I'd pulled myself together for her.

Callum might not be here now, but maybe – just maybe – he needed that too. Needed me to hold on. To believe in him when no one else would.

So that's what I had to do.

I had to hang on to the hope that once the police found Callum, he would clear everything up. There would be a perfectly logical explanation. A reason. Something that made this make sense.

Even if right now I couldn't imagine what that might be.

24

THEN

October

I threw my coat over the back of the sofa as I kicked my shoes off. 'We've just about got time to shower and change before we go.'

'Go?' Callum asked, looking at me blankly.

'To Lucy's engagement party,' I reminded him as I tugged my hair down from the tight bun I wore it in for work.

'Oh, I'd forgotten you'd got that tonight.'

'*We've* got that tonight,' I corrected him as I headed towards the bedroom.

'We?' Something about the wariness in his tone made me stop, and I turned slowly.

'Yes, we. They invited both of us. Maddie will be there too; you'll finally get to meet them at last.'

Callum shuffled. 'Yeah, but I don't want to intrude on your girls' night.'

'It's not a girls' night,' I assured him. 'The guys are coming too; it's an engagement party.'

'Yeah, but it's still your time with your friends. I know you don't see them much.'

He was right, I didn't, but that was my choice. I always made an excuse; a reason I couldn't see them for a meal or a night out. Not because I didn't want to go, but because as lovely as they were, the truth was, I wasn't like them. I didn't fit into their world. I never had. They'd welcomed me into their little group when I'd moved here from Portsmouth, but I still felt like an outsider, just as I had as the new kid at school.

Their lives had gone in different directions, and yet for some reason they kept reaching out to me. They'd gone to college and university, whilst for me, helping Mum at the café had become my full-time job. Their lives had moved on, whilst mine had stayed stuck. I had nothing, I had no one. Just a café. Although most of the time it felt more and more like it had me.

But things were different now. I had Callum. And I couldn't wait to show him off to the world. To prove to everyone that finally things were different. I was different.

'But it's—'

'Let's do something a bit more casual for the first time I meet your friends,' Callum interjected.

'It's just drinks, nothing fancy,' I assured him.

Callum shook his head. 'This is Lucy's night. She should have everyone's undivided attention focused on her.'

I laughed. 'And you think what? If you come you'll steal the spotlight?'

'No, of course not,' Callum replied. 'But it will shift the focus from celebrating her engagement to everyone assessing us. Assessing me.'

'They're not like that,' I objected.

'Not curious about who you're dating? Not worried about how fast our relationship is moving?'

'Well...' I hesitated.

'Precisely,' Callum said triumphantly.

'But most of their concerns are just because they don't know you yet. Once they've met you—'

'And they will,' Callum interrupted again. 'But not tonight, okay?'

My shoulders slumped. There was something so final about the way he said it. He wasn't angry or frustrated, and yet there was a familiarity to it.

For a split second as our eyes met, it wasn't Callum I saw. It was Dad.

I shook my head, dropping my gaze to the floor. It wasn't the same. *He* wasn't the same. But the panic fluttering in my chest didn't settle.

'Liv?' Callum's voice was soft and concerned.

I lifted my chin and met his gaze with a broad smile. 'Of course, it's okay,' I said with forced brightness.

Except it wasn't.

I wanted him with me. I wanted him to be part of my life. All of it. Or at least my present. Lucy and Maddie were the only people I had in my life; was it so much to ask for him to want to meet them? Was it so wrong for me to want him to see that I was more than just the café?

He's not the same as Dad, I reminded myself again. But I couldn't shake the feeling that Dad had never been able to see what was really important to me.

Or, for that matter, to even see me at all.

Was Callum doing the same?

I straightened my spine. Then again, perhaps the only thing that mattered here was that I wasn't the same. I couldn't make the same mistakes I made with Dad. Fighting him for everything. Constantly pushing against his decisions. Telling him he was wrong. Demanding more, whatever the cost.

I wouldn't do that this time.

Otherwise, Callum might leave too.

'You're not mad, are you?' There was a hopeful undercurrent to his voice.

I shook my head quickly and gave him a bright smile. 'No, of course not.'

His expression shifted. But instead of looking relieved, he seemed almost... disappointed.

I blinked.

It was almost as though he wanted me to be mad.

But that was a crazy thought. Of course he wouldn't. He probably just expected me to be and was surprised that I wasn't.

It wasn't the first time he'd bailed on our plans together. Usually, it was because of work. An urgent meeting. A trip that couldn't be avoided.

His unreliability was unsettling. It wasn't easy to handle the disappointment of being abandoned.

Then again, it couldn't be easy for him either, knowing he was letting me down. Work required sacrifices. And unlike me, at least he was following his career aspirations. A little disappointment here and there was a small sacrifice to bear for him to have that.

I knew what it was like to have passion and drive. When the pursuit of a dream overtook everything else. If I was in his shoes, could I truly say I'd do things differently?

After all, I had been once. And I knew the choices I'd made.

I envied him that clarity. The ability to know what you wanted from life and to fight for it. But I also knew not to stand in the way. In *his* way. People had done that to me, and bad things had happened. Lives were ruined.

And not just mine.

25

NOW

December

'Thank you for coming in, Ms Reed,' PC Monroe said, holding the door to the interview room open. 'We appreciate your assistance with our inquiries.'

I hesitated, fighting the overpowering desire to flee. His words were meant to reassure me that my presence was voluntary, but I knew as well as he did how quickly that could change. Inhaling deeply, I stepped into the room.

A man seated at the table turned as I entered, offering one short, sharp nod of acknowledgement before returning his attention to the open folder in front of him. His lack of uniform sent a ripple of panic through me. I should have anticipated this.

'Take a seat,' the man said without lifting his head.

Reluctantly, I lowered myself into the chair opposite him.

'We wanted to speak to you face to face to clarify a few things about your missing persons report,' PC Monroe said as he closed the door.

We. Somehow, the word felt reassuring, and I realised as he sat down beside his colleague that I was glad he was staying. He was still a police officer, but at least he was familiar.

'It's fine,' I assured him, fighting to keep my expression neutral while my stomach churned. 'I just want to find Callum.' That part, at least, was true.

'This is Detective Sergeant Harrington,' PC Monroe said. 'He's taken over the investigation now.'

My gaze shifted to the man beside him. He was older – mid-fifties, maybe – with a grim expression. But it wasn't the look on his face that unsettled me. It was his title. A detective sergeant meant this was serious now. No longer just a missing persons report. This was something more.

DS Harrington looked up and pressed a button beside him. 'This interview is being recorded. I'm DS Harrington and the other officer present is...' He paused, and PC Monroe said his own name. 'For the purposes of the tape can you please introduce yourself.' DS Harrington paused again, this time nodding at me.

'Olivia Reed.' My voice shook as I spoke.

'Thank you for coming in today so we can ask you some questions about the disappearance of your boyfriend. This is a voluntary interview, and we are grateful for your cooperation. We're recording it so we can get as much information as possible from you and we can listen to the recording again in due course if we need to.'

I nodded slightly, my thoughts drifting as he stated the date and time. It all sounded so reasonable and innocuous.

But it had last time too.

DS Harrington nodded. 'Right. Let's start with the basics. You reported that your boyfriend, Callum Hayes, went missing on Sunday evening.'

'Yes.' The question was implied rather than stated, but I felt compelled to answer.

'PC Monroe mentioned to you on the telephone yesterday that there is no record of a Callum Hayes with the date of birth you provided,' DS Harrington continued. 'We've expanded our search, but the results are the same.'

I frowned. 'That doesn't make sense. How can there be no record of him?'

'You're absolutely certain that the information you provided is correct?'

I nodded. 'It's what Callum told me,' I replied firmly, refusing to voice the question that still lingered in my brain. *What if I was wrong?*

I tried to shake the thought free. I couldn't have made a mistake. Not about this.

But doubt continued to niggle at me.

I'd thought that once before.

'Is it possible Callum is a nickname or a middle name?' PC Monroe suggested.

A wave of gratitude washed over me. He was trying to help, offering a logical explanation. I wanted to grasp at the sliver of hope he was giving me. But I couldn't.

I shook my head. 'I don't know.'

'There's a lot that you don't seem to know about your *boyfriend*,' DS Harrington said bluntly.

I flinched at the accuracy of his words.

Perhaps we'd moved in together too soon. Our relationship had moved too fast. We'd skipped over steps we should have taken time over: getting to know each other's world, meeting friends, talking about our pasts.

But then that was one step I'd been grateful we'd missed.

'I've never been very good at really knowing anyone.' The confession slipped unguarded from my lips, and I watched as PC Monroe's expression shifted.

I knew that look. Pity. I'd had enough of that in the past.

PC Monroe exchanged a look with DS Harrington, and a tingle of unease crawled up my spine.

'As part of our investigation we always carry out background enquiries on the person who reports someone missing, as they often hold vital information. In this case, your own background has been checked.' His careful, measured tone made my chest tighten.

'M-my background?' I stammered. 'What does that have to do with anything?'

PC Monroe shifted forward in his chair. 'One of the enquires we carry out is a PNC check – a search in the Police National Computer,' he clarified. 'I found that you were a potential suspect in an arson investigation eight years ago. You were also suspected of providing misleading information in an attempt to incriminate your piano teacher—' He glanced at the papers in front of him. 'Daniel Sinclair.'

'I don't understand,' I cut in. 'I was fourteen then. What does any of this have to do with Callum's disappearance now?'

The officers exchanged another glance before PC Monroe turned back to me. 'We have to consider background information on all parties when we're dealing with this type of investigation,' he said softly, 'especially where circum-stances may show a pattern in a person's behaviour.'

I shook my head. 'No. This is crazy. There must be a mistake in your system. I've told you everything I know about Callum.'

'Daniel Sinclair countered your accusations. He claimed you were lying...'

DS Harrington let his statement hang.

I swallowed. I knew where he was going with this. The same place the police had gone eight years ago.

'He alleged that *you* started the fire.'

My breathing quickened. This couldn't be happening again. I'd put all this behind me.

Or at least I'd tried to.

'He lied,' I said, fighting to keep my voice steady.

'Setting fire to his piano, his home, just because he suggested you find a new instructor,' DS Harrington continued as though he hadn't heard me, 'does suggest emotional instability. Which is relevant when we consider this situation.'

'I didn't do it,' I urged, repeating the plea I'd made so many times before.

No one had listened to me then either.

'Nobody's accusing you of anything at this stage,' DS Harrington said, though his words lacked conviction. 'But you have to see how this looks. We can't find any trace of Callum with the details that you've given us, and given your past, well, it raises questions.'

'We need you to help us understand what's going on here,' PC Monroe added more gently.

'I *am* helping. I've told you everything.'

DS Harrington shook his head. 'The lack of any traceable records for Callum, combined with your inability to provide explanations for the discrep-ancies, gives rise to some serious doubts about his existence.'

I blinked. 'His *existence*? Wait, you think I imagined him? That I made up a boyfriend?'

'Your prior history, along with the lack of records, raises questions about your credibility,' PC Monroe said carefully. 'There's also the matter of wasting police time.'

I stared at him, my eyes wide. 'Are you serious?'

Emotional instability.

Questions about your credibility.

I gripped the edge of the table as the room swayed. It was happening again.

Serious doubts about his existence.

Except this time it was worse. This time Callum was caught up in it too.

'Did you ever see any proof of his ID?' he continued. 'A driving licence, passport, anything official?'

'No, but...' I faltered. 'He's my boyfriend. Why would he show me any of that?'

'Did you take any trips together? Any flights?'

'No, we haven't been together long enough for that,' I said automatically.

The words stuck in my throat.

We hadn't been together long enough to travel. And yet, we'd lived together.

The contradiction jarred. Why was it too soon for one, but not the other?

Or maybe it had been too soon for both.

His moving in had been a practicality. A necessity. He moved in with me or he left Christchurch. Left me.

But that wasn't normal either. That wasn't how relationships were supposed to begin, urgent and pressured.

Had I rushed things?

Or had he?

26

THEN

October

The scent hit me halfway up the stairs. Soft. Sweet. Sickening.

Vanilla.

It seeped into my pores, suffocating me with the memories it brought with it.

I hesitated on the top step, torn between the overwhelming urge to run and my body's sudden inability to move.

The door to the flat was ajar. I stared at it, feeling betrayed. Inside was supposed to be safe. A cocoon from the past. But the door had failed to keep the memories out.

Before I could regain control and pull myself back to the present, the door swung open. Callum stood in the doorway, smiling. His sleeves were rolled up, beads of water glistening on his slightly damp hands, his eyes bright with anticipation.

'Hey,' he said. 'Perfect timing.'

He stepped aside and gestured for me to come in. 'Come on, I've got something for you.'

The scent was heavier now. My throat tightened with the reflex to gag as I stepped inside.

Tiny flames danced from candles positioned on every surface, their soft flickering light too delicate to chase away the demons they brought with them.

I fought to find my voice. 'W-what is this?'

'I ran you a bubble bath,' Callum said proudly, guiding me towards the bathroom. 'To make up for letting you down last night.'

'You didn't have to,' I murmured, forcing a smile, as though I was touched by his thoughtful gesture. I should have been. Any other woman would have been.

He pushed the bathroom door open with a flourish.

My breath caught. The bath was filled to the brim with bubbles. Candles lined the edge of the tub, their golden glow casting eerie reflections on the tiles.

He thought it was soothing. The bubbles. The candles. The vanilla. A warm rich scent that most people found relaxing.

But I wasn't most people.

Callum tugged at my coat, slipping it from my shoulders.

'Why vanilla?' I croaked.

His hands froze, my coat caught halfway, bunched around my elbows.

'Don't you like it?' His voice was small. Crushed.

I'd hurt his feelings. He'd tried to do something sweet. Something romantic. And I was ruining it.

I swallowed and forced a smile. 'I love it,' I said quickly. 'It's perfect.'

A flash of confusion crossed his face before he leaned in and kissed my cheek.

'Go, enjoy,' he murmured, taking my coat and giving me a gentle nudge further into the room. 'You deserve it.'

He drew back, and our eyes met. For the briefest moment, I had the strangest sensation that we were both lying.

27

NOW

December

'I can't believe we're doing this,' Lucy said, beaming at me as she met me outside the gallery. 'I can't even remember the last time we had lunch together.'

I smiled, pushing away the temptation to tell her that it was six months ago. Before Mum died.

We fell into step side by side, not even pausing to debate where we were going. She might not have been able to recall our lunchtime catch-ups, but her feet apparently remembered the way to our favourite café.

'I'm so happy you messaged,' Lucy chattered excitedly. 'I can't wait to tell you about this incredible new artist we have coming to the gallery next week. It's such a massive win for us to get someone so renowned.'

I nodded numbly, barely hearing a word as she carried on telling me all about him, as we ordered tuna melts and cups of tea.

Lucy paused mid-sentence. 'Liv? You okay?'

I shook myself out of my daze. 'Yeah, I'm...' For years I'd answered that question with the same reply. *I'm fine.* It didn't matter how I truly felt. What was going on at home. My response never changed.

But today that one little word felt impossible to say.

'Liv?' Lucy asked, taking a sip of tea.

'Do you think I'm unstable?'

Lucy lunged forwards, covering her hand with her mouth, her eyes wide as she tried to swallow the tea. 'What? Where did that come from?'

I shrugged. 'You and Maddie always tease me about the way I talk about Mum's café. Like she's still here. Like I've forgotten she's gone or something. I don't have any other friends except for you two. I don't have any interests. The Second Cup Café is my whole life. I'm hanging on to a failing café as though that's somehow going to save me.'

'Hey. No. Absolutely not.' Lucy reached across the table, placing her hand on my arm as she shook her head adamantly. 'That's crazy.'

I flinched.

'No, not crazy,' she rushed. 'I mean—' Lucy swallowed, looking flustered. 'You are the most loyal and committed friend and daughter. You stayed at that café instead of going to college and uni, instead of having your own life, because you knew your mum needed you.'

Guilt chafed at me. I hadn't surrendered my dreams because Mum needed me. I'd surrendered them because they'd destroyed us.

'And you're the same way with Maddie and me. You show up whenever we need anything, it doesn't matter what it is.'

I blinked. 'I don't think I've really done that much for either of you.'

'You do more than you think. You hold things together. Even when they're falling apart.'

There was a long pause.

Things were falling apart again now. *I* was falling apart.

'And it's not just us any more. You have Callum now too. I like him.'

'You've never even met him,' I said quietly.

Lucy shrugged. 'Don't get me wrong, Maddie and I desperately want to. But we can tell he's good for you. You're so vibrant when you talk about him. I know it's clichéd but it's like he lights you up.'

I took a deep breath. This was it. Time to tell her the truth.

Callum's missing.

The words circled in my brain, but somehow my lips wouldn't say them.

'Besides, it's kind of romantic. This mysterious boyfriend that no one has met.' She laughed. 'Are you sure he's actually real?'

I tried to laugh. But I couldn't.

Was he real?

28

THEN

November

The wail of a car alarm shattered the early morning quiet. I turned from the display case I was filling with freshly baked muffins and peered out the café window.

Across the street, the hazard warning lights on my Citroen blinked frantically.

I dumped the tray on the counter, hurried to the door and fumbled with the lock. Finally, I stepped onto the dimly lit street, my eyes scanning back and forth.

No one else was around.

I crossed the road and froze. Blades of jagged glass clung to the edges of the driver's window. I moved closer, staring at the shards scattered across the seat. But it wasn't my car I was seeing any more. It was another shattered window. Another time...

* * *

'Someone smashed the window on Daniel's car.'

'Someone?' PC Rourke said.

'I didn't see who it was,' I told him. His intense questioning expression didn't shift as he continued to stare at me. I shuffled, realising that he wasn't asking about the someone.

He was asking if it was me.

'I heard the crash when I was walking towards the house and then the alarm went off.'

'But you didn't see anyone?'

I shook my head. 'I couldn't see the car at that point. There are tall fir trees along the side of the drive.'

'Could you see the entrance to the driveway?'

'Yes.'

'And yet you didn't see anyone running away?'

I shook my head. 'I didn't see anyone until I was halfway up the drive and then Daniel dashed out of the house. He must have heard the alarm too.'

'Where were you standing at this point?'

I frowned. 'I don't know exactly. I guess beside the car.'

'Which side?'

'The driver's side.'

'And which window was smashed?'

I swallowed. 'The driver's window.'

'So, when Daniel came out of the house, you were standing beside the smashed driver's window?'

My eyes widened as I turned to Dad sitting beside me, and then back to PC Rourke. 'I wasn't standing there. I was just walking past.'

'I see.'

'The path is that side of the car,' I added, trying to justify my location.

'And yet neither of you saw anyone else?'

'Well, no.' I hesitated. 'But like I said, there's a lot of trees...'

'Hmm,' PC Rourke murmured. 'Did you see any movement or hear anything from that direction?'

I thought about lying. If I said yes, maybe he'd stop looking at me with that suspicious glare. I glanced up at Dad. He'd know if I lied though. He always knew. My shoulders sagged. 'No,' I admitted honestly. 'But the alarm was so loud.'

'Of course.' PC Rourke nodded. 'What happened next?'

'Daniel turned the alarm off and told me to go inside while he swept up glass.'

'So, you were alone in the house when the fire started?'

* * *

'We should call the police,' I said but made no move towards my phone. The idea of calling them, of filling in a report, made my stomach churn. But what choice did I have?

'There's no point,' Callum said quickly. 'It's just a broken window; it's not like they'll do anything.'

I stared at him, stunned by his response. He was always so rigid about following the rules. 'But the insurance company will need the crime number, won't they? Otherwise, they won't pay for the repairs.'

'It's not worth making a claim for this,' Callum said firmly. 'It'll bump your premiums up. Plus, they'd charge you for the excess anyway.'

I turned back to the car, surveying the shards of broken glass. I couldn't deny he was right, but... 'I can't afford to pay for a new window.'

'I'll take care of it.'

My head jolted back, and I stared at Callum again. 'You know a mechanic?' He'd never mentioned anyone before. He didn't even have a car. 'But even if they give you a discount—'

'There'll be no charge,' Callum said. His tone was so certain, as though he didn't have any doubt. But how was that possible? How could he know that someone would do the repair for free?

Why would anyone do that?

'But—'

'They owe me.'

I frowned as questions formed on my lips. Who was this person? What could they possibly owe Callum for? And why didn't I know anything about them?

But I said nothing.

He was right, I didn't have the budget for rising insurance costs or to pay the excess on a claim. But if I was honest with myself, it wasn't the money that stopped me from asking questions. It was the fact that if Callum took care of it then I wouldn't have to call the police.

* * *

'Is this really necessary?' I asked as I handed Callum the screwdriver he'd asked for.

He rolled his eyes as he looked down at me from the top of the ladder. 'Someone smashed your car window, Liv.'

'But I was in the café when it happened. I'm fine.' I turned in a slow circle, demonstrating I was unharmed.

'Precisely, you were in the café *alone*.'

I stopped pivoting as I realised he had a point. I was always alone in the café first thing in the morning while I did the baking for the day.

'I can't believe you didn't already have CCTV installed,' Callum said gruffly. 'Especially now it's just you running this place.'

The bluntness of his words winded me. I peered up at him, wondering why he'd been so curt, but his attention was completely focused on fixing the camera to the wall. He didn't even seem to realise how much his words had hurt me. I didn't need to be reminded that I was alone.

It had been nine months since I'd lost Mum, nine months of running the café alone, but still...

'I'm not taking any chances with your safety,' Callum said, his jaw taut with determination.

This time, though, I wondered if it was the unfamiliar DIY causing his tension, or perhaps, just maybe it was his desire to keep me safe.

I didn't like the feeling of being monitored and recorded, but I couldn't deny the fact Callum was doing this for me took away some of my discomfort. He wanted to keep me safe. He cared that I was okay.

An unfamiliar feeling of warmth descended on me, like snuggling into a warm blanket on a cold day. It was comforting. Safe.

'Well, that's the café and the flat covered.' The ladder creaked as Callum climbed down. 'Can you check the feed?'

I fiddled with the app he'd already downloaded on my phone, checking all three cameras were now working.

He peered over my shoulder at the screen. 'We'll need to upgrade your storage space before we can store more data,' Callum muttered. 'But for now it'll save data for forty-eight hours.'

I nodded as I inhaled his rich woody scent so close to me. Maybe I could get used to having someone taking care of me...

'Let me install it on my phone too,' Callum said, leaning closer as he copied the setting from my app.

A text message flashed up on his screen.

ACE

This needs to be handled in person. Immediately.

I instinctively glanced up at Callum as he inhaled deeply as though fighting to retain his composure.

'Is everything okay?' I asked.

'Just a work thing,' he said, swiping the notification away and slipping his phone into his pocket. 'I'll have to go and deal with it.'

My eyes widened. 'What, now?'

Callum nodded. 'I can't leave it.'

'But it's almost 8 p.m. They can't expect you to go into work now. Besides, we have plans.'

He shrugged. A sharp quick movement that dismissed my objections as though they were irrelevant. As though our plans were irrelevant.

'You can't be serious?' I stared at him, stunned.

'You don't understand how important this job is to me.'

I snorted. 'I have a pretty good idea,' I replied bitterly. 'It's more important to you than I am, that's for sure.'

'It's not like that,' he objected.

'Isn't it?' I folded my arms. 'You bail every time we plan something together. Work is your priority over everything else, including us.'

'I told you, I need this to work out. It's my only chance to—'

'To redeem yourself,' I finished for him. 'Yeah, I know. You told me that when we first met. I admired you for that. Your drive and determination. I wished I could have been more like you. But now I'm starting to realise that I was like you once. I focused on one thing above everything and everyone else. For me, the piano came first. For you, it's work.'

'That's not true,' Callum objected.

'Isn't it?'

He didn't answer. He just slipped out of the door, the bell jangling into the silence he left behind.

The problem with being so focused on certain parts of your life was that you had to sacrifice others.

And I was starting to question if I was part of that 'other'.

29

NOW

December

I staggered out of the police station, feeling drained. They didn't believe me. That much was obvious. It was only a matter of time before they called me back again.

I knew the routine. I knew how it worked. They weren't done with me.

The station doors clicked shut behind me, but I still felt claustrophobic. Even the bitter cold outside barely penetrated the thick blanket of panic that wrapped itself tightly around me.

Every time I spoke to the police it felt like I was disturbing old ghosts. Ones I'd worked hard to lay to rest. Or at least learned to co-exist with. But now the police were digging up the past.

My past.

I took a deep breath of the frosty air. What would happen if they kept digging? The case had been dropped due to lack of evidence, but eight years on, could they reopen it?

Sweat beaded at the back of my neck, despite the chill in the air.

If they couldn't find Callum, where did that leave me?

I pressed my hand to my chest, desperate to ease the pressure that was building inside me. It had been stupid to involve the police. I should have known better. They didn't help. They interfered. They destroyed.

They would again this time too.

I'd gone to them out of fear for Callum's safety, but there was another fear that drove me too, a more selfish one – the fear of being alone. If I allowed myself to believe that Callum had simply chosen to leave, then that was it, everything we'd built was over. But if he hadn't had a choice, if somehow he was protecting me, then there was still hope.

But if I couldn't prove to the police that he existed, being alone might end up the least of my fears.

* * *

I'd almost reached the café before I realised where I was. I stood on the street and stared in the window at the darkened room. It felt strange seeing it dark and empty at this time of day. There were usually a few people seated at the tables or hurrying in for a coffee to go.

I glanced at my watch. There was still time; I could open up for a couple of hours. And yet, I didn't move. The thought of dealing with customers, pasting on a smile, making small talk, and pretending everything was normal was unbearable.

I'd been doing it for years. I was a master at giving a convincing performance.

All those years on stage, projecting an air of calm, quiet confidence as I settled onto the piano stool had been good training. Albeit not for the purpose I'd anticipated.

Today, though, it felt too hard. I'd used all my energy already. I'd always crashed after a performance. I poured every fibre of being into the music, leaving nothing in reserve. But the police interview had been more intense than any solo.

I turned down the side alleyway to the flat instead, slid my key into the lock and pushed the door open. A lump rose in my throat, making it hard to breathe as I climbed the stairs, my heart pounding. Hope and dread swirled inside me as I silently prayed Callum would be there and yet at the same time knowing with unshakable certainty that he wouldn't be.

Lucy used to tease me for being contradictory; simultaneously hoping for the best while fearing the worst. She never understood how remarkable it was that I managed to hold out any hope at all. Not after everything I'd experienced. Being a suspected arsonist had a way of realigning your expectations.

The thought of Lucy made me want to call her. She was my closest friend. The one person I could always turn to.

Except...

What if she didn't believe me either?

I let myself in the flat and shut the door behind me, the familiar creak of the hinge slicing through my pounding head.

I was home. I was safe. I reassured myself as I tried to soothe the frayed nerves that vibrated through my body.

But it didn't help.

We can't find any evidence that Callum exists.

PC Monroe's statement replayed on a loop, drowning out whatever comfort being back in the familiar surroundings might have brought.

It was preposterous. The implication that I'd imagined everything. That I'd imagined Callum.

But it wasn't the first time I'd been accused of that. Of being delusional. Crazy.

I sucked in a deep breath and marched to the living room, anger and frustration propelling me forwards. They'd been wrong before. Just as they were wrong now.

Weren't they?

I stopped in the middle of the living room. I hadn't been able to prove it last time. And now...

My thoughts raced as I desperately searched my mind for something to prove Callum's existence. But there wasn't anything.

Nothing of his in the flat. No photos. Lucy and Maddie had never met him. And all of his family and friends were in Portsmouth.

But still, there had to be someone that had seen us together. Seen him.

I moved to the window. My gaze automatically scanned the street below, as though I'd be able to spot Callum on his way home. But the street was empty except for a couple walking hand in hand passing my parked car.

My car.

My eyes widened as I stared at it. Callum had installed CCTV cameras last week after my car window had been smashed.

I pulled my phone from my pocket and opened the app. There would be video footage of Callum coming and going. I could finally give the police an image to search for. But more than that, I could prove he existed. I wasn't crazy.

I drummed my fingers impatiently against the phone as the live feed loaded slowly.

I switched to the archive and scrolled back through the timeline. Last night. Yesterday morning. Monday night. Monday afternoon.

The scroll bar stopped moving.

I tapped the screen again. It couldn't freeze now. I was so close. Just another twenty-four hours further back and...

'We'll need to upgrade your storage space before we can store more data.' Callum's voice resounded in my memory. *'But for now it'll save data for forty-eight hours.'*

Forty-eight hours.

That was it. That was as far back as the video went. We hadn't got round to increasing the storage yet.

Callum had been missing for seventy-two hours.

How could I have been so stupid? I should have thought of it earlier. If I'd checked it the day he disappeared, or even just yesterday, he would have been there, captured on camera.

But now...

I dropped down onto the sofa. I still couldn't prove Callum was real, but that didn't mean he wasn't.

Yet I was the only one who knew him. Who'd even met him.

The truth jarred against me, undeniable now. It was odd. I'd always known it. But now, without Callum here to explain his absences or offer reassurances, it was just me and my spiralling anxieties, exacerbated by the police's questions.

As far as they were concerned, Callum didn't exist, which meant their investigation was now focused on me. The fact they couldn't decide if I was delusional or just desperate had bought me some time. But as soon as they made their minds up...

I squeezed my eyes shut. I needed to focus. To think. I should have known better than to go to the police in the first place. I'd never been able to count on them before. Why would it be any different now? I was on my own.

I should have been used to that. But somehow it felt lonelier now than it had before. It shouldn't have done. I'd spent so long being alone. It should have been second nature to me.

It was.

Until Callum.

If he even existed.

I drew back, caught off guard by that thought. Of course Callum existed. I knew that.

But I'd seen the way the police officers looked at me, the disbelief in their eyes, the doubt in their voices. It was starting to wear on me...

Could I really have imagined him?

I flopped back against the sofa as my strength evaporated. The idea was ridiculous.

And yet...

Grief did strange things to people. That's what people always said. It rewired your brain. Left you clinging to whatever gave you hope.

Was that what I'd done?

Had losing Mum carved such a gaping hole inside me that I'd filled it with a story, a person, who never really existed?

When I was five, I had an imaginary friend named Max. He'd sat beside me at the table, shared my toast, walked with me to nursery. I used to get so angry when Mum didn't set out a plate for him.

That was normal then. Expected, even.

But I wasn't five any more.

And this wasn't *pretend.*

Was it?

30

THEN

November

I paced past the living room, checking my phone every few minutes, even though the volume was turned up so loud it would have been impossible to miss a call or message.

Callum usually came by now. Even if he had a meeting that ran late, he'd send a quick 'Welcome home' or 'How's your day?'

Something.

It had been strange enough that he hadn't come to the café to help me close up. We worked well together. The rhythm we'd found together the day we met had become a routine. Not that I expected him to do so every night. There was no obligation.

But today...

I scrunched my nose. I thought at least he'd be here when I got home, with a welcoming hug and a 'Happy Birthday'. He'd dashed out early this morning, too sleepy and distracted to remember those two little words. But I knew he wouldn't completely forget. Not Callum.

I caught my reflection in the darkened window, my stiff back and folded arms emanating tension even in the distorted image. He might have missed other chances to meet my friends, but surely this was different. This was important.

'Don't get your hopes up too much.' Mum's voice whispered in the back of my mind. *'It's just not his thing.'*

She'd been talking about Dad. Trying to let me down as gently as she could that he was going to miss another concert.

But right now it felt like her words applied to Callum too. It was as though she was warning me he wouldn't come. That as much as I wanted him to be here, I couldn't count on it.

I let out a weary sigh. That niggling sense of disconnection was becoming harder to ignore. He was always busy when I needed him. He seemed to forget his commitments, his promises – they were just empty words. I couldn't count on him to be where he said he'd be, where I needed him to be.

Was I being unreasonable? I tipped my head to the side as I stared out of the window. It wasn't as though I resented him having his own plans. I didn't want to control him or dictate his movements. I knew from experience how claustrophobic it felt to be confined like that. I wouldn't do that to anyone. Especially him.

I just wanted to be involved. To feel like we were connected, not just in the moments that we spent alone together, but the way that our lives fitted together. Meeting friends. Having plans.

My fingers twitched against my phone. It was tempting to message and ask where he was. I set the phone on the coffee table, face down. I wouldn't let myself slip down that path. I wanted him to be here because he wanted it too, not because he felt he had to be.

I let out a heavy sigh. There was a kind of flatness to that realisation. Sadness mixed with resignation. If he made it in time, great. If he didn't... well, that would have to be okay too.

The intercom buzzed and despite my intention of nonchalance, for a split second, my body surged with excitement. And then, just as quickly, the realisation that he had a key hit me.

It wasn't him.

I shook myself out of my disappointment and pressed the buzzer to open the downstairs door. Pasting on my biggest smile, I greeted Lucy as she bounded up the stairs.

'Happy birthday!' she announced, holding up a bottle of wine and a box of cupcakes as she breezed into the flat.

I grabbed the wine glasses from the kitchen, while Lucy made herself comfortable on the sofa. She unscrewed the cap of the wine bottle and filled the glasses.

'I can't believe you still buy all this,' I said with a laugh as she handed me a glass.

'It's part of our tradition,' Lucy responded with a shrug.

I shook my head. 'A two-litre bottle of Diet Coke would be more accurate.'

'True, but the over-eighteen version of our tradition is more fun,' she said, raising her glass. 'Cheap red wine and chocolate cupcakes. No candles, obviously.'

I smiled. Lucy never forgot our tradition. Every detail of it, including the parts to omit.

* * *

'I know you said you didn't want to do anything for your birthday,' Lucy said as we sat cross-legged on her bedroom carpet after school. 'But...' She leapt up, grinning broadly as she rummaged in her wardrobe.

'What are you up to?' I asked, a bubble of excitement rising in my chest. Lucy was wrong; I hadn't said I didn't want to celebrate. I just said that I didn't do so.

Or more accurately, my parents didn't. Celebrating the birth of the person you blamed for destroying your life didn't really work.

I craned my neck. 'What is it?' I asked, unable to contain my curiosity.

'Close your eyes,' she instructed me.

I hesitated.

'You'll spoil the surprise,' Lucy objected, prompting me to comply.

I listened to the sounds of her shuffling around and then... 'Happy birthday to you, happy birthday to you,' Lucy sang loudly, as though determined to make up for the fact that she was the only one present.

I opened my eyes as she continued to sing. In front of me sat a two-litre bottle of Diet Coke and two chocolate cupcakes. But I barely saw them.

My gaze was locked on the two pink candles protruding from the cakes, with tiny orange flames flickering in the late afternoon light.

'Happy bir—' Lucy stopped, and the sound of my raspy rapid breathing filled the silence.

I knew she was staring at me. I wasn't reacting in the right way. She'd done some-

thing lovely, and instead of feeling grateful, I was spiralling. But I couldn't shift my gaze from the flames. I couldn't speak. Couldn't breathe.

'Liv?'

Suddenly the flames went out.

I blinked and watched as Lucy whipped the candles out of the cupcakes and threw them in the bin.

'Are you okay?' she asked gently.

I nodded as my breathing slowed.

* * *

I tipped my head to the left as I studied her. I couldn't help but wonder why she'd never questioned my reaction. But she'd never put candles in a cake again.

It was one of the things I loved most about our friendship. There was never any pressure.

Lucy opened the box, and I realised there was one amendment to our celebration. There were three cupcakes this year...

Lucy glanced around the flat, before her gaze settled on the two wine glasses. 'No Callum, again?'

I frowned. Was it my imagination or she had added extra weight to the word 'again'? There was nothing judgemental in her expression, though, only sympathy.

'Something came up at the last minute,' I said, keeping my voice level.

'It's always the last minute.'

Lucy's words caught me off guard. Blunt. Unfiltered. But I couldn't argue. She was right. It *was* always the last minute.

That was the problem. It made planning anything impossible.

'Sorry he missed your engagement party—'

'That's not important,' Lucy interrupted. 'It's not like he knows me.'

There was a lull.

It felt like the silence resounded with an unspoken question. After three months, shouldn't he know her, or at least have met her?

He hadn't really connected with anything in my life outside of the café. Or included me in anything of his life either.

He was evasive about his life before he'd arrived in Christchurch.

But then, if I was honest, so was I. I hadn't told him everything.

'We just don't want you to get hurt,' Lucy said softly.

'*We?*'

'Maddie and I.'

Of course. They'd been talking about me. About my relationship. My life.

'We're both worried about you,' she assured me, as though that made it better.

If anything, it made it worse.

I didn't want to be someone people felt they had to worry about. Someone incapable of making her own decisions. Someone not responsible enough. Not *adult* enough.

I felt like the kid of the group. They'd grown up. They'd *lived* while I'd stayed exactly where I'd been when I moved here at fourteen.

And we all knew it.

'He surprised me with a bubble bath yesterday. I guess it was an apology, for bailing.'

'That's something.'

'Yeah, very romantic.'

'You don't sound convinced.'

'There were candles. Everywhere.'

Lucy's eyebrows lifted.

'Vanilla candles,' I added.

She winced. 'Candles and vanilla, the two things you hate.'

I smiled weakly. 'Yeah.'

'Did he know?'

I shook my head.

'O-kay.' There was another beat of silence. 'Why not?'

'It never came up.' It wasn't a lie. Until that point, there hadn't been anything to prompt telling him.

'What happened when you explained?'

I didn't answer.

'Liv? You did tell him, didn't you?'

I swallowed. 'I didn't know what to say.'

'You told me.'

Her reply made it sound so simple. I'd told her, therefore I could tell him, but...' 'I didn't exactly tell you, you kind of figured out I hated candles from my reaction.'

Lucy shrugged. 'But you told me you have the same reaction to the scent of vanilla. I didn't know about that one.'

'True,' I admitted. 'You're different, though. You never asked questions.'

'And he would?'

I nodded. 'He *always* asks questions.'

It was the one thing that troubled me about our relationship. I frowned. One of the many things, I corrected silently.

'And that's a bad thing?' Lucy asked carefully.

'I'm not sure,' I admitted. 'I mean, it could be sweet, right? He's interested. He wants to know more about me.'

Lucy nodded. 'That would make sense. But?'

'How come you never asked?' I sidestepped her question.

She tilted her head. 'I got the feeling you didn't want to talk about it.'

I nodded. 'I didn't.'

'And now?' she asked tentatively.

I hesitated.

She was giving me the option to continue in the comfortable silence we'd always shared, or to break it. Somehow, I knew she wouldn't be offended either way.

It was only once she knew that things would change...

But living with it alone hadn't solved anything. Callum's questions, the pianist, the candles had highlighted that the past was still with me, whether I talked about it or not.

Perhaps Lucy deserved to know who I really was.

'Why do you do this every year?' I asked, signalling the bottle of wine and untouched cupcakes.

Lucy stared at me with a bewildered expression. 'Because you're my friend.'

'Yeah.' I shuffled awkwardly. 'But why?'

Confusion morphed into surprise. 'Because you're fun to hang out with,' Lucy said as though I should know.

I felt my face contort, the disbelief I felt inside seeping out.

'You don't believe me,' Lucy exclaimed, her stunned surprise practically tangible.

'I...' I tried to deny it, but the lie wouldn't come.

'Okay, then, let's try this; because spending time with you isn't tiresome.'
I laughed.

'Ah ha!' Lucy said triumphantly. 'Looks like we found a level of reasoning you're able to accept.'

'I'm sorry,' I murmured, with my laughter instantly fading.

'Why are you sorry?' Lucy's confusion was back.

'It's not that I don't believe you. It's…' My words floundered.

'That you don't believe it's possible?'

I didn't answer. I didn't need to. We both knew she was right.

'There was a fire,' I announced suddenly.

Lucy nodded. The movement was so slight I wasn't sure if I'd imagined it.

'It started from a candle. A vanilla candle.'

She nodded again, this time firmer. 'I wondered.'

'But you still never asked?'

'I figured you'd tell me when you were ready.' She smiled. 'Even if it took eight years.'

The corner of my mouth twitched, but guilt stifled the half-formed smile. 'There's more to the story.'

Lucy nodded again. 'I thought there might be.'

'You're still not going to ask?'

She shook her head. 'I'll be here whenever you're ready.'

'Even if it takes another eight years?' I teased tentatively.

'Even if it takes eighty.'

* * *

I put the empty wine glasses in the dishwasher and switched the radio on. The empty flat felt too quiet now Lucy had gone home.

With a sigh I glanced at the clock, wondering what time Callum would be back. I shook my head. What was I doing? I wasn't the kind of person to hinge my evening on someone else's movements. I had plenty of things to be getting on with besides waiting around for him.

I scrunched my nose as I glanced around the kitchen, suddenly drawing a blank as to what those things might be.

My gaze fell upon the laundry basket in the corner of the room, and I nodded firmly. That was something I could do.

I dug through the clothes, checking the pockets before tossing them into the washing machine. My fingers brushed something inside the apron I'd worn in the café earlier. I pulled out a crumped piece of paper from the corner of the pocket. I turned to throw it into the bin, but as I did so, the writing caught my attention.

It wasn't my writing.

I uncurled the edges, smoothing out the paper until it was readable.

Happy birthday, Liv
    Sorry I can't be with you to celebrate. I really wanted to be.
    X

My gaze shifted from the note to the apron and back again, a deep frown etched into my forehead.

I kept the clean aprons in a drawer in the café. Which meant Callum would have had to slip the note into the pocket last night, before I closed up. The thoughtfulness of the gesture, however, was buried by questions.

Had he meant he wished he could be with me during the day? Or had he known all along that he wouldn't be joining Lucy and me this evening?

Had he always intended to stand me up?

31

NOW

December

I threw the duvet off as I sat up and swung my legs out of bed. My head throbbed with a pressure that the movement made even worse.

Fumbling for the light switch, I closed my eyes against the sudden brightness as it flicked on. Squinting, I tugged open the drawer of the bedside cabinet and rummaged for paracetamol.

I found the packet, popped two caplets into my mouth, and took a gulp of water from the glass beside the radio.

Reaching to drop the packet back into the drawer, I stopped, my gaze locked on a small piece of paper protruding from beneath a tube of hand cream. I threw the paracetamol packet on the bed beside me and retrieved the note.

I knew what it was even before I read it.

Happy birthday, Liv
    Sorry I can't be with you to celebrate. I really wanted to be.
    X

I clung to it, reading it over and over again. Callum had written it. Which meant...

He *was* real.

My hands trembled as tears rolled down my cheeks. I hadn't realised how much I'd needed that confirmation. Not for the police or anyone else. But for me.

I finally had something of his. His writing. His words.

I'd forgotten I'd kept it. I wasn't even sure why I had. Did I treasure the sentiment of his words and wanted to keep it as a sign of his love? Or was it because of the unanswered question it raised as to whether he'd lied to me?

I'd never asked him about it. And he'd never mentioned it. It had just slid into the abyss of things that weren't talked about.

* * *

'And you're sure this is from Callum?' PC Monroe studied the note on the table between us.

'Yes,' I replied, not sure how many more times he needed me to confirm it. 'He must have slipped it into the pocket of my apron when we were closing up the night before my birthday. I found it the next evening when I was doing the laundry.'

'Where do you keep your aprons?'

'In a drawer in the café's kitchen.'

PC Monroe tapped his pen against the desk. 'Who has access to that area?'

'No one. Just me.' I shrugged. 'And Callum, when he helps out.'

'Is the kitchen kept locked?'

'Well, no,' I replied hesitantly.

'So, a customer could access it without your knowledge?'

'I... I guess,' I admitted reluctantly. 'If I was busy serving or clearing tables.'

PC Monroe nodded slowly, his expression full of doubt.

'But it's from Callum,' I insisted, growing frustrated.

'It's not even signed,' he pointed out.

'It's his handwriting.'

PC Monroe's brow furrowed. 'Do you have anything else with his handwriting on?'

'Umm...' My thoughts raced as I tried to think of something.

I'm a digital guy. Callum's voice echoed in my brain.

'He uses his phone or laptop for most things,' I admitted.

'But you have *seen* his handwriting before?'

There was something about his tone that made me feel small inside. 'What?'

'I'm just wondering given you said before that he sent you text messages, did he ever give you a handwritten note? A birthday card? Something?'

My mind was blank. I couldn't think of anything. But there must have been. How else would have I known it was his writing?

'Can't you do some handwriting analysis or something?'

'And compare it to what?' PC Monroe asked. 'We can't prove this was written by someone who doesn't even seem to exist.'

'But he does exist, the note proves it.'

'Anyone could have written this,' he said gently. 'Even you.'

'W-what?'

'I'm not saying you did.' PC Monroe paused. 'But you *could* have done.'

To me the note was proof of Callum's existence, his love for me, but to the police...

'So, it's useless?' I asked, already knowing the answer.

'I'm sorry, Miss Reed. I'll retain the note as potential evidence, but no action will be taken with it at this time. We need something more concrete than this.'

32

THEN

November

I was just making myself a coffee when my phone rang. Lucy's name flashed up on the screen.

I frowned. She didn't usually call during the day. We both worked ridiculous hours and didn't have time for unplanned phone calls, unless something was wrong.

I picked up on the second ring. 'What's up?'

'Oh, thank goodness you answered,' Lucy rambled the second I pressed the phone to my ear. 'I have an event at the gallery tonight and the caterer has completely screwed up. They somehow double booked.'

I blinked. 'What? How do you double book something like that?'

'I have no idea,' she groaned. 'But one thing's for sure, I won't be using them again.'

'What are you going to do?'

There was a pause. 'I told them if they could rustle up some savouries, I'd find someone else to handle the desserts.'

Another pause as Lucy let her statement hang.

Someone.

In other words, *me*.

'Lucy?' I said cautiously as nerves swelled in the pit of my stomach.

'Maybe you could rustle up some coconut macaroons and your amazing chocolate brownies?' Lucy suggested hopefully. 'You could cut them into cute little pieces so it looks fancy.'

I found myself agreeing even before I'd thought through how I would actually manage to meet her request.

I'd figure something out. I'd have to. I couldn't let her down.

She'd never let me down.

'And maybe you could help serve?' Her question was tentative, as though she was afraid she was pushing her luck.

'What's the dress code?'

'Black trousers, white shirt,' she said quickly.

I did a mental scan of my wardrobe before giving a short sharp nod. 'Got it. Text me with the details and I'll be there.'

I heard Lucy's exhale as though she was suddenly able to breathe again. 'You're a star, Liv.'

My body tensed, her words having a different impact than she'd intended. There was a time I'd wanted that statement to be true. When it meant stages, applause and my name at the top of a programme. I'd have done almost anything for that kind of recognition then.

But not now.

'Don't mention it,' I told her, dismissing her praise. The only thing that mattered now was the task at hand. Focusing on one practicality at a time was how I'd got through the last eight years, and it was how I would get through tonight too.

* * *

I slid the final tray of brownies into the oven and set the timer. Wiping my hands on my apron, I smiled as I watched Callum carefully dipping coconut macaroons into a bowl of melted dark chocolate. Concentration was etched on his face as he worked, methodically placing each one onto the baking paper with care.

Lucy's last-minute request had turned out to be easier than expected, thanks to Callum's perfectly timed arrival. He hadn't even hesitated; he'd just grabbed an apron and told me to put him to work.

The sound of him humming made the sterile minimalist kitchen feel warm and cosy.

'Thanks for helping me with all this,' I said gratefully. 'It means a lot.'

Callum grinned back at me. 'You know I'm always happy to pitch in.'

I grinned. I did know.

'You should come tonight,' I said suddenly. 'You can finally meet Lucy, and I know she'd be grateful for the extra help.'

Callum froze. For a split second I could have sworn I saw panic flash across his face. And then it was gone.

'I'd love to,' he replied with a beaming smile.

I felt my breath gush out as my body relaxed. Of course he hadn't been panicked by my suggestion. Maybe it had taken him by surprise. Maybe he hadn't expected me to want him there. Judging from his grin, he was as excited as I was for him to finally meet one of my friends.

I wrapped my arms around his neck. This was exactly the way I wanted things to be.

'Not that I'm not appreciating this hug,' Callum whispered against my neck, 'but what time did you say you needed to deliver these cakes?'

I groaned as I pulled myself away from him. 'In less than thirty minutes.'

Callum chuckled. 'In that case, you go and get changed and I'll finish these' – he jerked his head at the macaroons – 'and then I'll get ready.'

'Thanks,' I said, giving him a kiss. 'The last batch of brownies is almost done. Can you take them out of the oven when the timer goes off, please?' I asked before I hurried up to the flat.

* * *

The shrill screech of the smoke alarm hit me the second I stepped out of the flat. I veered towards the back entrance to the café a few steps away, thick smoke seeping through the open doorway.

I pushed the door wide and staggered back as the smoke engulfed me, stinging my eyes.

Callum.

That one thought propelled me forwards. I raised my arm, covering my mouth and nose in the crook of my elbow as I charged into the kitchen. 'Callum?' I choked, fumbling my way through the once familiar kitchen.

The oven light glowed dimly through the haze.

The brownies.

Somewhere in the back of my mind I knew I needed to reach the oven. Turn it off. Prevent a fire. But my brain and body felt disconnected.

I couldn't move. I was trapped in the smoke.

Again.

'Olivia?'

I heard Callum's voice calling me, but it felt so far away.

'What are you doing?' He barged past me, racing towards the oven. I watched silently as he twisted the dial off. He moved away towards the window. I heard the click of the lock before it creaked open. But my gaze stayed fixed on the oven dial.

I'd only caught a glimpse of it before Callum had turned it, but it looked wrong. Too high. Much too high.

But that didn't make sense. I baked brownies practically every day. I knew what temperature to cook them on.

Maybe I was wrong. Maybe the haze and my panic had distorted my vision.

'Why were you just standing there?' Callum asked, his eyes wide with fright as he waved a tea towel under the smoke detector.

I opened my mouth, but the words wouldn't come. How could I explain why my body had frozen without revealing my past? My chest tightened. But I knew it was from more than just the smoke-filled kitchen. It was fear, shame, and guilt all slamming against me, making it hard to breathe.

But this time the situation had nothing to do with me.

I'd left Callum to look after the brownies. This was his fault. 'Why didn't you take the brownies out when the timer went off?' I demanded, channelling the cocktail of emotions that surged within me into one short sharp question.

Callum frowned. 'It didn't go off.'

'How long were you gone for?' I demanded. He must have been outside when the timer rang.

'Not that long,' Callum assured me. 'I was just loading the brownies and macaroons into the car for you while I waited for the last batch. I checked the timer before I stepped out to make sure I had time.'

I shook my head. He must have been gone longer than he realised. The timer would have gone off twenty minutes ago.

'See for yourself,' Callum said, jerking his head towards the timer.

It was still ticking down.

I stared at it, bewildered. How was that possible? I'd never set the timer wrong before.

I glanced back at the oven dial. Did that mean I had done that wrong too?

* * *

Lucy spotted me the second I stepped through the gallery's back entrance, my arms laden with boxes of cakes.

'You made it!' she cried, hurrying towards me. 'I was starting to worry.'

'Sorry, I had to take another shower to get the smell of smoke out of my hair.'

'Smoke?' Lucy's eyes widened.

'I overcooked the last batch of brownies.' I scrunched my nose as I glanced down at the boxes. 'I hope there's enough without them.'

'We'll manage,' Lucy said. 'I'm amazed you managed to make all these in such a short space of time.'

'Callum helped,' I replied, feeling a surge of pride quickly followed by guilt as I recalled how short I'd been with him in the smoke-filled kitchen. How accusatory. 'He was going to come and help us serve too, but after the disaster with the brownies, he offered to stay behind and try to air the smoke out of the kitchen.'

'Aww,' Lucy murmured. 'That's so thoughtful.'

She was right. It was thoughtful. *He* was thoughtful. And he deserved better than my accusations and blame. The shock of being immersed in the smoke had triggered memories I'd tried to keep buried. But that wasn't an excuse to lash out at Callum. I owed him an apology.

But first, I had to get through this evening...

I peeked through the open door to the main hall. In the rush of preparation and the subsequent drama, I hadn't allowed myself time to dwell on how being here would feel. But now that I was, a wave of inadequacy crashed over me.

'I hope the cakes are fancy enough,' I said apologetically, eyeing the room full of clusters of people dressed in smart suits and long dresses. 'This is a bit different than my usual clientele.'

'They're perfect,' Lucy assured me, ushering me to a side room. 'Come on, let's get them plated up so we can start serving. The savoury items have almost gone already.'

We set the macaroons and bite-sized brownies on silver trays and then I followed Lucy as she waltzed into the gallery with grace and confidence.

I dawdled behind, silently taking in the polished floors, clinking glasses and hum of chatter. All of it made me feel out of place, but the worst part was the sound of Bach emanating from the string quartet in the corner. It was elegant, unobtrusive, and entirely too familiar.

* * *

'Stop.'

My fingers froze above the piano keys, the final note hanging in the air, unresolved.

I turned my head towards Daniel. He sat poised on the edge of his chair beside me, his dark eyes sharp beneath his frown. He exhaled, shaking his head slightly before tapping his pencil against the music.

Tap, tap, tap.

My gaze dropped to where he was indicating my mistake. Not that I needed him to; I already knew what I'd done wrong. A hesitation. A fraction of a second falter before the rapid scale. A tiny slip.

'You'll have to do it again.' His voice was firm. Expectant.

I sucked in a sharp breath, stifling my objections. The piece had been almost perfect. But then, that was the problem. Almost perfect wasn't good enough. Not for him. Which meant not for me either.

Daniel was the only person who believed in my abilities. He had faith I could be a successful pianist. I could be somebody.

But belief came with expectations. And those left no room for flaws. Success didn't come from almost perfect.

I swallowed hard, repositioning my hands. Mistakes weren't an option. Not for me. Not even little ones.

I could do better.

I would do better.

I took a breath, trying to steady the nerves that vibrated within me, before sinking back into the music.

* * *

I sucked in a deep breath. I was doing this for Lucy, I reminded myself as I moved further into the room. I focused on keeping my tray level as I moved through the crowded gallery with a smile I'd practised behind the coffee counter a thousand times.

People barely looked at me. Just reached for a cake, nodded, and moved on. I didn't mind. It was better that way. To be practically invisible. Forgettable.

My gaze drifted back to the musicians. I could have belonged here. Once.

I could have been the one performing, dressed in a floor-length black dress, fingers gliding across piano keys, commanding the attention of the entire room. I'd played events just like this – small recitals, cultural nights, spaces filled with quiet applause and refined expectations.

If I hadn't lost everything, this could have been my world.

Instead, I was circling the edges of it with a tray of food, trying not to flinch every time the music dipped into something I recognised.

* * *

The crowd had thinned, leaving the last few stragglers lingering with half empty glasses.

Lucy placed her hand on my elbow and guided me to the side room. 'You were amazing tonight,' she whispered.

'It was just a few cakes,' I said, setting my empty tray down on the table in front of us.

'I'm not talking about the cakes, although they were a hit, as I knew they would be.'

I frowned, feeling confused. Circulating in that room full of strangers had drained my energy too much to allow me to think clearly.

'I'm talking about in there.' She nodded towards the gallery. 'I know this kind of event isn't your thing.'

'Oh.' I nodded slowly. 'Right. It's a bit... formal,' I finished lamely.

'Difficult,' Lucy said at the same time.

I blinked. 'W-what makes you say that?'

Lucy gave a half shrug. 'I don't know, just a feeling, I guess.'

We stared at each other silently. I wasn't sure if she was waiting for me to confirm it or deny it.

I did neither.

33

NOW

December

I stood in the middle of the bedroom, surrounded by the contents of upturned drawers.

There had to be something here.

But the disarray around me implied the opposite.

I moved to the living room and started rummaging again. Just because I hadn't found anything yet didn't mean I wouldn't. I didn't need much. Just a sticky note. A discarded shopping list. Anything.

Nothing.

I let out a frustrated groan and moved on to the kitchen, but I already knew I wouldn't find anything in here. The tiny kitchen lacked storage space, and the worktop was cluttered by dirty dishes and cups that had been building up all week.

After spending all day cleaning mugs and plates, the last thing I felt like doing when I got home was cleaning another kitchen. It had been a relief when Callum had taken over that chore, but without him...

I scrunched my nose as I peered at the crockery soaking in a sink full of murky water. I'd barely eaten since Callum disappeared. I'd been surviving on cups of tea and snacks, otherwise it would have been even worse. I let out a sigh and pulled the dishwasher door open. Sliding out the top rack, I blinked in surprise.

Everything was clean.

A small smile tugged at my lips. Callum must have run the dishwasher before he left.

I froze.

That was odd, wasn't it? If Callum had left me like PC Munroe thought, why would he care if the dishes were clean? Surely you only did something like that if you were planning on coming back.

I fought the urge to grab my phone and call the station. To me, it felt like a sign that Callum hadn't simply walked out on me. But to the police?

My shoulders slumped as I realised it would be trivial. A clean dishwasher didn't confirm Callum's disappearance was suspicious. It just meant I had clean plates.

I took a deep breath, trying to quell the wave of disappointment before slowly emptying the dishwasher, absentmindedly sliding plates and dishes back into the cupboards where they belonged, while my thoughts drifted back to Callum.

I turned back to the dishwasher, reaching for the next item, but stopped.

I didn't recognise it.

My brain snapped back to attention as my gaze fixed on the black water bottle. Slowly, I lifted it out and held it in front of me, studying it carefully as I turned it in my hands. *Urban* was written in orange across the bottle, with white lettering below it, most of which had faded away.

There was a familiarity to it, but I couldn't place it. The only thing I knew was the bottle wasn't mine.

Which meant it must have been Callum's.

A lump formed in my throat, and I blinked furiously, trying not to cry. It was ridiculous. I was getting emotional over something as insignificant as a water bottle.

And yet, it wasn't just a water bottle. It was something of his.

I hugged it to my chest, clinging to it as though somehow it was a link to him.

But it wasn't enough. I couldn't take it to the police and present it as evidence of Callum's existence. It was just a water bottle. A clean one, at that. No fingerprints, no DNA.

It didn't bring me any closer to finding him.

And yet it felt monumental. To the police, it would be meaningless. But to me, it was proof I wasn't going crazy.

The police were right; I couldn't be sure how long the note had been in my apron pocket before I found it. I couldn't even be sure it had been written by Callum. The more I thought about it, the more I questioned if I'd ever actually seen Callum's writing at all.

Was it possible that I'd found the note on my birthday and just assumed it was from him, because that was the only thing that made sense?

I couldn't rule it out.

But someone had brought that bottle into the flat and put it in the dishwasher.

And that someone wasn't me.

So Callum had to be real.

* * *

I stood in front of the Arcado Lounge, a place I'd been to so many times, but today my gaze drifted upwards. The windows above were dark, making the orange lettering more pronounced: Urban.

No wonder the name had felt so familiar. I must have walked past it practically every week, and yet I'd never paid attention to it. But when I started searching for Urban after finding Callum's water bottle, everything clicked into place.

I veered into the arcade that led to the gym and my pace slowed as I approached the entrance. Gyms made me nervous. They always had.

Lucy had tried to tempt me into joining hers after Mum passed. She thought it would do me good to try something new. Something that wasn't connected to Mum. But one visit had been enough to tell me I didn't belong there.

The clank of weights. The designer gym gear that was way out of my budget. The shouts and laughter that always made me feel like I was on the outside of a joke I didn't understand. It all made me feel like I was intruding on someone else's territory.

It was all tied to the past. Everything was. Gyms reminded me of school sports. The popular kids. The bullies.

The gym had been their space. The music room had been mine. They avoided mine out of disinterest. I avoided theirs out of self-preservation.

Even now, crossing into the gym felt like I was trespassing. I may as well have worn a neon sign that said, 'I don't belong here'. I was an outsider still.

Back then, I'd told myself I didn't care. I had something they didn't: ambition, purpose, a future. But as I climbed the narrow staircase that smelled faintly of sweat, I couldn't help but wonder, what if they were the ones who had it right?

What good had all that ambition done me?

While I'd been practising every spare moment and stressing about exams and performances, they'd been having fun simply being kids. They'd still had room to grow. To try things. To fail. And then get up and try again.

Whereas I hadn't had that luxury. One mistake and my entire identity was torn apart. I'd invested so much of myself into that one dream, I didn't know how to do anything else.

I snorted softly. Now I was the one who was stuck. Trapped in a life I hadn't planned, trying to keep afloat a café I didn't want, in a town I didn't choose, constantly in the shadow of a past I couldn't fix.

As soon as I reached the top of the stairs, I realised the gym wasn't what I expected. No social media influencers filming themselves. No bright lights or thumping music. No tight designer gear. Just people. Normal people.

A guy in his fifties lifting weights in a baggy T-shirt. A young woman with her hair falling out of its bun as she pushed back and forth on the rowing machine, her face a contortion of determination and desperation. Two friends laughing as they jogged side by side on the treadmills.

It felt strangely calm and welcoming.

I exhaled a long breath, letting the scene in front of me fill me with something I hadn't expected: courage. I stepped forward towards the reception desk.

The woman behind the welcome desk looked up and gave me a warm, easy smile.

'Hi,' I said, hoping the wobble in my voice wasn't noticeable. 'My, er, friend, Callum Hayes, comes here, do you know him?' I asked hopefully. 'Early twenties, dark hair.'

She shook her head. 'Sorry, I can't think of a Callum off hand. But we have so many members.' She gave me an apologetic smile.

I felt my body deflate. Now what? I'd psyched myself up to come here, determined to find answers, and I'd been foiled straight away. I couldn't exactly demand she check her records. Privacy laws would stop her from telling me anything even if he was a member.

I needed to be more indirect. Talk to other members. People who weren't bound by rules. Maybe one of them would know something, but there was only way to get to them...

I forced a shrug, hoping the movement masked my disappointment. 'Well, anyway, he mentioned you have a ten-day trial running and suggested I come along and check it out,' I said, relaying the information I'd read online.

'That's great,' she said, full of enthusiasm. 'I'm Jenna, let me show you around and then I'll just need you to fill in a form with your details so we can get you set up on the system.'

I nodded; that sounded simple enough.

'As you can see, we have all the fitness machines here – bikes, rowing machines, treadmills – and over there we have our weights. Or if you're interested in trying our classes, you will find most of them take place in our main studio,' she said, leading me towards the large room at the far end of the gym. I peeked through the window at the Pilates class in progress. It was a mixture of ages and abilities; it felt like something even I wouldn't be totally out of place in.

'Were you looking for anything specific?' my tour guide asked.

'I, er...' My confidence wavered. 'I'm not really sure. I've never joined a gym before,' I admitted quietly.

'That's okay,' Jenna said reassuringly, as though my confession wasn't the horrendous admission I felt it was. 'Lots of our members had never even been to a gym before, or some had found them a bit intimidating and hadn't stuck at it.'

I stared at her, stunned. 'They did? I thought that was just me.'

She chuckled softly. 'Definitely not. The key is finding the right gym for you. I've worked at others in the past, but I have to say this is by far the friendliest. There is a lovely social side to it here. The members often go out for coffee together after a class. Or take part in our beach walks. All optional, of course.'

'Wow, that sounds really nice actually.' I caught the edge of surprise in my voice, and an instinctive need to apologise kicked in, but before I could even utter a word, she nodded.

'Yeah, I know, right? There's so much more than you'd expect here.'

I smiled tentatively. 'Maybe I could try a few classes.'

'Absolutely,' she replied with a beaming grin. 'Let's get you that paperwork.'

I followed her towards the desk, my gaze drifting back around the gym. Did Callum do any of the classes? And if so, which? How many would I have to try before I found someone who knew him?

My stomach somersaulted. *Would* I find someone who knew him? What if he only came to work out on the machines alone? He might come and go and barely exchange anything more than a 'hello' with the other members.

That was assuming he even was a member himself. Maybe he'd done the trial and never come back. Just like I intended to do.

A row of black and orange water bottles caught my attention, and I frowned. Why would Callum buy a branded Urban water bottle if he wasn't a full member? Surely that wasn't the kind of thing you bought unless the place meant something to you. Unless there was a sense of pride. Of belonging.

'If you could fill this out,' Jenna said, handing me a form. 'We can help you get started with an exercise programme if you're a little unsure where to begin with all the machines. But I can show you the basics today if you like?'

I nodded, feeling more of my unease slip away. 'Yeah, actually, that would be really great.'

I picked up a pen from the desk and studied the form. It was simple enough and yet I hesitated. It felt wrong. My shoulders tensed as I braced myself waiting for someone to stop me and tell me I was an imposter. This time it wasn't just the past that was making me feel uncomfortable; it was the fact my presence here was all a charade.

People here had been welcoming and friendly so far. But how would they feel when they realised I was only here for information?

But then, why did that matter? It wasn't as though I was going to join properly. I'd use the trial to do some digging, find Callum, and I'd never have to come back here again. Everything would go back to normal.

I paused as the pen pressed against the page. Did I want things to go back to normal?

I wanted Callum back, I knew that. But the rest...?

* * *

'Thanks so much,' I said as I walked by the reception desk on my way to the exit. In the last hour, I'd quizzed practically every member of the gym I'd seen, but no one knew Callum. Despite my disappointment, strangely the time here hadn't been horrendous. In fact, it had been kind of pleasant. I shook my head. Maybe not everything had to be defined by the past.

Maybe *I* didn't have to be.

'How did it go?' Jenna asked.

'Not as bad as I expected,' I replied automatically, and then immediately clapped a hand over my mouth as I realised how bad that sounded.

She laughed. 'Don't worry, for a first session, that's a glowing review.'

I chuckled softly, relieved I hadn't offended her. 'I'll have to thank Callum for telling me about you guys,' I added, giving it one last shot just in case his name rang any bells this time around.

'Please do, and point him out to me if you see him here. It would be nice to thank him for spreading the word about our little gym.'

'Who's this?' a lady asked behind me as she checked in on the screen in front of the desk.

'Callum Hayes,' I said, nodding as Jenna gave me a little wave goodbye and dashed off to help another member. 'I met him at The Second Cup Café,' I added, feeling the need to fill in the silence.

'The Second Cup Café? Oh, you must mean Cal.'

My stomach somersaulted.

Cal.

The name tore through me. It felt so casual the way it fell from her lips, as though it was nothing. But it wasn't nothing. Not to me.

It felt like a betrayal. As though she knew him better than I did. Well enough to shorten his name. To call him Cal.

I never had.

Not once.

'He's always talking about that café,' she continued. 'His girlfriend owns the place.'

I froze.

His girlfriend.

The words felt strange. Unexpected.

He'd talked about me. About my café. The guy who avoided my friends. Had left without any trace of his existence. Had talked about me.

What did it mean?

I shook my head. There was only one way to know for sure. I had to find Callum.

'Do you know what day he comes in?' I asked, forcing myself to focus.

The woman shot me a quizzical look. Probably wondering why I was chasing after a guy she'd just told me already had a girlfriend. It wasn't as though I could tell her that was me. After all, shouldn't his girlfriend know what day he worked out?

'Would be nice to say thanks for the recommendation,' I mumbled quickly.

'I'm afraid I'm not sure. I work shifts, so I'm here a bit sporadically. Don't often run into the same people.'

'Ah,' I said, unable to mask my disappointment. I couldn't help but wonder if she was being intentionally cagey.

'You know who might know more? Ian,' she announced suddenly. 'He's always in on a Monday evening for the Strength Fusion class. He's pretty friendly with Cal. Two of a kind, those two, always talking about their boats.'

'His boat,' I murmured in surprise as her words stirred my memory. I could almost see him standing in my living room the very first time he came to the flat. We'd talked about loss. Mum. His grandfather.

And the boat he'd left him.

How had I forgotten about that?

Then again, it was in Portsmouth. And neither of us wanted to think about that place, let alone go back there.

And yet, he'd talked about it here. To the people who called him Cal...

How long had Callum been coming to this gym? To these people who knew him better than I did?

He had told me its name, though. What was it called? The E... 'The Elusive,' I blurted out as the name suddenly sprang into my head.

'You know it?' she asked, clearly surprised.

I shifted awkwardly. 'He mentioned it, though I'd have gone somewhere exotic if I owned a boat.'

'I know, right?' The woman laughed. 'It seems a waste to leave a boat moored in the River Stour when you could be sailing the world.'

Moored in the River Stour.

Her words swirled in my head, repeating over and over. The River Stour was here. In Christchurch. Which meant...

I swallowed. *The Elusive* was here...

And maybe, so was Callum...

34

THEN

November

Rain drummed heavily against the windows, and I snuggled closer to Callum beneath the soft fleecy throw as we sat on the sofa, his arm draped over my shoulders. The final credits started to roll on the TV screen before us and I let out a contented sigh.

Callum shifted. 'Liv, I need to tell you something.'

My body tensed at Callum's anxious tone.

'It's about your dad…'

I drew back and stared at him. 'My dad?' What could Callum have to tell me about him?

'He regrets what he did.'

I froze. 'What?'

'Abandoning you the way he did. He—'

'You don't know that. You don't know how he feels. It's a naïve assumption to think that man has any remorse.'

'It's not an assumption.' Callum shifted awkwardly. 'I know.'

His words were so quiet I had to strain my ears to hear them. But even then, I couldn't have heard properly. He couldn't have said—

'I *know*,' he repeated.

My mouth hung open as I stared at him blankly. I wanted to question him, demand to know what he meant. But the words wouldn't come. Deep down I didn't want to know the answer.

'He told me,' Callum said.

I drew back, my body suddenly heavy and slow. 'You've spoken to him?' my voice croaked. Confusion battled with fear inside me. 'How?'

After all these years, had Dad finally come back? But why now? And why had he contacted Callum instead of me?

'I found him.'

The tiny flicker of hope was instantly extinguished with those three tiny words. Dad hadn't sought me out. He hadn't come back for me. Callum had done what I'd sworn I never would.

He'd searched for him.

He'd found him.

The floor seemed to shift beneath me. Everything felt unbalanced. Unstable.

My body vibrated with the force of emotions welling inside me. Grief. Anger. Betrayal.

'Why?'

The word tore from me full of pain and anguish, like a primal cry. Why would Callum do that? Why would he go behind my back? Why would he betray me?

'For you.' Callum's voice was gravelled with emotion. 'I found him for you.'

The room spun. How could it be for me when it was the last thing I wanted?

Dad's absence from my life had created a huge void within me that I'd spent years carefully sidestepping, knowing that it could swallow me whole if I let it.

Callum was supposed to be on my side. He was supposed to care about me. Protect me. Not dig up the past that I'd worked so hard to bury.

'He's your dad,' Callum said, as though that was an explanation.

I snorted. 'My dad who abandoned me.' My words were staccato – sharp and short.

'Everyone makes mistakes,' Callum murmured so softly it was almost a whisper.

'He abandoned me long before he left,' I said, finally voicing the anger and hurt I'd carried for years. 'Leaving the way he did destroyed me.' I dug my nails into my palms as I spoke. 'But a life without his constant disapproval, where I didn't have to witness his daily disappointment in me? That was the silver lining.'

* * *

'I knew that piano would be nothing but trouble.'

'That's not fair,' I objected. Why was Dad blaming my love of music for Daniel's actions?

'I told you she was too obsessed,' Dad continued to Mum, as though I wasn't even there.

'Olivia said she didn't start the fire,' Mum responded. Although the way her voice lifted at the end made it sound more like a question than a statement.

Dad scoffed. Mum may have had doubts, but he didn't. He was convinced of my guilt.

'I loved my lessons. Why would I sabotage them?' I demanded indignantly.

'You can't sabotage something that's already over,' he retorted. 'Daniel had finally come to his senses. There weren't going to be any more lessons. And you knew that.'

I shook my head in stunned silence. How could Dad believe Daniel over me?

'At least this'll be the end of that damn piano.'

My body tensed. 'What do you mean, the end of the piano?'

'Daniel was already done with you.' Dad's words were cold and final. 'And he certainly won't be recommending you to any other teachers now.'

I shrugged defiantly. 'I'll find a new teacher myself.'

He snorted. 'You think they'll agree to teach you?' Dad let out a loud, scornful laugh. 'No one will take that risk, and without a teacher, you'll never get into the Royal Academy of Music. It was always a slim chance, but now you've got nothing.'

I wanted to scream at him that he was wrong, but I couldn't.

He wasn't.

* * *

'I know what it's like to be alone,' Callum said quietly. 'To have lost everyone that mattered. That isolation. That pain...' His chest heaved. 'I just wanted to take some of that pain away from you. To help, in some small way.'

'Help?' I scoffed, my voice sharp with disdain, as I sprang to my feet. 'Help is what I did for you. I gave you a place to stay. Another option than having to crawl back to your family on *their* terms. But I didn't make the decision for you. I just gave you a choice. So *you* could decide what was best for you. What *you* wanted.'

'I... I...' Callum stuttered, looking uncertain.

'You took that decision away from me.' My eyes narrowed. 'What about Rob?'

Callum shifted forwards, perching on the edge of the sofa as he frowned. 'What's Rob got to do with this?'

'You want me to face the person who betrayed me, but you won't see Rob.'

'It's different.'

'Why?'

'He's not family.'

'Family isn't always blood.'

Callum swallowed.

'What's his number?' I asked, reaching for my phone.

'I deleted it.'

'His surname then?'

Callum didn't speak.

'The company where you both worked?'

He remained silent.

'It doesn't feel good, does it? Being confronted with the past you've tried hard to leave behind?' I said triumphantly. 'You ask all these questions about my past, even when you know it's difficult for me to talk about.'

'I just want to get to know you,' Callum objected.

'And I want to get to know you. All of you. The good and the bad. You can tell me.'

He shifted. 'It's complicated.'

'That's a cop-out, and you know it.'

Callum sank back against the sofa. 'You're right.'

'Talk to me,' I urged as I perched beside him.

'I wasn't trying to hurt you.'

Guilt tugged at my chest. 'I know,' I said, my tone softer now. 'But sometimes good intentions can be painful.'

'I'm sorry.' His gaze dropped to his lap. 'I thought—' He shook his head slowly. 'I just want you to have someone again. Have family again. I thought I was doing something good. Taking away the riskiness. That fear of being rejected, of being hurt again.'

'And you think that's what you've done?'

'He wants to see you. To apologise. To be part of your life.'

'If he wanted that, then why didn't he come back? He knew where I was. Exactly where he left us.'

'He was ashamed. And afraid you wouldn't want to see him.'

'He was right.'

'But don't you at least want to meet with him? Hear him out?'

'Hear him out? You think what he did was excusable?' My eyes narrowed. 'Or perhaps justifiable?'

Callum frowned. 'Why would it be justifiable? He abandoned you.'

'D-did he tell you why?' The question tore me apart to ask, but I needed to know. How much had Dad told Callum? Had he revealed the parts of my life that I'd been too ashamed to talk about?

If so, why was Callum still here?

Hope battled with dread, and I realised part of me wanted him to know. The part that hated keeping the past a secret from the person I wanted to share my future with. The part that longed for him to accept me for who I was, including my flaws. But another part, a stronger part, knew that some things were too big to come back from.

'He said when the business fell apart, he couldn't cope with feeling helpless and unable to protect and support his family. It was easier to leave you than to face up to his own failings.'

Easier.

The word ricocheted through me.

'It wasn't easier for *us*.' I spat the words out, sharp and bitter.

'Then tell him that. See him. Confront him. Say all the things you've been holding in for all these years.'

I rubbed my forehead. 'Did you find him to reunite us? Or to cause a showdown?'

'Maybe you can't have one without the other,' Callum suggested.

'Or maybe I don't want either.'

Callum tipped his head to the side. 'You're really not going to see him? You don't want any kind of closure, or retaliation?'

'Retaliation?' Now it was my turn to be confused. 'Why would I want to retaliate?'

Callum shrugged. 'He abandoned you. Left you and your mum with a struggling café and no support while he created a new life for himself. With a new family.'

I heard my gasp. Loud. Desperate.

'A new family?'

Callum's gaze didn't shift from my face. It was as though he wanted to capture my reaction. I closed my eyes, letting the darkness sooth me. I was being paranoid. Allowing the shock to distort my perception. Of course Callum was watching me carefully, fearful of how I'd take the news. His actions had been misguided, but he'd done this because he cared.

'He remarried. They have a five-year-old kid.'

I let out my breath and it gushed from me. 'I didn't even know he and Mum had divorced. She kept his name. Kept everything the same.'

'Almost as though she was waiting for him to come back,' Callum finished for me. 'Meanwhile, he moved on. A new wife. A daughter.'

A daughter.

He didn't just leave me.

He replaced me.

'I guess he found a daughter deserving of his love. One who was compliant. Good.'

'Weren't *you* good?' Callum stared at me. He seemed to almost be holding his breath, waiting for my reply.

This was my chance to tell him. Tell him what had happened. Who I really was.

I'd lived the pretence for so long. Trying to be the daughter my parents had truly wanted. One without music. Without dreams. Now was my chance to break free from it. To finally be myself again.

But I knew what had happened the last time I'd been myself.

People had almost died.

35

NOW

December

Cal.

The name repeated in my brain as I walked through the quiet grounds of Christchurch Priory. I'd never called him Cal. Should I have? Did he prefer that? But if so, why hadn't he told me?

Then again, I was starting to realise there were a lot of things Callum hadn't told me. How did he get the car window replaced for free? Or buy a CCTV system when he was broke? How had he found Dad? And why hadn't he told me he'd joined a gym?

And then there was *The Elusive*.

I reached the river, and my pace slowed as I scanned the water ahead. Was the woman at the gym right? Was *The Elusive* really here?

Callum had told me she was in Portsmouth. Why would he lie about that?

Her berth is in Portsmouth.

I froze as I recalled what Callum had actually said. He'd told me where her berth was. But that didn't mean the boat was there.

My request to see her had ended the conversation. Callum had changed the subject straight after that. He'd never actually said where *The Elusive* was.

I wasn't sure why that made me feel better. He might not have outright lied to me, but he'd still misled me. Had he misled me about other things too?

What if he'd known Wave Media didn't exist? What if he'd lied about them? Had I made a mistake with his date of birth? Or was that another lie, too?

How much did I really know about Callum Hayes?

My thoughts circled back on a loop. I certainly hadn't known his boat was in Christchurch. Here, somewhere along this river.

How many times had we walked along this path hand in hand? Or sat on the benches watching the swans? How close had we been to his boat? How could he have not said anything?

You can live on her if you need to. Not comfortably, but it's possible. I've done it.

Callum's words replayed in my mind.

He'd lived on her.

Was that where he was now? Living on his boat, hiding from me?

But why?

Everything led back to that question.

He could have left at any time, told me he wanted out. But he hadn't.

None of it made sense.

If his boat was in Christchurch, why not simply live on board when he couldn't afford the Airbnb? Then again, why rent an Airbnb at all when he already had somewhere he could stay?

Another question niggled at the edges of my mind. Had he even rented an Airbnb? I'd never been to his place. He always came to the café or the flat. I thought it had been sweet. He knew how busy I was so he came to me. But what if he'd had to? What if he'd been living on his boat instead?

Each question led to another 'why'?

If he had been living on his boat, why not just say so?

The answer screamed at me: he didn't want me to know his boat was here.

It felt illogical. What did it matter if I knew where his boat was? And yet somehow it also felt like the only answer.

If keeping the location of his boat a secret had been so important to Callum, then finding it was just as important to me.

My pulse quickened as I squinted at the names stencilled on the boats ahead of me. *Sea Whisper*, *Blue Moon*, and *Restless*. I walked further along the river path. *The Eloise.*

My heart sank.

Not *The Elusive*.

This was impossible. I didn't even know what it looked like. All I had was its name and some random details about how many berths it had. I could hardly walk around checking the name of every single boat in Christchurch. There must be hundreds, if not more. I couldn't even see them all from the path.

I pressed my hand to my head, but it did nothing to ease the throbbing that vibrated through my skull.

The knowledge that *The Elusive* was in Christchurch was the first real piece of information I'd had in days. I couldn't wait until Monday for the Strength Fusion class before I found out if this Ian knew the exact location.

More than two more days of waiting. Wondering. I shook my head. But what was the alternative?

Going back to the police hadn't done me any good last time. I couldn't prove Callum wrote the note. And I couldn't prove his boat was here either.

Relying on them to investigate and find the proof themselves felt risky. I had no credibility with them. How could I be sure they wouldn't write it off as another waste of their time?

My stomach lurched. Or accuse me of making it up?

No. I wasn't going through that again. They'd made me doubt myself, my sanity, enough already.

If I wanted to find *The Elusive*, I was going to have to do so myself.

The question was how.

'She's an IP24. An Island Plastics motorsailer, just under twenty-four feet.'

Callum's words ran through my head, and I grabbed my phone and hurried to a bench. Perching on the edge, I typed 'Island Plastics IP24' into Google. Images of boats filled the small screen. Small, sturdy vessels. I might not know where the boat was, but I finally had some idea of what I was looking for.

I nibbled my lip as I studied the river again. What I needed was someone I could ask. Someone who knew about boats. About *these* boats.

There had to be some kind of system. Some control over who moored here. A register? A boating association?

I searched again.

Christchurch Harbour Association appeared in the results. They seemed to be a voluntary organisation managing access to the harbour.

Perfect.

I clicked the link and scanned the website for anything useful – a list of moorings, a registry, a directory. Nothing obvious. Just details on how to apply for membership to the Christchurch Sailing Club.

Would Callum have had to join to moor *The Elusive* here? Would he have left a paper trail?

Everything I read blurred together. It felt so confusing. Like trying to play a sonata without having seen the music. I didn't even really know what I was looking at, let alone what I was looking for.

A phone number caught my attention, and I clicked on it, but as my finger hovered above the call button, I stopped.

Data protection.

Even if I managed to speak to someone, even if they knew the boat, knew Callum, they wouldn't help me. They wouldn't be allowed to tell me anything.

I slumped back against the bench, letting the phone fall to my lap. It all felt pointless.

If *The Elusive* had been here at some point, there was no guarantee that it still was. Callum could have sailed her out of my life and I wouldn't even have known.

But I couldn't just give up. Not without at least trying.

Maybe he wasn't here. But if I didn't look, then I'd never know one way or another.

I frowned. It was impossible to see the names of all the boats from the path. Some were moored in the middle of the river, side by side, their names hidden from view from here. Their owners must have used a tender to get out to them.

I glanced up and down the river. I needed to get closer. I needed to get out on the water.

The boat hire kiosks along the quay were all shut for winter. But maybe, just maybe, there was still a way.

36

THEN

December

The café had emptied early, the winter drizzle outside doing little to tempt anyone in for a late afternoon latte. The bell above the door jingled as the last customer left, and I flipped the sign to *Closed* with a relieved sigh.

'Closing up early?' Callum asked from behind me.

'One of the perks of being the boss,' I replied with a wink.

Callum stretched and rolled his shoulders, letting out a contented grunt as he looked around the quiet space. 'I can't believe it's December already,' he said.

I nodded, rubbing my hands together for warmth. 'Feels like September was five minutes ago.'

'It's going to be our first Christmas here together,' he added, like it was a casual observation, but something in his voice made my stomach flutter.

I'd spent the last few years dreading the holidays. The café became a retreat for those looking for a break in the midst of their Christmas shopping. They staggered in laden with bags, chattering excitedly about their festive plans. While Mum and I worked in silence, trying to ignore the constant reminders of what our family Christmases had once been like.

But this year, maybe it could be different.

Callum picked up a worn cardboard box from behind the counter and set it gently on one of the café tables. Dust puffed from the top as he peeled back the flaps. 'Found these in the stock cupboard. Looks like the ghosts of Christmases past.'

I chuckled. 'Back when we had the restaurant, Mum used to go overboard. Tinsel and fairy lights practically covered every surface. Moderation was not a word that applied to Christmas decorations.'

He laughed, holding up a string of fairy lights, already tangled into a stubborn knot. 'She sounds brilliant.'

'She was,' I said softly, taking the lights from his hands. 'When things were good.'

A silence fell between us as I slipped back into my memories. I turned to the counter and began gently untangling the lights. 'We never really bothered decorating since Dad left. It seemed a bit pointless.'

Callum moved behind me. 'Let's make it un-pointless, then.'

I looked up, surprised.

'Let's put them up,' he said, voice bright. 'Properly. Give the place some festive cheer.'

I hesitated. 'You don't have to—'

'I want to,' he said firmly.

Our eyes met and I realised that he was excited. I smiled, a warm rush sweeping through my body. His excitement was contagious. The kind of excitement I hadn't felt since I was a child. When Christmas was magical and carefree, instead of burdened with guilt and resentment.

* * *

Callum climbed down from the chair he'd been standing on and surveyed our work. 'Not bad, hey?'

I pivoted slowly, taking it all in. The fairy lights were strung across the windows and along the counter, casting a soft, golden glow. Red tinsel curled around the faded artwork on the walls, adding a burst of colour the café hadn't seen in years. And in the corner, the artificial Christmas tree stood proudly, its plastic branches dotted with mismatched ornaments.

'It's perfect,' I said, my voice catching as I fought the sudden lump in my throat.

Even with just the two of us here, the café felt warm and full of energy. Like it was finally waking up after a long sleep.

Callum frowned. 'Well, almost perfect,' he said, nodding towards the counter behind me. 'We missed one.'

I turned to see a stray bauble nestled in the corner like it had tried to make a run for it.

I chuckled as he retrieved it with exaggerated care, carrying it to the tree like a mischievous puppy being returned home. His expression was an irresistible mix of childish wonder and excitement.

I fumbled for my phone, desperate to capture the moment as he picked the perfect spot and hung the ornament on the tree. I wanted to preserve everything about our first Christmas together. My grin widened. The first of many.

'Erm.' Callum cleared this throat as he stepped out from behind the tree. 'I have bad news.'

My stomach lurched as I waited for Callum to continue. Silence stretched out between us. I hated the way he did that. Left me waiting. Wondering.

He licked his lips as if trying to summon the courage to speak. 'About tomorrow...' He cringed and my stomach plummeted.

'Tomorrow?' I clung to the word, praying he wasn't talking about the plans we had made to meet Lucy, Maddie and their partners for drinks after work. Surely he wouldn't bail on me again.

'Sorry, Liv, I'm not going to be able to make it.'

'But we arranged this for you, so you can finally meet everyone.'

'I know.' Callum shook his head sadly. 'I hate to abandon you. But if I don't go and meet this client the whole deal is going to fall through. If there was any way I could avoid it, you know I would.'

I nodded mutely. Of course he would. It wasn't as though he would choose to cancel on me again.

And yet, doubt niggled at me. His critical meetings always seemed to crop up at the most inconvenient times. Was that just coincidence?

Or...?

I shook my head, refusing to allow myself to finish that thought. I was so used to being guarded and let down that I couldn't tell the difference between instinct and insecurity any more.

37

NOW

December

'Thanks for this,' I said as I stood in Lucy's garage while she rummaged through the clutter.

'No worries,' she replied, glancing up at me, though her expression was more cautious than casual. 'You do remember how to paddleboard, don't you?'

I nodded. 'Yeah. I'll be fine.'

She raised an eyebrow. 'Like last time?'

* * *

I stood on Lucy's paddleboard, desperately trying to keep my balance as the river rocked us back and forth. I glanced at Maddie on her board to my left. She looked so graceful and poised as she effortlessly glided along the water.

Unlike me.

'Are you sure you wouldn't rather switch back?' I asked Lucy as she kneeled on the front of the board.

'I'm enjoying being the one chilling out while you do all the paddling for a change.' Lucy laughed. 'Even if you are determined to make me seasick with all the wobbling.'

'Sorry,' I muttered. 'I haven't quite got the hang of it yet.'

'Don't worry, you will,' she assured me. 'But you need to turn. Shift your weight back and paddle on the left.'

I moved careful, trying to stay upright.

'Move your right leg back.' Lucy's tone was becoming more urgent. 'Liv, you need to—'

Lucy squealed as the board tipped beneath us and we plunged into the cold water. I gasped for air as I resurfaced, my hair plastered to my face. The sound of Maddie's laughter filled the quiet morning air. She pointed at us before she squealed and splashed into the water as well.

* * *

A laugh escaped before I could stop it. 'You mean the time you tried to show me how to turn and capsized us straight into the river?'

Lucy rolled her eyes. 'You were about to run us into a moored boat!'

'We weren't *that* close,' I said, as my smile withered at the mention of a boat, and the present came crashing down around me.

'We were all laughing so hard we could barely get back onto the boards,' Lucy continued, still grinning. 'It was such a disaster. A hilarious one.'

We loaded the inflatable paddleboard, pump and oar into my car, and I closed the boot with a quiet thud.

'Got time for a coffee before I head into work?' Lucy asked hopefully, her voice lifting at the end. 'It's not often you take time off from the café these days.'

'Sorry,' I said with a shake of my head. 'I want to get out on the water before it gets busy.'

Lucy snorted. 'Busy? Liv, it's December. No one else is crazy enough to be paddleboarding when it's this cold.'

I ground my toe into the gravel driveway. She was right, of course. But this had nothing to do with the busyness of the river. Now that I'd made up my mind to do this, I just wanted to get out there and start searching.

She tilted her head. 'What's prompted this sudden desire to paddleboard anyway?'

I hesitated. 'I don't know, just wanted a bit of exercise, I guess.' The lie caught in my throat. 'I joined a gym,' I added. At least that part was true.

Her mouth dropped open. 'You? An actual gym?'

I shot her a look. 'Yes. A real gym.'

'Wow.' She shook her head in amazement. 'You know I'm not entirely sure if this Callum of yours is real or fictitious given I still haven't met him.'

My chest tightened. I opened my mouth to speak, but no words came.

'But real or not, he's clearly a good influence on you.'

* * *

I winced as the icy water stung my feet by Iford bridge. Lucy was right; this was a crazy idea. The water was cold enough even in August, but in December?

Wading further in, I pushed the paddleboard ahead of me, until the water reached above my shins. Scrambling on to the board, I stayed on my knees. There was no way I was attempting to stand today.

The board rocked gently beneath me as I tentatively found my rhythm – dip, pull, dip, pull. I glided slowly along the River Stour towards the boats.

There was a stillness to the air. It felt strange being out on the water, immersed in calm tranquillity while everyone else was heading to work. There was a strange sense of peace to it, despite what I was doing. For the first time in days, it felt like my thoughts could finally slow down. I had to focus on keeping my balance instead of all the questions I still had no answers to. Fast, racing thoughts and sharp movements didn't belong here. They would risk capsizing me again, toppling me into the water.

The only thing I could do was glide slowly down the river and hope that somewhere amongst all of these boats, I'd find Callum. It felt like a long shot. But at the same time, with the paddleboard, everything was accessible now.

I had no idea how long it would take me or whether my arms would withstand the unaccustomed exercise. My knees were already aching from the uncomfortable position. But I kept paddling.

Despite having the image of the IP24 firmly in my mind, I still found myself reading the name of every boat I passed.

Just in case.

* * *

I glided past Tuckton Tea Gardens. The picnic tables were all empty. But the memory of sitting there with Callum felt so vivid. Kids playing at their parents' feet, the last rays of autumn sunshine warming our faces on a lazy Sunday morning.

Lucy and Maddie had made that possible. Covering the café so I could take a day off. It had felt so indulgent, eating the Tea Garden's signature Brunch Baps as Callum and I huddled together on a bench, watching the river.

That moment had felt like a glimpse of what our lives could be like.

Together.

I dipped the paddle into the river again, my arms protesting with every pull.

But I had to keep moving.

I followed the bend of the river to the right and the Captain's Club Hotel came into view. I inhaled sharply as more memories tugged at me.

I shook my head. I had to stay focused. I had to keep moving forwards.

I shuffled cautiously on the board, the ache in my knees becoming unbearable, but I knew the consequences of making any sudden movements. I glanced at my watch. It had been over two hours already.

Another bend in the river and then up ahead, Christchurch Priory stood like a beacon. There were more boats now as I neared the quay. They lined both sides of the river and yet more were clustered down the centre, creating narrow channels for other boats to pass.

Coastal Cruiser.

Horizon Quest.

And then my gaze locked on one moored in the middle of the river.

I blinked. I read the name once, twice, three times, just to be sure. Even then, I couldn't look away. My paddling was becoming more frantic, and water slopped over my feet as the board rocked precariously.

Had I really found it?

Faded blue paint, scuffed on the sides, and in elegant calligraphy, *The Elusive.*

I stopped paddling, letting the board drift closer. I felt the thud as it bumped into the hull. Setting the paddle down beside me on the paddleboard, I grabbed the mooring line.

I wanted to call out, to shout for Callum, but my voice had abandoned me. I cautiously rose to my feet, desperately trying not to fall as the paddleboard wobbled beneath me.

Struggling, finally, I managed to haul myself over the stern of the boat, landing on the deck with a thud.

There was still no movement on board. I tried to shrug off the wave of disappointment that Callum hadn't rushed out of the cabin to greet me. My entrance had hardly been graceful or quiet. Surely he would have heard it.

I edged forward, across the deck towards the helm, my heart pounding. Desperate for answers and yet simultaneously fighting the urge to flee, afraid of what those answers might be.

I took a deep breath, bracing myself for the harsh truth. Because once I saw him, I would no longer be able to avoid it. If Callum was here, hiding on his boat, then it meant only one thing.

He had left me.

The door to the cabin sat off to the right of the wheel. I lifted my hand and knocked against the wood. What would I say when Callum answered the door?

Still nothing.

I glanced back behind me, suddenly realising there was no tender tethered to the boat. He wasn't on board.

I let out a frustrated groan. I'd come too far to turn back now. Even if Callum wasn't on board right now, maybe I could find something to prove who he was. To prove he existed...

I studied the door. There was no handle, just a metal lock and latch. I reached for it, expecting resistance, but the moment I pulled it, the hinges groaned and the door swung outward.

The smell hit me. Rank. Nauseating. But it wasn't the smell that welded me to the spot. It was what lay the other side of the shallow drop over the raised threshold that separated the helm from the cabin.

Callum.

His body was twisted and awkward. His eyes staring upwards.

I didn't scream.

I couldn't.

He was here.

He was real.

And he was gone.

38

NOW

December

I rocked back and forth in the chair staring at the stark white wall, unable to look at the two men in front of me. I'd known it would only be a matter of time before I was back here again. But I hadn't expected it to be for this.

'Tell us about the boat,' PC Monroe said, intruding on my thoughts.

'Callum's grandfather left it to him. When he lost his job in Portsmouth and had money problems, he said it was the only thing he managed to hang on to.'

'Why didn't you tell us about it before?'

'I-I didn't think of it at first.' I struggled to keep my voice from giving out. 'Callum mentioned it back when we met, but he said her berth was in Portsmouth. I thought that meant the boat was there too.'

'So, Callum never took you on board?'

I shook my head. 'I asked to see it, but...' My mouth opened and closed as I tried to explain what I still couldn't understand. 'I guess he didn't want me to.'

'Yet, you were on the boat today,' DS Harrington pointed out.

'I discovered that Callum had sailed here from Portsmouth. That *The Elusive* was here in Christchurch. It had always been here. I thought if I could find it...'

'Find it?' PC Monroe asked. 'You didn't know where it was?'

'No.' I shook my head again. 'But Callum loved the river. Loved seeing the boats. And I thought...' I swallowed. 'I thought maybe his boat was among them. I borrowed a paddleboard and just started looking. I knew it was a crazy idea. That I might not even find it. He might already have sailed out of Christchurch. But I just kept thinking if I could find it. If I could find him...' My shoulders slumped defeatedly.

'Then what?' PC Monroe prompted gently.

'Then he'd come home,' I whispered. I couldn't hold the tears back any longer. They flooded from me with heaving sobs as I buried my face in my hands. 'I-I just wanted us to be t-together.'

The pause seemed to stretch on endlessly as my mind filled with all the things that Callum and I would never get to do together now. The small things, like closing the café in the evening, walking by the river, celebrating our first Christmas. The things that made a life together.

'It seems when someone tries to leave you, bad things happen to them,' DS Harrington said as my sobs quietened.

'N-no, that's not true.'

'Isn't it? Daniel Sinclair told you he couldn't teach you any more and then his piano was set on fire. Callum Hayes packed everything he owned and left you, and then he's found dead on his boat.'

Dead.

The word dug into me, tearing me apart from inside.

Callum was dead.

I was alone.

Again.

'Why would I go back on the boat?' I glared at DS Harrington, my eyes burning. 'If I'd killed Callum already, why would I go back there today? Why wouldn't I just tell you about the boat and let you find it yourselves? Or say nothing about it at all? Why would I go there and see him like—' I couldn't continue.

DS Harrington nodded slowly. 'You know, that question occurred to me too.'

I took a slow, deep breath, allowing the air to fill my lungs.

'And then I realised, you needed to be there. You needed to be the one to find Callum. To call us from the boat. To give us a legitimate reason why your fingerprints would be found on board a boat you claimed you'd never been on.'

'No, that's not—'

'Then why didn't you call us the second you realised his boat was here?'

'Because I didn't trust you,' I snapped. 'I knew you thought I was delusional. That you didn't believe Callum even existed. So why would you check into anything I told you?'

DS Harrington leaned forwards, his gaze locked on mine. 'Because it's our job,' he said firmly.

'I didn't do anything wrong.'

'You've said that before,' DS Harrington said. 'When you were fourteen.'

I clasped my hands together tightly.

'You were at the scene of an arson, and now a man's death. We're waiting on the result of the post-mortem, but as soon as we have the cause of death confirmed...' DS Harrington let his sentence hang. 'Until then, don't leave Christchurch.'

I'd succeeded in proving Callum existed, but in doing so, I'd become the prime suspect in his death.

39

NOW

December

'Hey, Liv.' Lucy's bright, cheerful voice was so comfortingly familiar that I couldn't hold back the tears any longer as I clung to the phone against my ear.

'Olivia? What's wrong?' Her cheerfulness was instantly replaced by panic.

'It's – it's Callum,' I hiccupped through my sobs. 'He's dead.'

* * *

I sat in the passenger seat of Lucy's black SUV, barely aware of the streets passing in a blur.

She hadn't spoken since she'd picked me up from the police station. I was grateful for that. I didn't have the energy for more conversation. For more questions.

Everything had come unravelled. The more I'd learned in the last few days, the more I'd come to realise that even if I'd found him, Callum and I might not have had a future together. He might not have wanted one.

But it was something else to know that he wouldn't have a future at all.

And if DS Harrington had his way, neither would I. At least not one outside of prison.

'Liv?' Lucy said gently.

I didn't respond. I wanted to say cocooned in the silence.

'Liv, we're home.'

I blinked as I turned my head and stared at the darkened building.

'Are you sure you want to be here?' she asked softly.

I paused, uncertain how to answer. I didn't want to be here. Not like this. It felt emptier and lonelier than ever. But where else was there?

'You can come and stay with us,' Lucy suggested. 'Greg won't mind.'

It was so tempting to say yes. To let Lucy take me home. To pretend, just for a little while, that none of this was happening.

But this was mine. The café. The flat. At least for now...

I shook my head. 'I'll be fine here,' I assured her.

'Okay then,' she said as she unfastened her seatbelt with a click.

'What are you doing?' I asked.

'You don't really think I'm going to let you stay here alone, do you?' Lucy asked, reaching for my hand and squeezing it tightly.

Tears filled my eyes. I should have known she wouldn't abandon me.

'Lucy, about your paddleboard—'

'Don't even think about that,' Lucy said, swatting my words away with her other hand.

'I should have tied it up,' I murmured. 'You lent it to me, and I should have taken better care of it.'

She shook her head. 'It's just a paddleboard.'

'No,' I said. 'It's not. It was *yours*.'

'Moments like this really make you think about your priorities,' she said with a weak smile. 'The things that really matter in life. A paddleboard can be replaced. But people... Callum...'

We fell into silence again.

* * *

'He disappeared on Sunday,' I said finally as I rocked on the sofa, nursing a mug of hot tea.

'Sunday? But that's four days ago.' Lucy stared at me, her eyes wide. 'Why didn't you say anything?'

'I didn't know how to tell you,' I confessed. 'I didn't know what to say. Everything had been going so well between us. We'd decorated the café, we were excited about our first Christmas together and then, puff, he was just gone.'

'You know I wouldn't have bombarded you with questions or expected you to explain anything. Not to me.'

I swallowed.

'I'd have just been here with you if you'd wanted to talk. Or cry. You didn't have to go through that alone.'

I nodded. 'I know, but...'

'What?'

I peered at her through watery eyes. 'At first, I was just so in shock that I couldn't fully process that he'd really gone. I thought if I could just find him and talk to him, then everything would be okay. That we'd be okay.'

'I would have helped you search for him.'

I stared at my mug of tea. 'I think I was afraid to tell you. To tell anyone. It was like as long as I didn't say it out loud, then he wasn't really gone. He could just come back, and no one would ever need to know that he'd left me too.'

Lucy wrapped her arm around my shoulders. 'I would never have judged you.'

I shifted uncomfortably.

'You do know that, don't you?'

I nibbled my lip. 'There was nothing of his left. No clothes. No photos. Even his phone number was disconnected. It was like he'd never existed. The police didn't believe me. They thought I'd made him up. That I was delusional.'

Lucy closed her eyes. 'Oh, Liv...'

'I kept thinking, what if you didn't believe me either?' My voice broke again. 'You'd never met him. And you used to joke, remember? 'This "mysterious boyfriend" of yours.' Even you weren't really sure if he was real or fictitious.'

She flinched. 'I didn't mean it like that.'

'I know,' I said quickly. 'But all these questions started surfacing. The company he said he worked for didn't exist. His name and date of birth didn't tie up with any records. And the police looked at me like I was insane. I couldn't call you. I couldn't see that in your face too.'

'I don't understand why the police would jump to that kind of conclusion, though?' Lucy said, a frown creasing her forehead. 'When you report your boyfriend missing, you shouldn't have to deal with people questioning your sanity.'

I squirmed on the sofa. 'It's because of the fire,' I admitted quietly.

Lucy's head jerked upwards, and she stared at me. 'The one before you moved here?'

I nodded. 'It happened at my piano teacher's house. He was outside at the time and I was alone in his music room. It happened so fast; one second, I was setting my music on the piano, and the next the whole room was ablaze.'

'Oh my word.' Lucy stared at me, her eyes wide. 'Were you hurt?'

'Not badly,' I assured her. 'At least not physically, but...' I took a shaky breath, summoning my courage to go on. 'Daniel accused me of starting the fire and suddenly everything changed. Sympathy morphed into suspicion in an instant.' I tucked my knees up against my chest. 'I was completely trauma-tised after being trapped in the fire. I was suffering from smoke inhalation and minor burns. But it was as though none of that mattered. No one cared.' I let out a weary sigh. 'I was deemed crazy and dangerous.'

'But that's ridiculous.' Lucy shook her head. 'How could they think that?'

I shrugged. 'It was his word against mine. Daniel had a solid career behind him. He was a respected pianist. A popular teacher. Whereas me...' I shrugged, feeling as helpless now as I had back then. 'I'd never really fitted in anywhere. Daniel had always been the only person that truly got me. We spoke the same language. We were driven by the same passion for music. He was my only ally. And then suddenly, he was my biggest threat.'

'That's...' Lucy seemed to struggle for words. 'Awful,' she finished finally.

'If the police could have made an arrest on what they believed then I would be in prison.'

'But they never made an arrest? Not even Daniel?'

I shook my head.

'So that was it? The case was just dropped?'

'Yeah.' I nodded.

'Well, at least you were free, I guess.'

I snorted. 'I was hardly free. I might not have been arrested, but I still ended up imprisoned. This town. This café. They were my confinement.'

'And the piano?'

'It was the first thing Dad sold when the restaurant struggled after rumours about me started to circulate.'

Lucy's eyes widened.

'Not that it mattered,' I said, repeating the assurances I'd told myself at the time. 'I hadn't touched the piano since the fire. I'd tried, but every time I sat on the stool ready to play, my chest tightened, and I felt like I was back in that smoke again. I couldn't breathe. Couldn't move.'

'That's understandable,' Lucy said gently. 'You'd been through something traumatic. You needed time to recover.'

'Recover?' The word felt wrong. 'It was never about recovery. It was about survival. Trying to salvage what was left and start again. Not just for me, but for all of us. Except there's no such thing as a clean slate. The past sticks to you. As soon as I reported Callum missing, everything was dug up again. I guess it was just easier for the police to write me off than believe me.'

'But I wouldn't have done that to you,' Lucy assured me.

'I couldn't risk losing you as well,' I said, my voice barely audible. 'You're the only person I've got.'

'Don't you know by now, you can't lose me. You're stuck with me for good.'

I tried to smile, but I couldn't. I'd thought that about my parents too... There was still so much she didn't know. Would she still feel the same if she did?

'I can't believe the police dragged you to the station to answer questions today.' Lucy shook her head in disgust. 'What were they thinking, after everything you have been through?'

'They're just doing their jobs,' I replied, repeating the words Mum had once said to me.

'I understand that they need to file reports and everything, but they should have talked to you here, or at least called me so I could be with you.'

I appreciated her sentiment. Part of me wished she could have been with me. But another part was relieved she hadn't been.

It wasn't just the past I had to worry about now. Being accused of arson had been bad enough. But the way DS Harrington had looked at me told me they had a new accusation now.

Murder.

40

NOW

December

I blinked slowly, my eyes adjusting to the soft morning light. I pressed my hand to my head. I hadn't expected to sleep, not that I felt any better for it. My head was pounding, and my eyes were heavy and sore.

The soft clinking of a spoon against a mug told me Lucy was already up. I swung my legs out of bed and padded to the kitchen in bare feet.

'Hey,' she said, smiling slightly as she saw me. 'Did you manage to sleep at all?'

I nodded, but instantly regretted the movement.

'Here, drink this,' she said, sliding a mug of tea across the counter towards me. 'You look like you need it more than I do.'

I wasn't in a position to disagree.

'Liv...' She shifted her weight from foot to foot. 'Would you be okay if I pop into work this morning? Just for a couple of hours,' she added quickly. 'We have a new gallery install—'

'Of course,' I said.

'I can call them if you want me to stay.'

'No,' I said quickly. 'I'll be fine. You should go.'

'Really?'

I managed a tight smile. 'Honestly, I'll be fine.'

'Okay,' Lucy replied, though she didn't look convinced. 'But promise me you will call if you need anything. I mean it, anything at all.'

'I will.'

Lucy didn't move.

'Go,' I urged her. 'I'm just going to take some paracetamol and lie on the sofa till this headache has gone.'

'I know you,' she said, eyeing me warily. 'The second I leave you'll go downstairs and open the café.'

I couldn't deny in any other circumstances she would have been right. But today, I had other things to deal with.

Not that she would approve of those either. She'd tell me to leave the investigating to the police.

She didn't know I had too much at stake for that.

Lucy crossed her arms. 'You view the café as your safe haven. But it's not really safe at all. It's more of a confinement in a life that you hate. A business that's a constant struggle. At risk of going under at any moment and taking you down with it.'

'It's staying afloat,' I objected. *Barely*. Though I omitted that part.

'I'm not just talking about financially.' Her tone softened. 'I mean you, personally. It's like you view the survival of the café as some sort of proof of your worth. If it fails, you fail. Not just the business, but your mum and everything she worked for.'

I swallowed. She wasn't wrong. But I wasn't ready to admit that.

Not yet.

* * *

I waited for the click as the door closed before hurrying to the coat rack. I grabbed the coat I'd been wearing the other day and rummaged through the pockets, pulling out a crumpled napkin.

When I'd written this list I'd been trying to prove Callum existed. Now I needed to prove I hadn't killed him. Smoothing the napkin out on the coffee table, I gritted my teeth. I wasn't going to take the fall. Not this time.

The best place to start was by figuring out who Callum really was. I stared at the napkin. There was one person who knew the answer...

Rob.

Something told me he was the key. The one who'd started this whole chain of events off. His allegations had led to Callum being fired, which had led him to come here. To me.

It had never made sense why Rob would make up claims of corruption. Callum had to have been holding something back.

He wouldn't tell me, but maybe Rob would.

I grabbed my laptop and typed *marketing consultancy, corruption* into Google, searching for any stories from the summer in Portsmouth.

There it was.

A link to a newspaper article about corruption in a firm called Gunwharf Communications. I clicked it, but the link went to a dead page.

I searched again. This time I found a retraction and an apology for the same company.

It all tied in with what Callum had told me when we first met. Rob had passed him information, and Callum had run with it, taking it to the press, trying to expose the truth. But it had fallen apart. The firm covered their tracks. The newspaper had retracted the story, and Callum had been fired.

At last, I had something. I grabbed a pen and added Gunwharf Communications to the list on the napkin before trying another link. This time Instagram opened with a post about the original article. I smiled. There was a photo of the article attached.

I clicked on it, enlarging it. It didn't show the full article, only the headline and journalist.

William Calloway.

My heart raced. He would have the answers. He could talk to the police.

I found the newspaper's phone number and called.

'I need to speak to William Calloway,' I said.

'He's no longer with the paper,' a woman's voice informed me.

I stiffened. 'What do you mean, "no longer with the paper"? Where did he go? What paper did he move to?'

'I'm afraid I can't share that information.'

'At least tell me when he left.'

A pause. Then, reluctantly, she answered, 'August.'

August.

The call went dead.

I checked the date on the original newspaper article. The fifth of August.

Callum had been right. There was something bigger going on. He and William Calloway had both lost their jobs. And the trail led back to one person. The one who had started it all.

Rob.

I pulled up the website for Gunwharf Communications. The site was sleek and professional, filled with testimonials from household brands even I recognised. Everything about it inspired confidence. Exactly what you'd expect from a high-end marketing firm.

I clicked on the 'Team' page and scrolled through the staff directory.

Callum had said he and Rob were marketing consultants. But there were two Robs listed as marketing consultants.

The first was in his mid-50s. His profile mentioned his wife and kids. Not him.

I scrolled down.

The second one looked the right age, about the same as Callum. It had to be him.

I glanced at my phone. I should call the police. Tell them this information, let them follow up and talk to Rob.

Or...

I took a deep breath as I realised what I needed to do.

I was going to Portsmouth.

41

NOW

December

The steady hum of the engine usually felt calming. I'd always loved long car journeys. The quiet stillness inside the car, whilst the landscape blurred past the windows. As though somehow, I was straddling a space between the two. Suspended between where I'd left and where I was going.

Our love of travelling was the only thing Dad and I had ever had in common. There was always a sense of excitement and adventure in a trip together. It felt like an escape; from the restaurant, from the piano, from everything that divided us. There was nothing to do but sit side by side and talk as he drove. We were just us: father and daughter. No judgement, no disappointment.

Yet today, instead of bringing me comfort, the miles stretching before me felt daunting. What if the police stopped me? DS Harrington had been very clear that I wasn't to leave town.

Then again, what if they didn't?

The problem wasn't really my fear of the police, or even the reminder of Dad.

It was the destination.

In the eight years since we'd left, the only thing I'd known for sure was that

I'd never go back. Never *could* go back. Not to Portsmouth. Not to the life I'd had there. It had changed me too much for that.

But now Portsmouth was exactly where I was heading.

Not for myself. For Callum.

And yet something about it felt too coincidental. As much as I wanted to believe this was only about him, his lies, his death, I couldn't shake the feeling that confronting the past was inevitable.

Portsmouth held the answers.

Maybe not just to Callum's disappearance. But to my own.

* * *

I sat in the corner of a café I hadn't stepped into since I was fourteen.

It looked almost exactly the same. The cracked tiles, the mismatched wooden chairs, the table that rocked back and forth at the slightest touch. And yet somehow, it worked. What could have easily been classed as tired and old anywhere else was charming and atmospheric here.

No wonder Mum had loved this place.

* * *

'Two hot chocolates with everything and one chocolate brownie, please,' Mum said to the barista, without even pausing to ask what I wanted.

She didn't need to.

We always ordered the same thing. It was our little ritual after every concert. A mini celebration. Just the two of us.

'Ooo, look,' Mum said, nudging my arm. 'Our favourite table is free. Go and grab it quick.'

I laughed as I obediently dashed to the far table, nestled in the corner by the window.

I settled into my chair and watched as Mum weaved her way towards me, manoeuvring a tray through the crowded café. She set the tray down on the table slowly, anticipating the sharp movement as it instantly swayed.

'There,' she said, stepping back with a flourish. 'I didn't spill a drop.'

'I should think not,' I teased as my mouth watered at the sight of the hot choco-

lates topped with whipped cream and marshmallows. 'It would be a crime to waste any of these.'

'Absolutely,' Mum agreed. 'Besides, I have my reputation to uphold. You can't own a restaurant if you don't know how to carry a tray properly.'

I rolled my eyes and let out a groan.

Mum picked up a knife from the tray and cut the brownie in half. 'We really shouldn't,' she said, her eyes dancing with mischief as she slid a piece towards me.

'You say that every time, and yet you still order it,' I pointed out.

'Oh well, if you don't want it.' Mum reached her hand out towards my piece of brownie.

'No way,' I said, quickly snatching it from the plate before she could reach it. 'We always share.'

Mum laughed. 'We do,' she agreed. 'It tastes better that way, don't you think?' she asked with a wink.

* * *

I wrapped my hands around the tall glass mug of hot chocolate. It hadn't felt right to order a different drink. Not here. Though I didn't order a brownie. Not now Mum wasn't here to share it with me.

I glanced around the busy café, buzzing with chatter and movement. Why had Mum and I never been able to pull off the same level of popularity? On the face of it, The Second Cup Café wasn't that dissimilar. That's what had attracted Mum to it in the first place. She'd been so determined to replicate our favourite spot, as though she was trying to take just a little bit of our lives in Portsmouth with us.

But it had never quite worked.

Everything was just a little off. The wrong location. Too much competition. Too little capital. Or maybe it was simply too many ghosts.

* * *

My phone buzzed. A new email notification lit up the screen.

I tapped on it, holding my breath.

Dear Ms Hammond,

Thank you for your message. Your café expansion sounds exciting, and I'd love to meet with you to discuss how we can assist with your developments. I understand that you are only in town today, so I've rearranged my schedule and can be available at noon to meet with you at your requested location.

Please could you confirm if this is acceptable.

Kind regards,

Rob Weston

I exhaled slowly, relieved and surprised that it had actually worked. Rob had taken the bait.

Using a fake name and posing as a potential client with a thriving business that was expanding into the area had seemed like the best chance to get him to meet with me. But it had still been a long shot.

I typed a quick reply, confirming the meeting, and then paused as I remembered Lucy's promise to leave work as soon as she could slip away.

> Hey Lucy, I just needed to get away for a day or two. I've gone to Portsmouth to speak to one of Callum's old friends. I'll message when I'm back xx

I hit send and shoved the phone into my pocket quickly. There was no way Lucy would simply accept that message without calling me back to check I was okay. Heading out of town without telling her beforehand when she was already worried about me felt cruel, but what was the alternative?

If I'd told her, she would have tried to talk me out of it. Or worse still, she'd have insisted on coming with me.

I was here in search of answers, not to deal with more questions from someone else.

42

NOW

December

My head jolted up as the door opened again. It wasn't noon yet, but I couldn't help checking every person who entered the café, just in case.

The guy who'd entered this time lingered by the door. As he turned slowly, surveying the café, my stomach lurched.

It was him.

If this was a normal meeting, I'd raise my hand and signal to him without a second thought. I hesitated. This *wasn't* a normal meeting.

Right now I had the upper hand. I recognised him from his photograph on the company website, but he had no idea who he was meeting. Not even my real name.

I could walk straight past him and slip out the door without him ever knowing I'd been here. I could give his name to the police and let them investigate. They could find the answers, the ones that until two minutes ago I'd been so certain I wanted. But now...

What if I was getting in over my head here? Callum was dead. Was Rob involved? If I asked the wrong question, would I be next?

Rob started to move towards an empty table, clearly deciding that he was the first to arrive.

I lifted my hand and waved, before I'd even consciously decided to do so.

My common sense might know this was a bad idea, but apparently the rest of me wasn't listening.

Rob nodded, and changed direction. It was too late now, I realised as he headed towards me.

This was it.

'Ms Hammond,' Rob said, offering his hand.

I shook it briefly. 'Thanks for meeting me at such short notice.'

'No trouble at all,' he replied. 'I'm excited to hear more about your expansion plans.' He pulled out his laptop. 'You said this is one of the cafés you'll be acquiring,' Rob said, nodding approvingly. 'It's certainly a dynamic spot. What timescale are you looking at?'

'Actually.' I hesitated. 'There's a different matter I need to discuss with you.'

Rob arched an eyebrow.

'Callum Hayes,' I said, and I braced myself for his reaction.

Rob stared at me blankly. 'Who?'

'Callum Hayes,' I repeated firmly.

Still nothing.

I took a shaky breath. This was going to be more difficult than I'd anticipated. I'd thought the element of surprise would catch him off guard and give me an opening.

I drummed my fingers against the table. 'Your best friend. The guy you went to university with. Your colleague.' I paused. 'Or he was, until you got him fired.'

'What are you talking about?' Rob asked. His bewilderment was so intense it was almost palpable.

But how could that be?

'What is all this about?' There was an impatient edge to his voice.

I pulled my phone from my pocket. Ignoring the three missed calls from Lucy, I pulled up the image I'd saved to my photos. 'You sent Callum an email detailing corruption in the firm,' I said. 'Callum took it to the press. They ran the story.' I placed my phone on the table between us, the screenshot of the article facing him. 'And then you backtracked. The paper printed a retraction. Callum and the journalist both got fired, and you?' I leaned towards him. 'What did you get, Rob?'

'W-what?' Rob shook his head. 'I keep telling you, I don't know who—'

'Stop lying!' I shouted. The café stilled around us, but I didn't care. I just wanted answers. I wanted the truth.

I sucked in a deep breath, trying to regain my composure before I spoke again. 'Callum was your best friend,' I said. 'And then you sent him an email that threw his life into chaos.'

'I never sent that email,' Rob objected.

That email.

Now we were getting somewhere.

'Look, I don't know what you think you know, but you have everything all screwed up.'

I snorted. 'No, Rob. You're the one who screwed up. You manipulated your best friend, and for what?'

'I told you, I didn't send that email,' Rob insisted. 'If he'd come to me and talked to me instead of jumping in headfirst, I would have told him that. But no, he had to go and blow everything up and then he had the nerve to get mad at me, like it was my fault.'

'It was your fault. Callum trusted you and—'

'Who the heck is this Callum you keep going on about?'

'Your best mate,' I reminded him again. Why did he keep denying it?

'Okay, you're right,' he said. 'I did go to uni with my best mate.' He tapped the name on the byline. 'William Calloway.'

I couldn't move. Couldn't breathe.

'But Callum...'

Rob glided his finger across the trackpad on his laptop as I stared at him, my mind racing. 'Look,' he said, turning the laptop to face me.

My gaze shifted to the photo on the screen. Rob stood in the middle of the picture. His arm draped across the shoulders of a girl to his left. And on his right...

'That's Callum.'

Silence stretched between us until Rob finally spoke.

'No,' he said softly. His expression was almost pitying now. 'That's William Calloway.'

43

NOW

December

'William Calloway.' I repeated the name slowly. It felt wrong on my lips. Like I was speaking a language I didn't recognise.

He was Callum.

My Callum.

Except the truth was, he wasn't actually either.

'Why did he lie to me?' I asked Rob, my vision blurring as I gazed at him, pleading for an answer. One that would make sense. One that would salvage something of the relationship I'd thought we'd had.

Rob shook his head. 'I don't know. Will's done a lot of things in the last few months that didn't make sense to me.'

Will.

The ease with which he spoke that name jarred against me. I wanted to protest. To correct him.

He drew in a breath. 'It all started with that email.'

'I thought you said you didn't send it?' I questioned.

'I didn't. But Will was so sure I had.' Rob shrugged, helplessly. 'I thought maybe my account had been hacked. I changed my password and checked my sent mail, but there was nothing. Besides, it felt too specific. Hackers would be after something of value, like tricking you into making a bank transfer to their account, not concocting some conspiracy theory where the only result was Will getting fired. It was too personal.'

I frowned. 'It wasn't the only outcome, though, was it? It destroyed your friendship too.'

Rob nodded. 'In the end I spoke to our IT department. Part of me was afraid to do so. I mean, if Will was right and the false information had come from my email...'

'You could be fired too,' I finished.

'Anyway, they couldn't retrieve the actual message, but there was a log of messages received and sent. An email had been sent to Will on the fourth of August at 11:57 p.m.'

'And that wasn't you?'

'No way,' Rob said, rolling his eyes. 'I don't do late-night work emails.' Rob snorted. 'I'm not that dedicated.'

'But then who...'

Rob rubbed his hand across his face. 'The only thing I could think of was that my girlfriend stayed over that night.'

I drew back. 'Ace? The girl that dumped you after the article came out?'

'That's the one,' Rob said ruefully.

'Why would—' I stopped.

'Ms Hammond?' Rob frowned as he studied me. 'Are you okay?'

I shook my head. 'My name's not really Hammond. I was afraid if you were involved with whatever was going on, then you might know my real name and—'

'I wouldn't meet with you,' Rob finished for me.

'My name is Olivia Reed,' I said, scanning his face for the slightest flicker of recognition.

Nothing.

'I'm C— Will's girlfriend.' I paused. 'Or at least I thought I was.'

'What do you mean?'

I swallowed. I wasn't ready to explain that yet. I wasn't even sure I could. 'Your girlfriend is the one who told Will about the job at Wave Media. She's the reason he came to Christchurch. The reason we met.'

'Wave Media?' Rob shook his head. 'I don't know them.'

'They're a marketing consultancy. Or at least that's what Will told me. But then he also told me that you and he were colleagues, and he was a marketing consultant too.'

'Seriously?' Rob said, scratching his head. 'That's such a random claim to make. I mean, Will has no clue about anything marketing related.'

I shrugged. 'I guess he didn't need to. It turns out Wave Media doesn't actually exist.'

'W-what? Why?' Rob looked as confused as I felt.

'I don't know. But somehow Ace seems to be connected to all of it. The email. The fake company.'

'You think she intended to get Will fired?'

'I don't know. But it's like she wanted him in Christchurch.'

Rob's gaze dropped back to the laptop screen, and he stared at the blonde-haired woman in the photo. 'I just don't get what Avery would get from that, though.'

Avery.

It was an unusual name, but there was something familiar about it. Like the fragment of a song that I hummed along to even though I didn't know the words.

'Avery? That's Ace's real name?'

'Yeah,' Rob replied. 'Avery Quinn.'

I sighed. The name didn't mean anything after all.

'I'm just not sure how she fits into all this.' Rob reverted back to his chain of thought. 'I mean, you said you were his girlfriend,' Rob continued. 'So, it's not like she lured Will away to date him. And even if she had wanted that, why would she need to go to those extremes? Why ruin his career?'

'And why did Will tell me his name was Callum Hayes?' I added to Rob's list of questions. 'Why did he move in with me, start planning a future with me, and then one day just pack all his stuff and disappear?'

'Wait, what?' Rob lurched forward. 'Will's missing?'

I shook my head as I met his gaze. 'Will's dead.'

44

NOW

December

The house looked the same as I remembered. The fir trees were taller, and the car on the drive was new, but the rest...

I took a shaky breath, no longer sure why I was actually here. I could turn around now, drive back to Christchurch, and stick to my original plan to never see Daniel Sinclair ever again.

My feet didn't move.

It seemed stupid to walk away now. I'd come all this way for answers. I couldn't leave without them.

So far Portsmouth had simply led to another dead end. Rob wasn't involved after all. All I had to go on was another name: Avery Quinn.

Googling her hadn't revealed anything. Rob's attempts to call her had been met with the same out-of-service message that I'd encountered for Callum's number.

It felt too coincidental. There had to be a connection. Maybe the police would have more luck figuring it out than I had.

But in order for them to take me seriously, I needed to disprove their belief that I was unstable and dangerous. And for that I needed the truth from the one person who knew what that was.

I pushed my shoulders back and marched down the driveway with renewed determination.

I rapped my knuckles against the familiar solid wood door I had knocked on so many times before. It felt like an eternity stretching out while I stood on that doorstep, my thoughts racing, wondering what I'd say, how I'd react when I saw him again.

As the latch clicked, a new thought suddenly occurred to me. What if he didn't even live here any more?

The door swung open and in that instant I knew the answer to that question. He looked thinner, frailer. His face was pale, his eyes duller than I remembered, as though their spark had been extinguished.

I knew how that felt.

Yet what froze me in place were the scars. Angry, twisted patches of skin trailed along his neck and jaw.

My breath hitched. I'd come here ready to accuse him. Ready to demand the truth. But in that moment, all I could see was the evidence that he'd lived it too.

He'd rushed into a burning room and saved me.

And yet, I couldn't let myself feel sorry for him. There would never have even been a fire if it hadn't been for him.

I dug my fingernails into my palms. His well-being wasn't my concern, just as mine had never been of any consequence to him.

'Hello?' Daniel said, his voice lifting slightly as he looked at me enquiringly.

He didn't recognise me.

Despite the changes in his appearance, the resemblance was still sufficient. But I'd grown up. I was no longer a teenager seeking his approval, idolising him, memorising his every word.

He was the enemy now. My enemy. And it was time he knew it.

I wasn't here for a happy reunion. I wasn't here to reconnect with the man I once admired, the man I'd once tried to emulate. I was here for one reason: the truth.

I lifted my chin and met his gaze. 'I'm Olivia Reed,' I said, bracing myself as I waited for his reaction.

He physically recoiled, as though the sound of my name hurt him. There was something satisfying in that. Powerful. Invigorating.

My name had meant nothing to Rob. But Daniel? He knew. He *knew* who I was. What he'd done.

'Olivia, I...'

He was speechless. I had never known him to be speechless. He was always so poised and in control.

But I wasn't here to reminisce. I wasn't the girl who hung on his every word any more. Who believed he was the key to her success.

In the end, he had been the key to my downfall.

'What are you doing here?' he asked. His voice trembled with something close to fear.

As much as I hadn't wanted to see him, it seemed he was even more disturbed by seeing me.

'I thought it was time we talked,' I said flatly. My own calmness surprised me. I'd always been too emotional; at least, that's what Dad said. I let my feelings consume me.

Daniel had told me differently. He'd said emotions were the key to creativity. That playing music wasn't about hitting the right notes, but *feeling* them. And sharing that feeling with the audience.

I'd listened. I'd focused on tapping into that, drawing it out, excelling at it.

Yet in the end, he was the one who taught me to disconnect. That emotions made you weak. Susceptible. Malleable.

It was a lesson I was quite willing to share with him now. It was time for the student to become the master.

* * *

I stepped across the threshold and Daniel closed the door behind me. My gaze drifted instinctively to the door on the left.

It had always felt like a portal to another world. One filled with music, warmth, and acceptance. My chest tightened at the sight of it now. The memories of the last time I had stepped through that doorway were as thick and heavy as the smoke that had once filled my lungs.

Daniel turned without a word, heading to the right, down a long, narrow hallway towards an open door at the end.

I hesitated for a moment before I managed to break free from the grip of the past.

I followed him into a bright and airy living room. My gaze swept the unfamiliar space. Before, I'd always entered this house as a student confined to the music room. Now, I was a guest, it was like getting a glimpse of a different chapter of Daniel's life.

He lingered in the centre of the room, looking awkward and uncomfortable, as though he didn't know what to do now. I strode towards an armchair without waiting to be asked to sit. I didn't need his permission for anything any more.

Instead of perching on the edge of the chair, straight backed and poised, the way Daniel had taught me to sit at the piano, I eased back against the soft cushions and crossed my legs. The tension in my body held in with calm control and an air of confidence I hadn't felt in years.

Daniel dithered for a moment before perching on the edge of the sofa opposite. 'I'm surprised to see you back in—' He clamped his mouth closed.

'Your house?' I finished for him.

'In Portsmouth,' he mumbled. 'I heard your family had moved away after the restaurant closed.'

'After the restaurant failed, you mean,' I corrected him.

'Er, yes, I was sorry to see that happen.'

I tipped my head to the side. 'But not sorry enough to prevent it?'

Daniel swallowed. 'What are you doing here, Olivia?'

'I want the truth,' I told him evenly. 'After all these years, all this pain, you owe me that much.'

'We've been through this before.' Daniel's voice sounded weary. 'I told the police everything at the time.'

'You told the police lies. Now it's time to try the truth.'

Daniel shook his head. 'It's good to see you looking so well, Olivia. I often wondered what became of you, where you ended up, and I would love to hear about your family and your career, but you don't get to march into my home and start throwing around these crazy accusations again.'

Hatred oozed from every pore at his condescending dismissal.

'You want to know about my life?' I leaned forwards as I spat the words at him. 'Everything that happened was because of you. If you hadn't lied about me, if you hadn't destroyed my reputation, my family's business, then we would never have left Portsmouth. I'd have been the musician that I'd always dreamed I'd be. I'd still have my family. Dad wouldn't have left and maybe

Mum wouldn't have got sick, or maybe if she hadn't had to work so hard, if she hadn't been through so much stress and heartbreak, she would have been stronger, she'd have fought harder.

'And I'd have never met Callum. I'd never have got caught up in his lies. I wouldn't have been betrayed again.'

Daniel stared at me, clearly taken back by my outburst. 'Your parents... I... I didn't know,' he finished lamely.

'Why would you? You didn't care what happened to me. What happened to us.'

He shook his head. 'No, that's not true.'

'Then why did you do it? Why did you destroy us?'

'I didn't mean to.' A flicker of panic lit up his eyes as his words hung in the air.

Anticipation vibrated within me. After all these years it felt like there was a chink in his armour. A sliver of remorse. Something that I could build on.

'Look, I'm sorry to hear about your parents, and whoever Callum is and whatever he's done. But none of that has anything to do with me.' Daniel's body language shifted as though he suddenly closed himself off. 'And you have no right to come into my home, yelling and making these wild accusations again.' He stood up abruptly. 'You need to leave now, Olivia.'

I shook my head. 'I'm not going anywhere. Not without the truth.'

'You either leave of your own free will, or I'll call the police and they can remove you,' he said, his tone harsh and cold. 'Is that really a route you want to go down again?'

My body vibrated with disdain. Daniel had betrayed me when I was a kid. He'd lied to everyone about me. And I'd been powerless to defend myself against his accusations.

But I wasn't a kid any more. I couldn't be intimidated and cast aside. I had nothing left to lose. Everyone I loved had either died or left me. They'd never know the truth. That I wasn't unstable or dangerous. They'd never get to know the real me.

'Why did you do it?' I demanded, without moving from the armchair. 'Why did you start the fire?' My voice cracked, but I held his gaze. 'Was it the money? Did you need the insurance payout?'

Daniel shook his head slowly, tiredly. 'You don't know what you're talking about.'

'Then tell me.' My voice softened. 'Explain it to me. I *want* to understand.'

He didn't respond.

Rage boiled inside me, like a volcano ready to erupt.

'You were my teacher. You were someone I admired. Someone I trusted. You got it. You understood what it meant to have this passion, this dream, that no one else could understand. Not the kids at school. Not my parents. Not *anyone*. Just you.'

My body trembled as I fought for breath. 'And then you *lied*. You made me out to be some unstable, unhinged kid. You told them I was dangerous. That I was obsessed. Disturbed. You turned me into what all those kids at school already thought I was.'

I shook my head. 'How could you do that? You knew what it was like. To be the outsider. To fight every single day for the one thing that made you *you*. And you took that from me.'

Daniel shook his head. 'You have to let it go, Olivia. It's done. It's in the past.'

I leapt to my feet. 'The past?' I spat. 'It might be behind *you*, but it's never been behind *me*. You took everything from me. My future. My family. My name. You just thought I'd go away. That I'd disappear.'

He looked at me blankly.

'I was fourteen and my parents believed I was an arsonist. They blamed me for losing the restaurant. For everything that came after. Because *you* made them.'

'I'm sorry for the way things have turned out for you, I really am,' Daniel assured me.

'Then help me. Tell the police the truth. Confess.'

'I didn't start the fire, Olivia,' Daniel insisted earnestly.

I understood why the police had believed him. Everything about him exuded sincerity.

His certainty almost made me doubt myself. But I knew I was innocent. I would never have done that.

Would I? The question whispered softly in the recesses of my mind.

Even now, I wasn't sure.

He turned to the desk behind him. 'If there's ever anything you need, anything I can do to help...' Daniel tore a bright yellow Post-it from the pad and scribbled something quickly. 'I want you to call me,' he finished as he thrust the note towards me.

I stared at it.

'I need to you to clear my name,' I whispered, my quiet desperation filling the room.

He didn't respond. Instead he stepped forward, grasped my hand and pressed the note into my palm, closing my fingers around it.

I wanted to throw it back at him. It was an empty gesture. He was just trying to make himself feel better. Feel as though he'd done something useful. Something good. I snorted. That was assuming it was even his real number.

He didn't care about me. He'd proved that already.

'Just take it,' he urged softly.

I didn't have the strength to argue.

Coming here had been a long shot, I'd known that. But the disappointment was overwhelming.

This had been a mistake.

He was never going to confess. Never going to clear my name.

Perhaps it didn't even matter any more. There wasn't anyone left who would care.

I turned mutely towards the door.

I froze.

My gaze locked on one of the framed photographs above the fireplace. I'd seen that face before. The smile. The long blonde-curls.

Not here. Not that photo.

But the one Rob had shown me.

'Who is this?' I demanded as I pointed at the girl. 'Who is it?'

Daniel blinked, visibly thrown by my reaction. 'Avery,' he said finally. 'My daughter.'

45

NOW

December

I clambered into my car, slamming the door shut. The scrunched-up yellow Post-it note dropped onto the passenger seat beside me as I grabbed the seatbelt, yanked it across my body and fumbled with the buckle.

Daniel stood on his doorstep, watching me. His pretence of stunned confusion at my accusations of her involvement with Callum and Wave Media had been as flawless as his denial of starting the fire. It has been foolish to come here hoping for honesty. All I'd found was more deception. Deeper, darker and more far reaching than I could ever have imagined.

A loud grating vibrated against my hand as I fought with the gear stick. I had to get out of here. Out of this neighbourhood. This town.

Callum, Rob, Avery, Daniel. They were all connected. Everything led back to the fire.

I felt like I was fourteen again. Trapped in a nightmare with no way out. Everything I thought I knew was spiralling out of my grasp.

Nothing made sense.

Daniel had already destroyed me with his allegations eight years ago. Why would he send his daughter to intervene in my life now?

Did Rob know who Avery was? Had he lied about her surname, as I'd lied about mine? And how did Callum fit into all this? What had really brought him to Christchurch? A job opportunity?

Or me?

* * *

I barely saw the road ahead of me. Everything was a blur. The only thing I could see with any clarity were the orange flashes of the flames that tormented my brain.

The past I'd fought so hard to move on from was pulling me back, seeping into my present. Or perhaps it had never really let go.

Callum had lied about so much. His name. His job. But this... I swiped at my cheek, roughly brushing away my tears with the back of my hand. This was so much more insidious that I could even conceive.

His questions about my life, my family, my dreams, all had a different meaning now. It wasn't innocent curiosity from a man who cared about his partner's life. It was...

I searched my brain, desperately trying to find the right word. But I couldn't. I didn't even know what it was. I only knew it wasn't normal.

Wasn't right.

My gaze flicked to the passenger seat. The discarded Post-it note taunted me. Bright and colourful, it kept drawing my attention. Or maybe it wasn't the note itself. It was because of who it was from that kept it encroaching in my thoughts.

I let out a low growl of frustration as I snatched it up. The paper crinkled as I shoved it into my jeans pocket.

Out of sight, out of mind, as Mum used to say.

Except we both knew that never really worked.

* * *

Familiar landmarks registered at the edges of my consciousness, and I realised I was almost home.

Home.

The word felt so wrong.

The café. The flat. They weren't safe havens. They were caught up in it too. Remnants of what was left of my life. Tarnished by Callum's deception.

But I had nowhere else to go.

I couldn't go to Lucy's. Not like this. She would ask questions. How could I even begin to explain when I didn't understand it myself?

I couldn't drag her into the midst of this mess. Mum and Dad had got caught up in it and they'd suffered as a result. I wouldn't let that happen to Lucy too.

And the police? My grip tightened on the steering wheel. They wouldn't believe me. They'd thought I was delusional from the start. I couldn't charge into the station rambling like a lunatic, making allegations that sounded preposterous even to my own ears.

I had nowhere left to go.

46

NOW

December

My trainers crunched against the gravel path as I walked slowly down the alleyway beside the café. I tugged my coat tighter around me, but the cold evening air still cut through to my bones.

I reached the door that led up to the flat. *Our* flat.

I froze, my hand hovering in front of the lock, key poised and ready. But the thought of stepping inside the space that had finally started to feel like home filled me with dread. Without Callum, all that waited for me on the other side was an empty stillness that would swallow me up.

William.

The correction slammed into my mind silently, yet it felt deafening.

My hand dropped to my side, the cold metal of the key numbing my fingers as the name drained away the last threads of energy.

I wanted to push him from my thoughts, to swing the door open and move on with my life. But I couldn't. The knowledge that I would never get to come home to him again bore into me. I'd never hear his cheerful voice as I stepped inside. Never see him rushing towards me, his arms wide before enveloping me in a big bear hug, full of warmth and love.

But was any of it even real?

I pivoted, turning away from the flat, and veered back towards the café's side entrance. Fumbling with the keys, I tried to ignore the irony that the space I'd once loathed was now the only space I could bear to enter. And yet, even here, the memories were overpowering.

The lock clicked and I stepped into the dark kitchen. My hand instinctively reached for the light switch, and I blinked as the florescent light flickered on.

The door clunked closed behind me, the sound shattering the silence.

I hesitated. Now that I was here, I wasn't sure what to do.

I felt hot and dishevelled from the long drive. The long day.

Not that it mattered.

There was nobody here to see me. It was too late to open up. Not that I had any inclination to do so. But maybe I could deal with a few things. Make myself a cup of tea. Throw out the stale pastries. Get things in order for tomorrow. Be useful.

I dumped my keys and phone on the counter, flicked the kettle on and threw myself into mundane tasks. Desperately trying to distract myself from the ache of loneliness that throbbed in my chest and the endless questions that swirled in my mind. I opened the fridge, reached for the milk and scrunched my nose as I debated what could be salvaged.

'I hear you've been looking for me.'

I gasped as I swung round at the voice behind me. Sharp and unfamiliar.

Avery.

I'd only seen her in photographs, but her face was etched into my memory.

She stood in the doorway, glaring at me with contempt. I'd been so lost in my thoughts I hadn't heard the door open as she let herself into my haven.

Without shifting her gaze, she reached back and closed the door behind her.

Click.

The sound of the lock snapping into place was unmistakable as it sliced through the silence.

She'd locked us in.

Together.

I clung to the bottle of milk in my hand, the cold air from the open fridge biting at my skin as I stared mutely at her. Emotions surged within me. Fear and anger both screaming at me to do something. Anything.

But what could I do?

All I had in my hands was a half empty bottle of milk. My phone was on the counter by the door. I couldn't even call for help.

She was the last person I wanted to see.

And yet, she was the person I most needed. The only one who had any answers.

I swallowed and set the milk down on the worktop beside me as I closed the fridge with quiet control.

Turning back, I took a deep breath before meeting Avery's gaze dead on. She might have the upper hand, but this was my space.

My café.

Avery's gaze swept over the room. 'I hunted for restaurants, but it never occurred to me to look for a tiny café.' She sneered. 'A bit of a comedown, isn't it?'

My skin bristled. I'd resented every moment I'd spent here, trapped in this failing café, comparing it to the restaurant and the life we'd had before. But hearing her dismiss it as inferior triggered something unexpected, a sense of pride I hadn't even known existed.

'It may be smaller,' I said quietly. 'And not as fancy. But it's ours.'

'Ours?' Avery laughed. 'Hasn't it sunk in yet?' She stretched her arms wide, encompassing the empty café. 'There is no one else. Just you. You're completely and utterly alone. Every single person you cared about has gone.' Avery stepped forward, closing the gap between us. 'Because of you.'

I clenched my jaw. I wanted to protest, but I couldn't.

She was right.

It had been *my* passion that had led us here. That brought Daniel into our lives. That drove a wedge between Dad and me. It had derailed the restaurant. Resulted in us fleeing the lives we had worked so hard to make successful. It had caused my parents to resent me. And Dad to leave.

But the one thing my passion had never done was start that fire.

'I didn't destroy everything,' I said at last, my voice steady now. 'Your father did.'

Avery's expression hardened. 'My father saved your life, and you repaid him by destroying his career. His reputation. His life.'

I shook my head. 'It wasn't like that.'

I didn't know what had happened to Daniel after the fire. I didn't care. I only knew what his lies had done to us. To *me*.

Avery snorted. 'You and your family packed up and disappeared. You got to leave while I was stuck in that house. It was like the scent of burnt ash lingered over everything. I couldn't escape it. Not at home. Not at school. No one would let me.'

She took a breath as she pressed her palms against her thighs. 'That fire destroyed Dad's precious piano, but it was the rumours that destroyed him. Everywhere he went, people whispered about him. Watched him. Judged him. He's never played since. Music was his whole world, and you took it from him.'

'It had been mine too,' I said flatly. There was something bittersweet about knowing his lies hadn't fully worked. They hadn't protected him. He'd tried to pin everything on me, but he hadn't been able to escape the fall out either.

I wasn't the only one who'd lost their dreams.

'It was all I had,' I said quietly. 'It was who I was. And his lies ensured my career was over before it began.'

'I'm glad,' Avery gloated. 'Why should you have success and happiness when the rest of us couldn't?'

The vindictiveness of her tone seared through me.

'You know, I tried to find you for years,' she said, softer now, but still venomous. 'I needed to find you. But I didn't have the knowledge. The skills.' Avery shook her head sadly. 'I thought you were going to elude me forever. I tried to move on; to fill the void you'd caused in my family, my life. But there was always this lingering feeling that I never quite fitted in, that I was never fully accepted.'

I knew that feeling. It was eerie to hear her describe it so accurately. To describe me.

'I started dating a guy a friend knew from uni,' she continued, drifting slowly around the kitchen, her fingers skimming across the counter, as if claiming the space. As if she belonged here. 'It wasn't serious. He wasn't serious.' She shrugged. 'But it was something.'

I pictured the photo Rob had shown me, his arm casually draped over Avery's shoulders. He hadn't sounded heartbroken when he'd talked about the way she dumped him. The way she'd taken William's side over his.

'One night, we were at the pub, hanging out with his friends,' she said. 'I was on the outskirts of their group, feeling out of place, like usual. But this time I wasn't the only one.' She smiled, yet there was a sadness to it still. 'There was a guy there I hadn't met before. Sitting in the corner, frantically typing on his laptop, in the middle of a noisy pub. I mean, who does that? Brings their laptop on a night out?' She shook her head with a soft chuckle, but there was a hollowness to it.

'He was so focused, he didn't even seem to notice the guys teasing him. Or maybe he just didn't care. The thing was, he wasn't just mindlessly scrolling or pretending to be busy. He was working. Like, properly working.'

She turned back to me, her eyes meeting mine. 'Turned out, he was a junior reporter desperate to prove himself.'

My stomach lurched.

William.

'The others said he was crazy, obsessed even, the way he chased after any story, pushing past every obstacle, regardless of the risks. But he was on his own too, just like me. Trying to carve out a place in the world that had never made room for him.'

Her gaze didn't waver.

'That's when I knew Will was exactly the kind of person I needed.'

47

NOW

December

I felt the ground shift beneath me, as if I was back on the paddleboard, fighting to keep my balance.

'You used him,' I said, the words catching in my throat.

Avery gave a faint shrug. 'I gave him a story.'

She made it sound so simple. So transactional.

'But the one thing I've learned is that no one will help you without something to gain. If you want something, you have to make them *need* to help you. It wasn't enough to just give him a story. He needed to be desperate enough to take it.'

'The email he thought was from Rob...' My voice faltered. Rob had suspected Avery had sent that email; that part wasn't a surprise. But her reason for doing so... 'You intended to get Will fired.' I stared at her, stunned.

Part of me understood her hatred of me. She believed her father's version of events. She thought I'd hurt her family.

But Will? He was innocent.

Or at least he had been.

'It was so easy,' Avery sneered. 'He was reckless, overeager, and willing to bend the rules if it meant a chance at success. All I had to do was leak him information for a story that wasn't real. And he fell for it. He believed it. Every word, every half-truth. He was so eager to find his big break, so desperate to prove his journalistic abilities, that he cut corners. He didn't check his facts. Rob had confided in me that his carelessness would be the ruin of him one day, I just made sure that day was now.'

'Why go to those lengths? Why not just take him the story?'

Avery rolled her eyes as though my question was foolish. 'Nobody was going to touch this story. It was too old, too convoluted, required too much effort. But someone with nothing left? Someone who needed a story – any story – to claw their way back?'

A slow grin spread across her face. 'Without a job and his reputation in tatters I knew he wouldn't be able to resist the chance of solving a case the police couldn't. There was no way an editor would turn down a story like that. He'd be redeemed. And if his career wasn't enough motivation, of course it didn't hurt that he'd be my hero. Getting justice for my father. Finding the evidence that cleared his name and led to the arrest of the person who set fire to our home.'

Her smile faded and her eyes narrowed as she turned back to me. 'I just had to make sure he understood what kind of person you were. How dangerous and spiteful a fourteen-year-old could be. I showed him the effect of the injustices Dad had suffered. What you had done to him.'

My breath caught in my chest as Avery closed the gap between us. 'You escaped accountability back then, but I knew with the right motivation, Will would make sure that didn't happen again.'

Will's interest in my life, his probing questions about my family, about the piano, all shifted in their meaning. He hadn't innocently been trying to get to know his girlfriend. 'He was using me,' I said flatly.

I wasn't sure why that surprised me. The last few days had made me realise that nothing about our relationship, or for that matter about him, was real. But hearing Avery describe his deception so bluntly still stung.

Perhaps the truth was that some part of me had still been holding on to a tiny sliver of hope that I was wrong. That what we'd had meant something.

Avery had taken that from me. And from her gleeful expression, she had relished doing so.

'Why?'

She was the wrong person to ask. I knew that. Avery was hardly reliable. But at the same time she was the only person I could ask.

Will was gone.

'Why did he need to go to those lengths?' I demanded. 'Why insert himself into my life the way he did? Why pretend to be my boyfriend?'

I felt like I was fourteen again. Everything I'd believed in was crashing down around me. Just like before. Except this time, it was worse.

Falling for Will had been a risk. One I'd consciously decided to take. This time I hadn't been caught off guard out of naivety and blind trust. I'd been manipulated from the beginning.

This was Will. The man I'd been planning my future with. The man who'd given me hope to dream about a future at all. A life outside the confines of the safe little corner that Mum had created for us.

'The plan was for him to get close enough to earn your trust. Get you to open up about the past. And encourage your confession.' She smiled. 'The perfect exposé.'

I frowned. 'He never tried to get me to confess.'

Her smile wavered.

'He didn't need to,' Avery said, but her dismissive tone didn't match the tension radiating from her body. Her arms were stiff at her sides, her fists clenched as though fighting to retain her composure. 'That's why I picked him,' she added. 'Someone willing to do *anything* to prove you were guilty. Someone so fixated on getting the story at any cost. Heck, if he didn't bother to check sources, he wouldn't even need a real confession. I just needed him to find something – anything – he could use against you.'

Silence filled the space between us as Avery watched me, as though waiting for my reaction. Perhaps she'd hoped her confession would break me.

My jaw tightened, but I held her gaze.

You couldn't break what was already broken.

The reasons for William's presence in my life had been laid bare now. But they still didn't explain one thing...

'What happened to him?'

Avery tilted her head, with a bemused expression. 'Do you care?'

The question repeated like an irritating jingle that had got stuck in my head even though I didn't want it there.

I shouldn't care, should I? They'd been conspiring against me. Manipulating me. Using me. Whatever had happened to him shouldn't be any of my concern. He wasn't who I'd thought. *We* weren't who I'd thought.

And yet...

'As far as the police are concerned, you killed him,' Avery said with a shrug, as though their perception was all that mattered.

'But I didn't,' I said firmly.

My eyes narrowed as I studied her reaction to my words. Or more importantly, her lack of reaction.

She hadn't flinched. Hadn't disputed my proclamation of innocence.

'You *know* I didn't kill him.' The realisation hit me like a shockwave. 'Which means you know what really happened. And the only way you could know that is if you were there. If you—'

'You think you know everything, don't you?' she cut in, her tone laced with condescension. 'You think you're superior to me. The replacement daughter. The replacement girlfriend. The one they really wanted.'

The one they really wanted.

What did she mean?

It was clear she envied the relationship I'd had with her father. But William? That was all fake.

Wasn't it?

Why did my heartbeat quicken at that question?

I shouldn't care, I told myself again.

And yet, I knew I still did.

48

NOW

December

PC Monroe replayed the CCTV footage again. 'See?' he said, pointing to the screen. 'When she closes the door, she's standing right in front of the lock. It's impossible to tell if she locked it or simply closed it.'

I bristled. 'She locked it. She trapped me in my own café.'

He stood up, shaking his head. 'I'm afraid this isn't enough to warrant further action.'

'I *heard* the click of the lock,' I insisted, refusing to give up.

'I'm afraid without evidence—'

'You're not going to do anything,' I interrupted.

'Nothing in this video indicates threatening behaviour,' DS Harrington said behind me. He'd remained silent since his arrival. His body language spoke for him. He thought I was wasting their time again.

'But she admitted she manipulated everything,' I said, my voice unsteady. 'She set me up so that even my own boyfriend wasn't real. He was just investigating me.' My voice cracked. 'Everything we had was a lie. Even his name.' I took a shaky breath. 'Callum...' I struggled to say his name.

Callum.

The name that had once felt so natural as it slipped from my tongue now felt alien and wrong.

I hadn't just lost him. I'd lost *everything* about him.

Even his name.

'His name isn't Callum, it's William Calloway.'

I waited.

Waited for their surprised reactions, exchanged glances, the scribble of their pens and the flood of questions that would follow.

Nothing.

'We're already aware,' PC Monroe said quietly.

I blinked. 'You knew?'

'Of course we knew,' DS Harrington said, his tone clipped and dismissive. 'The registration documents for *The Elusive* listed his legal name. We've since verified his identity with his family.'

It made perfect sense.

And yet, somehow that didn't take the sting out of the fact that they had discovered his identity so quickly and easily, whereas I, the person who'd lived with him, loved him, had been so completely clueless.

'How did you discover this?' DS Harrington demanded.

I tried not to let my guilt show on my face. I'd been given strict instructions not to leave the area. My trip to Portsmouth could land me in more trouble.

'I searched online,' I said evenly, 'and found a story about corruption in a Portsmouth marketing consultancy. There was a retraction the next day. That led me to his friend, Rob.'

'And how does Avery Sinclair fit into all this?' PC Monroe asked.

'She was Rob's girlfriend. That's how she met Cal— William,' I corrected myself. 'She used him to track me down.'

'So this is all connected to the fire?' PC Monroe asked, scribbling notes as he spoke.

I nodded. 'And William was using me for a story.'

'Which gives you an even stronger motive for his murder,' DS Harrington interjected.

I'd been so focused on making sure they understood Avery's betrayal, I'd failed to consider the implications of Callum's – of William's – betrayal. I'd failed to consider what it meant for my perceived guilt.

'*If* I'd known,' I pointed out, 'but I believed him. I believed everything he told me.'

DS Harrington studied me dubiously. 'You know the thing that's never made any sense to me?' he said slowly. 'Why file a missing persons report for someone who appeared to have simply packed up his belongings and walked out?'

'I was worried about him,' I replied.

'Hmm,' DS Harrington murmured. 'Or you were trying to misdirect us. We can't be sure that you didn't already know William Calloway's real identity. Or that he had been actively deceiving you. Investigating you.'

I shook my head, but the words wouldn't come. I couldn't deny how it must look. But it wasn't true.

'I didn't know,' I whispered.

His eyes narrowed. 'That's not just betrayal, Miss Reed. That's motive.'

PC Monroe stiffened, looking almost as uncomfortable as I felt.

'We'll need you to come down to the station tomorrow for further questioning,' DS Harrington said firmly.

I flinched. He didn't believe me. Everything about his body language screamed that he would arrest me right now if he could. But he didn't have any real evidence.

Not yet.

Time was running out.

Avery's plan was falling into place and DS Harrington believed it without hesitation.

I turned to PC Monroe. 'You have to find Avery.'

He nodded. 'We will.'

It was the only hope I had. I could tell he wasn't convinced I was innocent, but unlike DS Harrington, at least he wasn't convinced of my guilt. 'We'll make some inquiries to follow up the connection to William,' PC Monroe conceded.

I let out a weary sigh. It was something, at least.

DS Harrington turned and left without another word, but PC Monroe lingered. 'Give me a call if you remember anything else.' He pulled a card from his pocket and handed it to me. 'Or if Avery comes back.'

* * *

I locked the door after PC Monroe and DS Harrington left, triple-checking it, my nerves still vibrating. Even the presence of the police hadn't settled them. If anything, it had added a new dimension to the tension.

I wasn't sure who to be more afraid of now; Avery or them.

They were both banking on my impending arrest.

I needed Callum.

Not the investigative journalist. Not the lies. But the guy I'd fallen in love with.

The one who'd stopped by to help close up, just because he knew I'd be tired. The one who gave me a big hug after a long day. The one who had installed the CCTV because he was worried about my safety.

I frowned. Why had he done that?

His deception had changed everything. It was like looking back on our relationship through a different lens. Everything I thought I knew, everything that had once been familiar and clear, was now distorted and blurred. Every sentence, every action had a different meaning.

And yet, if everything had been fake, why had he been so concerned about my safety?

My car being broken into had been unnerving. His reaction had seemed normal. A guy concerned about his girlfriend's safety. But if our relationship was fake, then that concern should have been fake too. So why take it so far?

He'd bought the CCTV, paid for it, installed it himself. Why go to the expense and time, unless...

Bile rose in my throat.

He was concerned I was in danger.

The car window being smashed had rattled him as much as it did me. I was spooked because it brought back memories. But him...

Was it possible we were afraid of the same thing? The connection to the past?

But if he was working with Avery, why would he be afraid of her?

49

NOW

December

I paced the living room. It was late, but I was too wired to sleep. How could I, knowing Avery was out there, plotting against me?

I could call Lucy. She'd drop everything and come back round if I asked. She'd listen, sympathise, and try to help. But the reality was she *couldn't* help. She couldn't unravel this mess. She couldn't prove my innocence. She couldn't bring Callum back.

She couldn't even mourn with me. Not really.

She'd never met him.

But then again, neither had I.

Only one person knew what had really happened. And she clearly wasn't going to confess. Not for me.

I slipped my hand into my pocket, fumbling for the scrap of paper I'd stuffed there earlier. I pulled it out and smoothed the creases, staring at the familiar writing.

Daniel Sinclair.

I didn't have any sway over Avery. But did he?

I nibbled my lip. Even if he did, would he really help me? The tiny note felt heavy in my hand. He was the last person I wanted to reach out to for help. I'd done that once before, for all the good it had done me.

Would this time be different?

'Hello?' Daniel answered on the first ring. 'Hello?' he repeated. There was an unfamiliar edge to his voice. Almost apprehensive expectation.

'It's Olivia,' I said at last.

'Are you okay?'

My spine stiffened. His concern jarred against me. It felt fake. Patronising.

'Avery was here,' I said, ignoring his question.

'Where are you?'

'At home.'

'In Christchurch?'

'Yes.'

'I'm about an hour away.'

'What?'

'I'm in the car on my way to you. I just passed Southampton.'

'You're coming here? Already?' I frowned. 'Why?'

'It's better if we talk when I arrive. I found the address of your café online. Are you there?'

50

NOW

December

I stood at the window, watching the street below. Waiting. A pair of headlights slowed as they approached, and my breath snatched in my chest.

The lights moved past.

I glanced at my watch. Almost 10 p.m. Daniel should've been here by now.

My fingers tapped restlessly against the side of my mug. The tea inside had gone cold long ago, but I clung to it anyway, as if the weight of it in my hands could anchor me.

I puffed out my cheeks as another set of headlights approached. This time the car pulled up against the kerb.

He was here.

Even though I'd been waiting for his arrival, the moment he stepped out of his car my stomach twisted.

This was the man whose lies had shattered my life, and I was about to welcome him into my home and beg him to help clear my name.

* * *

He sat perched on the edge of the sofa, his body angled forward as though he was ready to flee at any moment.

I stayed standing. Debating whether he would bolt first, or whether I would throw him out.

The hospitable thing would have been to take his coat and offer him a drink after his long journey. But he didn't deserve hospitality. The most I could manage was civility.

Just about.

He might be key to clearing my name, but he was also the reason it had ever been tarnished.

'You said you wanted to talk,' I reminded him, breaking the brittle silence.

He nodded. 'I called Avery after you left. She was' – he swallowed – 'evasive when I mentioned your name.'

I waited for him to continue.

'She hung up on me, actually.' Daniel frowned. 'Not that that's unusual. We don't have the best relationship.'

He let his words hang as though waiting for a response. For sympathy.

I had none.

'I called her boyfriend, Will.'

Will.

So, William hadn't just been chasing a story to save his career. He'd been here for her.

'When he didn't answer I reached out to some of her other friends,' Daniel continued, oblivious to my inner turmoil. 'Eventually, I spoke to her previous boyfriend, Rob...'

I nodded. 'And he told you how Avery had got William fired and manipulated him into coming to Christchurch?'

Rob didn't know her motive had been to find me. But Daniel would.

Daniel nodded mutely. 'I didn't know,' he said, peering up at me with watery brown eyes. 'If I had...'

His words fell away.

'You'd have done what?' I asked. 'Helped her?'

'No!' he snapped, recoiling as though my accusation had physically hurt him.

'Your lies caused this,' I pointed out. 'They ignited her resentment towards me, her anger, her blame. She did all this because of you.'

Daniel hung his head, the weight of his actions finally settling in.

'Did Rob also tell you that William is dead?'

He nodded again. 'How did he...' Daniel looked up at me as he spoke, his half-formed question like a weight pressing on my heart.

'I found him on his boat.'

'You found him?' Daniel's face twisted in horror. 'I'm sorry, that must have been awful.'

I swallowed. I didn't want his sympathy. I didn't need it.

I only needed answers.

'Don't you think it's time you told me what really happened eight years ago? Why did you set fire to your music room? Why did you do it when I was inside?'

He shook his head.

'Enough,' I yelled.

Daniel flinched backwards at the sharpness of my voice.

I strode towards him. 'I'm sick of your lies. I deserve the truth. I *demand* it.'

'I didn't start the fire,' Daniel said, his voice barely a whisper.

I sucked in a shaky breath, rage vibrating through my body.

'Avery did.'

51

NOW

December

Avery did.

I stared at Daniel as he sat on my sofa, his body crumpled as though the words had aged him.

His gaze was fixed on his hands, palms open on his lap.

'Avery?' That didn't make sense. 'She was just a kid.'

'She was twelve,' Daniel said without looking up.

'But...' My brain couldn't form a response. It felt too absurd. 'Why would she do that?'

'Because of you,' he said without hesitation.

The accusation sliced through me. 'What?' I shook my head, feeling dazed. 'No, that can't be right. We'd never met before today. I didn't even know you had a daughter until Dad mentioned you brought her to the restaurant sometimes.'

Daniel shrugged. 'She hated you.'

'How could she hate someone she'd never met?'

He lifted his head then, his eyes peering at me as though willing me to understand. 'Because you had what she never would.'

I blinked, confusion making my head throb.

'Music,' he said quietly. 'You were like me. You lived for it. You breathed it.

But you were better than me. You were gifted in a way that made teaching you a privilege. I could see the spectacular career you were destined to have, and I was so proud to be the one guiding you towards it.'

I said nothing. I couldn't.

'Avery didn't understand,' he continued. 'Not the music. Not the connection I had to it. *We* had to it.' A shadow passed over his face. 'She didn't just hate the music. She blamed it. She blamed *me*. She thought I'd chosen it over her. Over her mother.'

'And so she blamed me,' I said slowly.

He nodded. 'She resented me, but she needed me. Whereas you...'

'Were an easy target,' I finished for him, finally understanding.

'When I saw the car window, I knew it was Avery who had smashed it. She did things like that when she was mad. When she thought I was choosing music over her. Choosing my students over her. I was sweeping up the glass when I saw the flames in the music room. I-I couldn't breathe,' Daniel stammered. 'Couldn't think. I just charged inside.' He paused, his hands trembling now. 'I was so scared. Scared that I would lose her, too.'

Too.

The one word pierced through my daze.

'Who else?' I asked.

'Eleanor, my wife,' he replied quietly. 'Avery was the one who found her.' He swallowed. 'She took her own life the year before.'

For a moment all the anger I had towards Daniel, towards Avery, was suspended. Overpowered by grief and sorrow for the agony they had been through.

That kind of loss changes you.

'She found her in the bath,' Daniel said softly, 'surrounded by the vanilla candles Avery used to light for her.' He paused, his voice breaking. 'It was their symbol of love.'

I sank onto the edge of the sofa, the image draining me of strength. Avery must have only been eleven. That was too young to experience that kind of trauma.

I looked at Daniel, rocking gently on the far end of the sofa, lost in the weight of memory. Then again, maybe age couldn't protect you from something like that.

Maybe nothing could.

'When did you know?' My voice cracked. It felt selfish to drag the conversation back to me after everything he'd just shared, but I *needed* to know. 'When did you realise she started the fire?'

Daniel closed his eyes. 'I always knew.'

His admission winded me.

Some part of me, however small, had still hoped he hadn't known what he was doing when he accused me.

That he'd truly believed it.

That it was a mistake. A misjudgement.

Misguided distrust was better than intentional betrayal.

'She was in the hallway when I ran inside. Just standing there, staring at the closed music room door. It threw me for a second. Part of me was elated that she was safe. She was alive. But another part...' He swallowed. 'I heard screaming, choking. I thought it was her, but—'

'It was me,' I finished before he could say the words.

'I grabbed the door handle, the heat...' He lifted his right hand, scarred and deformed. 'It didn't move.' He turned his palm down, as though he couldn't bear to see it any longer. 'And that's when I realised, Avery was holding the key.'

52

NOW

December

I grabbed my phone from the coffee table.

'What are you doing?' Daniel asked, panic tightening his voice.

'Calling the police,' I said bluntly. 'You're going to tell them everything.'

He shook his head. 'I can't.'

I froze as I stared at him in disbelief. 'You have to.'

He didn't respond.

'I've spent so much of my life fixated on what other people think and believe, until I doubted myself. Doubting what really happened, even though I was the one who was actually there, the one who lived it firsthand.' I could hear my voice shaking as I spoke. 'If people question you enough, eventually you start to question yourself. What if your view of reality was skewed? What if something about you was off?'

'I'm sorry that you experienced that. That I caused you to. But she's my daughter. I had to protect her.'

'Despite the cost?'

Daniel shrugged weakly. 'That's a father's job.'

Anger bubbled inside me. I wanted to scream at him, but he was so wrong. Avery had tried to kill me. She didn't deserve his protection. I did. But the words wouldn't come.

Beneath the rage was something else. Smaller, but sharper.

Jealousy.

Daniel knew who Avery really was. He knew what she'd done. And he'd fought for her. Was still fighting for her.

Whereas my dad had simply left.

'She tried to kill me.'

'No, she just wanted to...' Daniel couldn't finish. Even he didn't believe his words.

'I didn't start that fire. And I didn't kill my boyfriend. But unless you tell the police the truth, they will never believe that I'm innocent.'

Daniel didn't respond.

'You owe me.'

He nodded. 'I know, but what you're asking...'

'She needs help. The kind of help she could have got if you hadn't lied. I know you thought you were protecting her, but do you really think it helped her? Look where it has led.'

Daniel's shoulders sagged; I could feel his defeat.

I turned my attention back to my phone as I tapped the keys.

'But I want to talk to my daughter first.'

'No,' I said quickly, shaking my head. 'You can't. You need to tell the police now.'

Daniel stood with quiet purpose. 'I'm not saying anything until I talk to Avery. I will convince her to turn herself in. It will be better for her that way.'

'You can't keep protecting her.'

'I'm always going to try,' he said simply. 'She's my daughter.'

* * *

I stood over him, monitoring every word he typed.

'It would be better if I called and spoke to her,' Daniel urged.

'No,' I replied adamantly. 'I don't trust you not to warn her to run.'

He nodded, reluctantly. 'I understand.'

'Not here,' I said firmly as Daniel typed a message asking Avery to come to the flat in the morning. 'We'll meet at the café. Before it opens at 7 a.m.'

We needed privacy, and no distractions so I could make sure Daniel didn't double-cross me again. But that didn't mean I was going to let Avery set foot inside my home.

'Do you mind if I use your bathroom?' Daniel asked, standing up slowly.

I nodded towards the door. 'It's at the end.'

Daniel gave a small nod of acknowledgement and took a step forward.

'Leave your phone,' I added, holding out my hand.

He froze, just for a second. Then, without a word, he placed his phone in my open palm and turned away.

I waited.

As soon as I heard the soft click of the latch as he closed the bathroom door behind him, I grabbed my own phone and rushed to the coat rack. Rummaging in the pocket, I pulled out the card PC Monroe had given me earlier.

My hands shook as I typed the number into my phone. I couldn't risk making a call. If Daniel heard me he'd get spooked and leave. If he and Avery disappeared, I'd forever be deemed to be guilty, certainly of the arson, maybe more.

I typed a hurried message.

Daniel Sinclair is here. He's confessed everything. Avery started fire. He won't make a statement until he talks to Avery. Meeting her at 7am in the café. Please be there. I don't trust him.

53

NOW

December

'I saw her once.'

Daniel looked up at me, startled by my sudden interruption to the silence that had stretched between us.

'Your wife,' I added when he didn't respond. 'She was standing in the doorway watching me play one day. She looked to sad.'

He nodded. 'Music made her sad. Or rather the absence of it.'

'I don't understand,' I said, frowning as I tried to make sense of his words.

'Eleanor was a pianist, just like me.' He shook his head. 'No, she was better than me. Much better.'

'What happened?'

Daniel took a deep breath. 'Avery.' He said it like it was an explanation. Like *she* was an explanation. 'We hadn't even talked about having kids. Neither of us were ready for it. Not then. We were so focused on our careers. Our music. And then suddenly we were going to be parents.'

He smiled ruefully. 'The weird thing was, when Eleanor told me, I was excited. I mean, I was going to be a *dad*. I knew it would change things, of course. Some of our plans would have to adapt. Our dreams would have to shrink a bit. But still, I was going to be a dad.'

His words were so full of wonder, as though even now he still couldn't quite believe that they'd applied to him.

'Eleanor planned to finish her current tour and then we'd both head home as the due date drew nearer. But' – he shrugged – 'Avery had other ideas. It was a difficult pregnancy. Difficult for both of them. There was a time when we weren't sure Avery would make it. Eleanor was put on bed rest. And all of those plans didn't just change, they stopped.'

'But after Avery was born—'

Daniel shook his head, sensing where my question was going.

'Somehow Eleanor never quite found her way back to who she'd been. I think nearly losing Avery tormented her with guilt. What if she'd endangered her somehow by continuing to tour? All the stress, the hours of practice, what if that had taken a toll? Or worse still, what if Avery had sensed she hadn't really wanted her?'

'That's a lot to carry,' I said softly.

'When Avery was little, things seemed okay. Eleanor threw herself into motherhood. It was like being needed gave her purpose. But then as Avery got older, more independent, Eleanor started to struggle. I thought I was doing the right thing, giving up performing and touring. I thought if I was around more, she would be okay. She'd get better. Teaching from the house seemed the perfect solution. I could earn and still be there for her. Besides, it wasn't as though I knew how to do anything else. Music was my life.'

I bristled. It had been mine once too.

'I hadn't realised how hard it would be on her. Listening to my students. Hearing them play the pieces that she used to play. Especially you.'

'Me?'

'You were so good. Not just technically. Anyone can learn that with time and dedication. But you had something else. Something that can't be taught. That passion. That connection. It was like the piano came alive beneath your fingers. Eleanor had that touch too. Perhaps that's why I became so focused on pushing you to reach your potential. I saw her in you.'

'Dad thought it was because you were using me to try to recapture what you'd lost. The performances. The success.'

'He was probably right,' Daniel admitted softly. 'At least partially. But mostly, it was her. For what she'd lost. I couldn't give that back to her, but you...'

His voice faded away and his gaze became distant, as though he was lost somewhere in the past.

'Avery adored her,' he said finally. 'But it was as though she felt her mother's happiness was her responsibility. I should have intervened. I should have made sure she understood no one has that kind of power. But I guess perhaps I wanted to believe it too. That their bond would be enough.'

He paused. 'In the end it was that bond that took Eleanor from us. She left a note. Said she finally realised how she'd been holding Avery back. That watching the passion you had when you played reminded her of how it felt to be truly alive. She'd lost that. And in doing so, she'd prevented Avery from finding her own passion.'

My throat tightened.

'Avery thinks her mother abandoned her because Avery wasn't good enough. But the truth is Eleanor left because she thought it was the best way to save Avery. To stop her from becoming like her. From losing herself. From giving up.'

'You didn't tell her?'

Daniel shook his head. 'How can you tell that to a daughter who's lost her mother?'

54

NOW

December

I checked my watch again.

'What time is it?' Daniel asked.

His voice startled me. I thought he was asleep.

We'd stayed in the living room all night, a strained silence looming between us. There was a sadness to it, knowing how connected we had once been, the understanding and passion that we had shared that no one else around us truly got. And now, all that was there was distrust and caution.

We'd talked until the early morning hours. He'd offered to leave, said he could go to a hotel. But I'd told him to stay.

Not because I cared. Because I didn't trust him not to disappear.

People had a way of doing that.

Even the ones I did trust.

I could've gone to my room, wrapped myself in my duvet and hoped for sleep. But how could I, knowing the man who had once destroyed me, who still held the power to do it again, was here, in my home?

He might not have been solely responsible, but he'd known the truth and had betrayed me to protect his daughter. Who was to say he wouldn't do the same again this time too?

He'd nodded off a couple of hours ago, his body twitching and lips murmuring words that I couldn't decipher.

'It's almost 5 a.m.,' I replied as he shuffled up on the sofa, rubbing his eyes and pushing his coat aside.

'Did you sleep at all?' he asked, his voice edged with concern, as though he cared for my well-being.

I snorted. He'd already proved he didn't.

'No,' I said simply. There was no need to explain.

He knew why.

I stood up and stretched, my body aching from a night on edge.

'I should make a start in the café,' I said. 'I've got muffins and cakes to bake for the day.'

The normality of it sounded weird to my own ears, and given Daniel's stunned expression, he thought so too. 'You're opening the café today?'

'I don't have a choice,' I replied flatly. 'I already lost a day's trade yesterday. I can't afford to stay closed.'

He nodded, the financial burden understandable even in the current circumstances. 'Can I help?' he offered.

The question caught me off guard.

This wasn't a man I was used to receiving help from. Nor did I want it. But I found myself nodding anyway.

At least if he was in the kitchen, I could keep an eye on him. There were still two hours before Avery would arrive.

A sharp ping made both of us jump and I fumbled for the phone in my pocket. I let out a deep breath as I read the message from PC Monroe.

We'll be there.

* * *

I unlocked the café door, my nerves on edge as I scanned up and down the dark alleyway. Every shadow felt like a threat.

Daniel followed me into the kitchen and I quickly locked the door behind us. After last night, I wasn't about to get caught off guard again.

'Do you want a coffee?' I asked. I never usually drank it. Even the smell turned my stomach. But today I needed the caffeine. I needed something to get me through the next few hours.

'Please,' Daniel replied. The gratitude in his voice told me I wasn't the only one barely holding it together.

As I dropped my keys on the counter, I hesitated, then slipped my phone into my pocket. *That* I would keep on me.

I led the way across the kitchen towards the café. The moment I opened the door and stepped inside, I froze.

A thick, bitter, nauseating scent filled my nostrils, overpowering the usual rich aroma of coffee grounds.

My head snapped towards the front entrance. The door was still shut. I charged towards it and grabbed the handle.

It didn't move.

It was still locked.

'What's wrong?' Daniel called from behind me, unnerved by my sudden panic.

'Can't you smell it?' I asked, turning to face him.

He paused, sniffed. 'It smells like—'

'Fuel,' I finished for him, my voice flat.

The scent was unmistakable.

Even the faintest hint of petrol could take me back. But this? This was thick. Lingering in the air like a threat.

I turned back to the door as I reached instinctively for the keys in my pocket, then remembered I'd left them on the counter in the kitchen.

'We have to get out,' I said, already moving across the café back towards the kitchen. I passed Daniel, who stood frozen in the middle of the floor, then heard him fall in behind me.

A slight creak to my right caught my attention. I turned my head just in time to see the bathroom door beside the kitchen swing open.

Avery.

I lunged towards the kitchen door, but she was already closer.

She stepped into the doorway, blocking the exit.

I froze.

Her expression was unreadable. Calm. Poised.

'How did you get in?' The questions was irrelevant. The how didn't matter. The fact was she was here.

She fished in her pocket and held her hand up, a set of keys dangling from her fingers. The distinctive keychain was instantly recognisable.

'I borrowed Will's keys,' she said with a smug smile.

My stomach lurched at the reminder of him. Something so small and insignificant, and yet it was his.

And *she* had it.

Resentment tore through my body. She dangled his keys like some sort of trophy. I wanted to tear them from her fingers. She'd taken enough from him.

Daniel moved forward. 'Avery, please—'

Her smile vanished. She shoved the keys back in her pocket, and I saw it—

The lighter.

A small, sharp click broke the silence and a bright orange flame danced to life in her hand.

From her other pocket, she pulled something small and familiar.

A candle.

Vanilla-scented.

She brought the two together, lighting the wick in a single practiced movement.

I took a step back, my heart hammering.

One candle.

That's all it took.

That's all it had taken.

* * *

I heard the click of the door behind me and turned, a beaming smile on my face, ready to start my lesson.

The door only opened a fraction and then stopped.

I frowned.

Something flew through the gap. Small and orange. My gaze followed it, but before I could even identify it, fire leapt up around it. And then...

Woosh.

I was surrounded.

* * *

I fought to swallow. I could still hear the sound of the flames cracking. Smell the burning.

Avery smiled faintly. 'I thought once would be enough,' she said, lifting the candle just a little higher. She shrugged. 'But like Dad always says, if at first you don't succeed...'

'Why?' I whispered.

Her eyes didn't meet mine. They shifted past me, to Daniel.

'Because he chose you.' Her voice dropped to something colder. 'He always chose *you*.'

'There was never any competition between you and Olivia,' Daniel said gently.

Avery's jaw tightened.

'You're my daughter. You always came first for me,' he insisted.

'Music always came first,' Avery replied with a snort. 'Mum knew it too. That's why she...' Her voice broke and she blinked rapidly. 'She knew she could never compete with your precious piano, and neither could I.'

'That's not true,' Daniel objected. 'I was passionate about it. Maybe a little too much, but—'

'A little?' Avery scoffed. 'You were obsessed. You were fixated on performing. And when you weren't good enough any more you wanted someone who could carry on your legacy. When I couldn't, you found somebody who could.' Her gaze snapped to me. 'You replaced me.'

I shook my head. 'It wasn't like that. I never wanted to take your place. I didn't even know—' I clamped my mouth closed shut, but it was too late.

The colour drained from Avery's face as understanding dawned on her. 'You didn't even know he had a daughter.'

I shook my head sadly. 'But it's not like we talked about family stuff. My lessons were focused on the music.'

Avery nodded. 'So focused on the music that my own dad forgot I existed.'

'That's not true,' I said quietly. 'Just because he didn't mention you to me doesn't mean he forgot about you.'

'I didn't,' Daniel said, his voice thick with emotion. 'I never forgot about you.'

Avery's gaze remained locked on me as though she hadn't even heard him. 'Maybe,' she conceded. 'Except he always talked about you to me.'

I swallowed. 'I was just his student.'

'You were his prodigy,' Avery corrected. 'You were everything I could never be.'

'So you tried to kill me? Just because I could play the piano better than you?'

'You make it sound so insignificant.'

'Because it is.'

'No,' Avery snapped. 'That piano was everything to him and so were you. As long as you were around, there would never be room in his life for me. You had to go.'

I stared at her, stunned. I'd never understood why Daniel would want to harm me. But the truth was equally unbelievable.

My passion for music had made me an outcast among my classmates. They didn't understand my dedication and discipline to practise. To them it made me boring and weird. I'd hated that part of it. The knowledge that who I was would never be fully accepted.

But I'd never imagined it would almost get me killed.

Daniel took a slow step towards Avery, palms raised. 'Let Olivia go,' he said gently. 'We can talk. Just you and me. The way it always should have been.'

Avery's gaze didn't move from me. The fuel-soaked air clung to us like a warning.

'You always say that,' she said. 'You always say it's about me. But it never is.'

Daniel took another step. 'Please, sweetheart. I'm here now.'

I registered the shift in her expression. I knew what she was going to do a millisecond before she opened her fingers, allowing the lit candle to fall to the floor as she stepped back.

'No—' I screamed. But it was already too late.

'*Run!*' Daniel shouted.

This time the flames didn't weld me to the spot and I bolted for the kitchen door.

But Avery lunged.

She slammed into me, her full weight driving me sideways.

Something cracked.

I screamed. The sound tore out of me as white-hot pain shot through my ankle. It buckled beneath me. I hit the ground hard, everything spinning as Avery landed on top of me.

Agony pulsed through my body, the café swimming in and out of focus.

Smoke thickened around us. Heat surged.

Daniel's voice rang out, sharp and desperate. 'Avery, no!'

Avery shrieked.

Then the weight lifted from me.

Through my blur I saw Daniel pulling her off me, wrestling her away.

This was my chance.

I forced myself onto my elbows, dragging my body towards the door.

Another scream, a thud and then Daniel was above me. 'I've got you,' he assured me as he scooped me up into his arms.

Just like he had before.

I clung to him, burying my face against his chest as flames roared around us.

Cold sharp air hit me as he carried me outside into the alleyway. He set me down on the gravel path and then turned to go back inside.

'Don't go,' I croaked, grabbing his sleeve.

'I have to,' he said, his voice breaking. 'She's my daughter.'

An anguished whimper tore out of me as I watched him disappear into the smoke.

'Are you okay?' A voice I didn't recognise called out to me.

I turned, trying to focus on where it was coming from. 'You have to help him, he went back inside,' I pleaded into the darkness.

Strong arms wrapped themselves around me, and I was lifted again. 'We need to get away from here,' the voice said urgently.

I whimpered as I jolted up and down as the stranger carried me down the alleyway and out onto the street.

'Daniel—'

My plea was drowned out as the café exploded in a blast of heat and light.

55

NOW

December

The air smelled of antiseptic. I smiled slightly. It was better than fuel and smoke.

'We've reviewed the CCTV footage,' PC Monroe informed me as he sat beside my hospital bed. 'It clearly shows Avery letting herself into the café and pouring fuel, before you and Daniel Sinclair arrived.'

At least this time I wasn't reliant on them to believe my words. They could see it for themselves.

I had William to thank for that.

'I'm sorry we weren't able to reach you in time,' DS Harrington said quietly from the doorway.

I nodded. 'Avery was early.'

'Yeah,' he said, rubbing his chin. 'But if we'd believed you sooner...'

The implication of his words was heavy between us. Maybe Daniel would have survived. Avery too.

'If he hadn't gone back for her...' PC Monroe said wearily.

'She was his daughter,' I replied sadly. 'A dad – a good dad – never stops trying to save his daughter.'

PC Monroe arched his eyebrow. 'Sounds like you admire him.'

I hesitated. 'I guess part of me does.'

'After everything he put you through?'

'It was eight years ago,' I said quietly. Perhaps it was finally time to let the past go.

'He should have told the truth about what really happened back then. He could have got Avery the help she needed. You would have had a completely different life.'

'I know.' I nodded. 'My family could have stayed in Portsmouth. Stayed together.' I let out a heavy sigh. 'I'd be lying if I said all that hadn't occurred to me. So many negative events stemmed from that one moment. I hated him for a long time. Not just because I believed he'd started the fire, but because of his lie.' I shook my head sadly. 'In a weird way, that lie was more destructive than the actual fire. It took more from me.'

PC Monroe didn't speak. He just waited.

'But I'll never know for sure what would have happened. Would the restaurant have thrived without the bad publicity? Would Dad have allowed me to pursue music? Would he have stayed? Would Mum have been happier? Healthier? Maybe.' I shrugged. 'But businesses fail all the time. So do marriages. If it hadn't been the fire, maybe something else would have caused Dad to leave. Maybe Mum would still have needed my help, and I might have abandoned music for the restaurant. Who knows?'

PC Monroe nodded slightly as I paused.

'I've spent enough of my life looking back. I don't intend to waste any more time.'

They'd taken so much from me already. I had every right to be hurt and angry. But they were gone. The only person that anger hurt now was myself.

They didn't deserve the power to take more.

I was done blaming myself and hiding from life. It was time I decided what I wanted, or, more importantly, who I wanted to be.

'What will you do now?' DS Harrington asked.

I hesitated, contemplating his question. 'I'm not sure,' I replied finally.

My gaze drifted around the room, settling on the balloon gently bobbing beside a scattering of cards. The one I would have expected, but the others... I reached out, my fingers brushing the gift tag tied to the balloon.

From your new friends at Urban. Looking forward to seeing you back at the gym soon.

I swallowed, blinking back the tears that sprang to my eyes every time I read that note.

'But what I do know,' I said quietly, 'is that you've gotta take a few risks in life to get what you want.'

I smiled ruefully as I repeated Callum's words. They'd seemed so naively simplistic at the time.

But now...

Mum's café was her legacy, but so was I. I didn't need to try to fill her shoes to keep her with me. She already was.

56

NOW

May

'I can't believe you've done this,' Lucy said, her eyes wide with wonder as she pivoted in circles in the centre of the room.

'You helped,' I said, laughing at her reaction. 'It's not like you've never seen it before.'

'I haven't,' she said adamantly. 'Not like this.'

I glanced around at the crowded room, allowing the sounds of excited chatter and laughter wash over me. She had a point. I'd never seen it like this either.

I spotted a small group of familiar faces from the gym, clustered around a table near the back, laughing loudly at something someone had just said. One of them caught my eye and gave me a wave. I lifted a hand in return, a smile tugging at my lips.

'I really thought you'd sell the café after everything that happened,' Lucy said quietly. 'I mean, it was never really your dream.'

I shook my head. 'It wasn't. But moving forward doesn't necessarily mean letting go of the past, of everything. It did mean making some changes, though,' I said with a smile.

'I'll say!' Lucy agreed. 'Turning the place into a wine bar, with live music, just feels more you.'

I nodded. 'It felt like it was time to bring music back into my life.'

Lucy jerked her head towards the piano in the corner. 'Does that mean you'll play something for us?'

I smiled. 'I will, in time.'

She nodded but didn't push.

I chuckled as I watched a couple of teenagers move through the crowd carrying trays, concentration etched in their faces, as though they were afraid to screw up on their first day. 'Hiring a few staff, especially a chef, was definitely a good call.'

Lucy pouted. 'Does that mean I won't get any more of your amazing brownies?'

'I'm sure I can—' My words evaporated as a figure in the doorway caught my attention.

'Liv, are you okay?'

I heard the question, but I didn't answer. I couldn't.

All I could do was stare, open-mouthed, at the man who was now walking towards me.

'Hi, Olivia. I'm—'

'I know who you are.' I cut through his introduction. The eight years had aged him, but I still recognised him.

He attempted to smile, weak and hesitant. 'I wasn't sure whether to come.'

It was on the tip of my tongue to tell him he'd made the wrong decision, but something stopped me. Or, more accurately, Callum stopped me.

I just wanted you to have someone again. Have family again.

This was what he'd wanted. For me to see my dad. To talk to him.

'I saw the news about the fire. I wanted to come then, but...'

'You were afraid I might need you?'

'No,' he said firmly.

I scoffed as I walked towards the counter. 'Really? My business, my home, my whole life burnt down, and yet you only show up now that I've started again.'

He followed me but stayed on the customer's side of the counter. I liked that. The barrier between us. Something solid.

'I was afraid that I was the last thing you needed.' He paused. 'I failed you. I know that now. Not just by leaving you the way did, but long before that. I should have trusted you. I should have known that you would never have started that fire. Just like William knew.'

'William?' My voice cracked.

'He came to see me.'

I nodded. I knew that. 'But...'

'He told me who he really was. William. William Calloway.'

The room dipped, and I grabbed the edge of the counter tightly.

'Are you okay?'

The concern in his voice was like a bucket of cold water being dumped on me. I couldn't remember him ever speaking to me with such concern before. Not when I was a kid. Not when I'd needed him. But now, here he was.

My father.

'He told you his real name,' I muttered through clenched teeth. After all the deception, the loss, the pain, I didn't think anything could hurt me any more.

I was wrong.

The man I'd loved had lied to me about everything. Even his identity. Yet he'd told my dad the truth.

It felt like yet another betrayal.

'He told me everything,' Dad said softly.

I heard the gasp, but it wasn't until I realised everyone was looking at me that I understood the sound had come from me.

'He wanted me to know the truth.'

I closed my eyes. Not wanting to hear any more.

'About you,' Dad finished.

My eyes flew open. I stared at him. 'About me?'

'He wanted me to know you were innocent. That you'd never started the fire.'

My mouth opened and closed. 'No. That's not right. He was investigating me. Using me for a story. He was trying to prove my guilt.'

'At first.' Dad nodded. 'Until he spent time with you. And he realised what I should always have known. You don't have a vengeful bone in your body.' He paused. 'But William explained how he tried to test you, provoke you even, into losing control. Bailing on plans. Letting you down at the last minute. Messing with the oven temperature and timers, filling the kitchen with smoke. Lighting vanilla candles to trigger your memories of the fire.' He looked at me, regret clouding his face. 'He thought if he pushed you enough that you'd be unable to keep up the act, and you'd confess. He was so convinced of your guilt that he thought what he was doing was justified. It was right. Except... you never cracked. No matter what he put you through, you were still *you*.'

I fought for breath. Everything about our relationship had been a lie. I'd known that already from Avery. But hearing it from Dad, learning every detail, every manipulation...

It was different.

It was worse.

'Why are you doing this to me?'

Dad shook his head. 'I'm not doing it to you. I'm doing it *for* you.'

'So I can be reminded of what an idiot I was to trust him? To love him?'

He grabbed my hands. I tried to pull away but he squeezed them tightly. 'So you can know how much he loved you.'

I blinked. 'What?'

'Olivia, he came to me because he wanted to try to make amends.'

'No. He wanted to destroy me. He wanted to bring an arsonist to justice.'

'But when he realised he'd made a mistake, that you were innocent, he wanted to try to fix things. He knew once he told you who he was, and what he'd done, you would probably never speak to him again. So he wanted you to have someone. To have me. To help you through it.'

'He packed his stuff. He left.'

'No,' Dad said firmly. 'He told me he was going to pack and move back onto the boat to give you space once he'd told you. But he wasn't leaving you. Not unless you wanted him to go.'

'But...' My thoughts swirled together, leaving me unable to form a rebuttal.

'He was going to tell you that night.'

'He hadn't left me?'

Dad shook his head. 'He wasn't me,' he said slowly. Sadly.

'Why didn't you tell me sooner?'

'William told me you didn't want to see me. Said I should give you time. And then when I read the news about the fire, and his death...' Dad shrugged helplessly. 'I didn't want to make things worse for you, when you were already going through so much.'

'So you waited until now, tonight, when things are starting to come together, when I have all these people here...'

Dad hung his head. 'It was selfish of me, I know, coming tonight, encroaching on your celebration, your success. But I couldn't miss seeing this. Seeing you. I had to be here, even if you threw me out. I needed to see that you were okay, but mostly I needed you to know that I'm sorry.'

He started to turn towards the door, but stopped. 'Your mum would have loved this, you know,' he said as his gaze drifted around the wine bar. 'You've done what neither of us could manage to do. You've brought life and joy into this place.'

I stood behind the counter in the middle of the bustling wine bar, staring at the door as it clicked closed behind him.

Lucy stepped up beside me and linked her arm through mine.

'He's right, you know,' she said softly. 'You've created something really special here.'

'Mum named it The Second Cup Café because it was her second chance,' I said, almost to myself. 'A place to start again.'

'And the new name?' Lucy asked, her gaze drifting up to the sign above the bar: *The Coda*.

'A concluding passage,' I said softly. 'Separate, but connected.'

She tilted her head. 'I like that. You've made it yours.'

I nodded slowly. It finally felt like home.

* * *

MORE FROM ALEX STONE

The next book from Alex Stone is available to order now here:
https://mybook.to/AlexStone6

ACKNOWLEDGEMENTS

Writing a novel can be a lonely process, but I've never truly done it alone, and for that, I'm incredibly grateful.

To Ahl, thank you for always supporting me, even when that means sharing a holiday with me *and* my deadline.

To Kathleen McGurl, your impeccable timing is a mystery in itself. You always seem to check in just when I need your advice the most. You have a remarkable knack for solving problems that torment me for months – in minutes. Your skill and ease make me envious, but above all, deeply thankful to call you my friend.

To Yvonne Hazell-Webb, thank you for patiently sharing your knowledge about boats when I knew absolutely nothing. Your insights brought authenticity to the story that I could never have achieved on my own.

To Stuart Gibbon, your continued expertise and generous advice on all things police-related has been invaluable. Thank you for always being on hand to answer my questions, no matter how obscure.

To Emma, thank you for stepping in when life (and a few building issues) pulled me in too many directions. Your tremendous support gave me the space I needed to meet my deadlines.

A huge thank you to my writing mentor, Jonathan Eyers from Cornerstones Literary Consultancy. Your encouragement and thoughtful feedback are always spot on. You somehow make sense of the chaotic early drafts and help me shape them into stories that flow.

To the incredible Author Events community – what began in 2024 as a small coffee morning during a time when I was struggling has grown into something far more than I ever imagined. One year on, it's a thriving community of authors, with regular coffee mornings and monthly author talks at the fabulous Sobo:Sommelier. Thank you for joining me as I veered into the unknown, planning events I wasn't sure anyone would turn up to. You did. And more than that, you made them a success.

To my readers – especially those of you who've been with me since the beginning – thank you. Your support, messages, and kind words have carried me through the toughest writing days. It's always a delight to meet you at a book launch, a library talk, or even unexpectedly at Café Riva (thank you, Deb, for coming all the way from Australia!). Knowing the characters I create live in your hearts is the greatest privilege of all.

And lastly, to my incredible editor, Emily Ruston – thank you for your insight, your patience, and your honesty. Your feedback is always what the book needs (even when it hurts!), and your belief in my work makes my stories what they are.

ABOUT THE AUTHOR

Alex Stone, originally an accountant from the West Midlands, is now a psychological suspense writer based in Dorset. This beautiful and dramatic coastline is the inspiration and setting for her novels. She was awarded the Katie Fforde Bursary in 2019.

Download your exclusive bonus content from Alex Stone here:

Visit Alex Stone's website: www.AlexStoneAuthor.com

Follow Alex on social media here:

ALSO BY ALEX STONE

THE *Murder* LIST

THE MURDER LIST IS A NEWSLETTER DEDICATED TO SPINE-CHILLING FICTION AND GRIPPING PAGE-TURNERS!

SIGN UP TO MAKE SURE YOU'RE ON OUR HIT LIST FOR EXCLUSIVE DEALS, AUTHOR CONTENT, AND COMPETITIONS.

SIGN UP TO OUR NEWSLETTER

BIT.LY/THEMURDERLISTNEWS

Boldwood

Boldwood Books is an award-winning fiction publishing company seeking out the best stories from around the world.

Find out more at www.boldwoodbooks.com

Join our reader community for brilliant books, competitions and offers!

Follow us
@BoldwoodBooks
@TheBoldBookClub

Sign up to our weekly deals newsletter

https://bit.ly/BoldwoodBNewsletter